George Alexander Peltz

How to Make Home Happy

Vol. 1

George Alexander Peltz

How to Make Home Happy
Vol. 1

ISBN/EAN: 9783337407346

Printed in Europe, USA, Canada, Australia, Japan

Cover: Foto ©Andreas Hilbeck / pixelio.de

More available books at **www.hansebooks.com**

THE HOME CIRCLE.

To Make Home Happy

—A—

HOUSEKEEPER'S HAND BOOK.

COMPRISING :—Eminently useful and practical suggestions upon Home Furnishing; Cheerful Decorations; Economy in Necessities; Rules of Polite Deportment; What to do in Emergencies; Taking care of Children; General Hints upon Various Subjects; Social Games; Amusements, Entertainments, etc., etc., with

COPIOUS VALUABLE ILLUSTRATIONS.

EDITED BY

A SKILLED CORPS OF AUTHORITIES.

PREFACE.

NOT every place where one may sleep and eat is worthy
to be called a home. About home there are the ideas of
comfort, repose, peace, content. Where these are wanting
none can be at home. So ill-furnished and ill-managed may
be one's abode that it is more a prison than a place of rest.
Such a place is not a home.

No external surroundings can guarantee a soul at rest.
Some people are unhappy amid the greatest luxury. Many
a sleepless night is passed on a bed of down. Many a life
of misery is passed in royal mansions. But yet it remains
true that other things being equal, those persons are happiest
whose wants and tastes are most fully met.

The problem of making home happy cannot be solved by
any one line of answers. Many sources must contribute to
that coveted attainment and these sources are considered in
this volume. There are *Necessities* for every happy home,
and these are first discussed. There are *Furnishings* also,
some essential and some otherwise, but all these need our

attention.   There are *Decorations* also for homes, by which they may be so embellished and beautified that their charm is greatly increased.   There is *Deportment*, that mysterious but mighty manner which at a glance discloses the true gentleman, or the clumsy clown.   There is *Hygiene*—that care of children and of others whereby health, the foundation of happiness, is assured.   There are *Emergencies* to be met that needless suffering may be shut out, and wise treatment secured promptly.   *Games and Amusements* form an important part of all real Home Life also, and if after all these points are considered anything remains unsaid, *General Hints* can happily cover it.   This broad sweep of needed knowledge is covered in this comprehensive volume.

That a book treating all these points will do much to make Home Happy, and will therefore be heartily welcomed, is fully believed by

THE PUBLISHERS.

TABLE OF CONTENTS.

LIST OF ILLUSTRATIONS.

THE HOME CIRCLE.—FRONTISPIECE.

x

At night returning, every labor sped,
He sits him down the monarch of a shed;
Smiles by his cheerful fire, and round surveys
His children's looks, that brighten at the blaze;
While his lov'd partner, boastful of her hoard,
Displays her cleanly platter on the board.

OLIVER GOLDSMITH.

HOME NECESSITIES.

Now stir the fire, and close the shutters fast,
Let fall the curtain, wheel the sofa round,
And, while the bubbling and loud-hissing urn
Throws up a steamy column, and the cups,
That cheer but not inebriate, wait on each,
So let us welcome peaceful evening in.

COWPER.

HOME NECESSITIES.

WHAT some regard as a necessity others consider a mere superfluity. The old story tells of a boy who did not want shoes in summer time as he could go barefoot, but he was actually suffering for a breast-pin. His conceptions of things did not accord with the common sense of the world however. He was a crank. He pined for the useless. Much that is brought into our homes is not needful in any sense,—much less is it needful as ministering directly to health or comfort.

That which exposes a household to open or insidious influences which damage health should be at once eradicated. This riddance is certainly a necessity. Ventilation, warming, illumination, and sanitary care in general, with all the work and help needed to preserve them in most effective operation are necessities. Without these home becomes a feeder to the hospital, or a minister to disease. It lays foundations for useless and miserable lives, rather than for those of robust activity and wide beneficence.

It is a shame that home should ever become the helper to harm, damaging those who dwell in its sacred precincts. Rather should it minister to all that is pure and healthful to body and to mind, and to such considerations all who control home affairs should studiously address themselves.

15

I.—WORK AND HELP.

THERE is no housekeeper who will not weary of the household work if she attempt to do it in person; nor is there one whose patience will not be sorely tried if she attempt to do it by proxy. Physical exhaustion on the one side, and mental exhaustion on the other, are the Scylla and Charybdis between which the good housewife struggles to guide the domestic craft. Some make fairly good progress in the effort, but more are sorely tried and buffeted, while many finally go down in the whirlpool of boarding-house or hotel life, or are shattered and scattered as families.

The comparatively new method of "flats," as conducted in New York, Chicago, and San Francisco, is a Parisian idea adapted to American necessities. In immense structures, with eight or ten floors, apartments are fitted up usually in sumptuous style, with every convenience and luxury. Elevators carry the residents and callers to any floor, so that the ninth floor is virtually as good as the first. The hall ways and apartments are heated and cared for by house servants; the meals are served *a la carte*, in a general dining-hall or restaurant, or are served in the rooms if desired; so that the only care the occupants have is the incidental charge of their own rooms and their social duties. This method avoids all personal labor and all care about servants, and yet each family has its own home.

Of course there are no yards or gardens in such places. When there are little children in a family the opportunities

16

are rather restricted. The old home idea is wholly lost in such a dwelling-place. Domestic duties are in utter disuse. Home cooking has no foothold. Home decoration may be practiced to a limited extent, and home courtesy may prevail; but after all, the home life barely exists.

In the old-fashioned home life, regularity is a prime factor. Without it all will speedily run to disorder. To do things regularly requires forethought and planning. What to do and when to do it, must both be clearly understood. Then the predetermined plans must be rigidly adhered to and carried through. Servants see at a glance whether the head of the house " means business " or not. Any number of orders may be issued, but if the servants know that it means nothing, they do not concern or bestir themselves. Orders should be few as possible, but they should be well considered and explicit, and when once issued they should be conformed to absolutely.

Vaporing, scolding, fretting, and storming about the house only lower the lady of the establishment in the esteem of her employees. Her superiority must appear in her calm deliberation and her intelligently formed decisions. But these need not be issued in an arbitrary, dictatorial form. The American spirit does not brook much of this. Help worth having can suit itself readily in other places, and such help will not submit to arbitrary or tyrannical treatment.

One of the best advisers of young housekeepers says to them: " Never, except in cases of extreme emergency, allow Monday's washing to be put off till Tuesday, Tuesday's ironing till Wednesday, or Wednesday's finishing up and setting to rights till Thursday. Leave Thursday for extra work; or when that is not required, for a resting day or a half holiday, and as a preparation for the up-stairs sweeping and dusting of Friday, and the down-stairs baking and scrubbing of Saturday." In this advice all good housewives will concur, though the men of the house, to quote one such, "cannot see why so arbitrary and inflexible a rule should be imposed upon the domestic economy."

Forethought will prove a great help in saving time, fuel, labor, and temper. For example : Mix bread at night, and it will be ready to bake with that "first fire," which always makes the oven hot in the morning.

Prepare fruit over night, so that pies or other preparations for dessert can be quickly made, and baked immediately after the bread.

Prepare hash for breakfast over night.

Have the kitchen and dining-room put in order before going to bed.

Have kindlings and whatever is requried for building needed fires laid out ready, and the fire in the kitchen raked down, so that it can be started in the shortest possible time. This is not only a saving in the morning, but it will be found very useful in case of illness in the night when a fire may be required at a moment's notice.

Much work is saved by forethought in purchases. If possible, lay in winter supplies ; buy starch, sugar, soap, tea, etc., etc., in quantities reasonably large, and deliver them to the kitchen as needed ; it may be by the week, or twice a week. It should not be so often as to become irksome, not so seldom as to lose sight of what is going on. Dried soap will prove an immense saving by its hardness, as compared with the soft, fresh bars for which the servant runs twice or thrice a week. Money and labor both are saved by such forethought as this.

Constant supervision is essential to securing good work. Eye-service is the bane of our laboring classes. See that orders are obeyed ; see that things are put to proper uses ; see that house-cloths do not become dish-cloths, or *vice versa ;* that hand-towels do not become cup-towels, or *vice versa ;* that combs, brushes, etc., etc., are kept out of the cooking apartment ; that the cellar broom is not used on the parlor carpet, or *vice versa*. Indeed, there is no end to the points that the housewife must supervise, if she be determined to have her work well done.

Accountability for articles belonging to each department must be insisted on with every servant. No article must be allowed to disappear without a sufficient reason. Nor must anything be out of its proper place, except as necessary. Explain to each new servant the nature of this accountability and hold every one steadily to it.

It is said that American kitchens are the worst in the world. Work is very materially promoted by means of a good kitchen. It should be roomy, light, and capable of good ventilation without sending its odors and its steam through the house. It should have plenty of good, convenient closets for all that pertains to the work there done. It should have direct access to the fuel, store-rooms, or cellar where provisions are stored, and convenient access to the dining-room. A window communication is best between kitchen and dining-room, using a waiting-maid to receive.

The conveniences of range, hot and cold water, sink, etc., are desirable, of course, but in some places they are not attainable. A dish-drainer is a great convenience. It may be made of a grooved board, slightly inclined so as to drain the water back into the sink or dish-pan. Dishes laid upon this as washed, that they may drain a few minutes, will be found in much better condition for wiping, and so labor will be saved. An elevated strip must surround all but the lower edge of this drainer to prevent the dishes from slipping off.

Kitchen company seriously interferes with work and service. The employees of a house are social beings. They have their associations and must continue to have them, but much visiting destroys effective management. It demoralizes servants and delays work. Company should be restricted to certain convenient hours. The indiscriminate furnishing of meals to their visitors by servants should not be permitted. Permission at that point should be asked of the lady of the house, and she, not the servant, should judge whether the case is exceptional and allowable. Interference in the presence of the "guests" would probably create a scene, but a good understanding at the outset would be as likely to preclude all trouble. Indeed, so few housewives know their own minds in domestic management, that the servants are little to blame if they too are ignorant of "the lady's" mind. Be reasonable with servants; yea, be generous; but be explicit and decided.

After this extended discussion, it still remains true that the thoughful, self-poised, kindly, but decided housewife will be the only one who will get the needed work done, and will find all her "help" really helpful. It seems wise to conclude this chapter with a few carefully selected

HINTS ON HOME WORK.

Aprons.—Have a good assortment of full-sized aprons which can be washed. They should be long and wide.

Brooms.—Four brooms should be in simultaneous use in a house. The best for the parlor and best rooms; the second best for the sitting-room and dining-room; the third for the kitchen; the last for the cellar, yard, etc. When the best broom shows wear, replace it with a new one, and "retire" the worst, moving the others back one place. Hang up brooms by a loop, or better, by a broom holder. (See Chapter xxi, Part I.)

Closets, etc.—Scrub them out thoroughly and frequently. Cover dish-shelves with clean white papers; the edges may be scolloped, or "pinked," if desired.

Dish-cloths.—Old towels, crash, napkins, table-cloths, etc., make splendid dish-cloths.

Dusters.—Feather dusters throw dust from one place to another. They are poor tools, except for the lightest kind of work. Cloths are preferable. These should be shaken out-of-doors frequently, or washed. Damp chamois skins are best for articles not liable to damage by dampness.

Fuel.—When cooking is not going on, the fire should be slacked by closing the dampers, etc. Coal should never be piled high in the stoves. It chokes the draft, makes heat where it does no good, burns out the stove tops, and wastes willfully. Ashes should be sifted and picked over. A large saving will be effected thus.

Holders.—Iron-holders, and others for hot pots, kettles, etc., will save time, labor, and burns. If such conveniences do not exist, towels will be substituted by the " help."

Ironing Tools.—Keep the cloths, etc., in good, orderly shape in a clean, dry place. The irons must be kept free from moisture.

Paper and String.—Lay all such together in a convenient place, nicely straightened out, ready for use at any time. If too much accumulates, sell it or burn it.

Pie-board.—This, with the roller, should be put away clean every time, in a scrupulously clean place.

Pots and Kettles.—Put away thoroughly cleaned and well dried. Scald out coffee and tea-pots frequently with soda-water. Keep each in its proper place.

Refrigerators.—Scrub and air these frequently. The purest and best makes need such treatment.

Water Coolers.—Scrub and air these. Sediment will collect which must be unwholesome and unsavory.

Whisks.—Use a clean, fine whisk for upholstered furniture. Have others for the stairs, corners of rooms, etc. All these in addition to whisks used for clothing.

II.—VENTILATION.

FRESH air is essential to healthful and happy human existence. It is so free and abundant that there should be no lack anywhere or at any time. Out-of-doors we get it without care or planning; but to get it in-doors, and so to get it that nobody is harmed, that nobody catches cold or gets the rheumatism, that is the problem.

Every living being gives off the deadly carbonic acid gas continually, and at the same time consumes the vitalizing. oxygen. Lamps, fires, combustion of all sorts, does the same, some forms of these being more active than others in the emission of carbonic acid gas. For every apartment where people live and fires burn there must be ventilation. Fresh air must come in, and foul air must go out.

In cold weather, this must be so done that a reasonable warmth in the room shall be maintained, and it must always be so done that chilling drafts shall not strike persons in such way as to check perspiration and produce sickness.

Ventilation in large buildings is usually provided for by forcing fresh air through all its ramifications. The air is admitted in such ways as shall most effectually diffuse it through the building, avoiding all blasts or sensible currents. If mechanical means are employed to force air, the problem is comparatively simple. Drive in enough air and distribute it with judgment, and it is all done.

But dwelling-houses do not admit of these elaborate

22

arrangements except in rare cases. How can they be ventilated? The commonest way is to open the window. If a
wind be stirring, or if the temperature within and without the
room vary much, currents of air will at once set in, and an
open window will do the desired work. But if the atmosphere be still and sultry, the windows may be open, and yet
no interchange of air take place. The top of the window
allows egress to the heated air. The bottom allows ingress
to the colder, external air. To ventilate a room, both openings of the window are needed. If windows are only on
one side of a room, a door upon the other side must be
open to do the work properly. Currents which would be
too strong, may be well broken by the ordinary shutter
blinds, the angle given the slats determining the direction
of currents to a great extent, and so breaking their volume
as to render them practically harmless.

An easy adaptation of ordinary windows for a good ventilating purpose is secured by inserting
on the sill, where the bottom sash shuts
down, a piece of wood the thickness of the
sash, and long as the sash is wide, but
about three inches high ; the effect being
that the sash, shutting down on this strip,
shall stand three inches above the sill and
yet the bottom will be closed tight. The
displacement between the upper and lower
sash will leave an opening by which currents of air will pass in and out, ventilating
the room very fairly, and that, too, without any perceptible draft.

A CHEAP METHOD
OF VENTILATION.

Another simple method is to tack muslin or ornamental
cloth across the bottom of the window frame, inside the
room, but not against the sash. The window may then be
raised. The muslin should rise three times the height of
the opening of the window. The effect of this is to produce

an interchange of air, with positively no perceptible draft, even when the wind without is high.

From the summit of the hallway, or open stairway of a house, it is well to carry an open pipe high above the roof, capped so as to keep out storm, and capable of being closed in the coldest weather. It will draw off the heated air of the house and render good service.

A ventilating shaft is a great accessory to a house. It should be like a large flue, say two feet square, and by inserting glass at the top it may be used for light also. Into such a shaft openings from the several rooms may be made, also from water-closets and reservoirs. This shaft should be placed next to a chimney flue which is always in use, so that the shaft itself will be warm enough to produce movement in the air. Or a surer way is to have at its base a heating apparatus of gas, oil, or steam, by means of which the current of air may be moved in the shaft and the entire house be ventilated. The outlet of such a shaft must be so constructed that snow and rain will not drive in even when the windows in it are open. It should be capable of entire closing also by means of cords and pulleys.

Every fire drawing its oxygen from a room, carries air out of the room, and this consumed air must be replaced through cracks or crevices, if by no better means. Some ventilation is always gained where such fires burn, therefore. But when they burn low, it is a chance that they will emit more injurious gases than the fresh air drawn in can counterbalance.

All heating methods which throw warmed air into the room may become valuable methods of ventilation. If the air be drawn direct from a foul cellar they will be injurious. If the air be baked by contact with red-hot surfaces, it will be dry and to a great extent stripped of its oxygen. But take the air from without, if possible from the top of the house, by means of a cold-air flue ; heat this air by contact with steam pipes or hot pipes, but not those which are red-hot, and you will have warm air and good air at one and the same time. Apertures or registers near the floor are needed in this case, by means of which cold air passes away. Near the floor the foul, heavy air settles also, which is driven out by the same means. Registers opening into a ventilating shaft, as just described, form the best escape for impure air, as they carry it entirely out of the house.

Some authorities recommend that ventilating openings be made directly into smoke-flues. Even if smoke and soot can be kept from entering the room where such a device is employed, which is doubtful, notwithstanding "traps" and other warranted contrivances, still every opening of this kind subtracts from the draft power of the fire below the opening, and hence is a disadvantage. The independent ventilation shaft is the most valuable help.

To enforce the need of ventilation, it may be stated that a pound of coal burned requires for its combustion one hundred and forty-eight cubic feet of air. Every gas-burner consumes about thirty-six cubic feet per hour. A candle consumes about eleven cubic feet per hour. A healthy adult requires two hundred and fifteen cubic feet of air per hour. Combining these facts, the absolute necessity of a large supply of fresh air to every living-room is an easy demonstration.

III.—WARMING.

IN the last chapter some points on the warming of houses
have been touched. Ventilation and warming are subjects so closely related that they cannot be considered
fully when apart. As in cooking, so in warming, the simplest method is the open fire, the mere bonfire in short. But
from such a fire, it is an easy step to an inclosing structure
which cuts off radiation of heat in useless directions and
conducts smoke where it will do the least harm. On this
principle the old-fashioned fireplaces were constructed.
They did very little work in proportion to the fuel consumed,
but where fuel was abundant that mattered little. Then, too,
in such fires, at least one-half of the heat goes up the
chimney, and some good authorities say that fifteen-six-
teenths is thus lost. Such fires heat by direct radiation.
Heat is thrown from them directly on the persons in the
room, on the walls and other objects. These become heated,
and in turn reflect heat so that all the contents of the room,
atmosphere, and solid bodies.are thoroughly warmed at last.
Until this completeness of heating is attained, however, one
may be blistering his face while cold creeps run down his
back. Then, too, such heat quickly falls off. It is irregular,
expensive, unsatisfactory.

Benjamin Franklin made an improvement on the old warming methods in the stoves which bear his name. He saved
much of the heat which formerly escaped by making his
stove to sit in the room, and the smoke to reach the chimney
by a circuitous passage, as in a stove-pipe. This compelled

26

much escaping heat to give off its power in the room. The fireplace of this stove was inclosed with another casing of iron, through which air circulated and passed into the room in a heated condition. So he had all the direct radiation of the fire and of the heated parts of the stove, plus the air which was heated by passing through the hot chambers.

Grates are simply an adaptation of the old fireplace to the later discovery of coal as a fuel. They are less open and therefore less wasteful, but all the side and back power of the fire is lost to the room so far as heating it is concerned. It passes off by conduction, and is lost in the walls.

Low-down grates are a favorite feature for fall and spring uses in sitting-rooms, offices, etc. They heat by direct radiation only, but for the lighter purposes in warming they are desirable as being both beautiful and sufficiently useful.

A fine specimen of these grates is shown in the accompanying cut. It is made with handsome nickel-plated frame and trimmings. In its "throat" is a double valve arrangement, shown in the cut, which can be used as a blower in starting the fire, as a damper in reducing the draft, or as a reflector to throw the heat into the room. These grates have indeed become so popular that improvement upon improvement has been made, and decoration

LOW-DOWN GRATE.

has been added to decoration, until they seem absolutely perfect, and certainly they are very beautiful.

Closed stoves heat the air by its contact with their heated surfaces. They are now made with mica doors or windows, through which the direct radiation also passes, and air chambers are added in which air is heated, so that stoves of an immense warming power, and withal very easy to manage, are now the standards.

A specimen of such heating stoves is shown in the adjoining engraving. Externally it is not at all displeasing to the eye. On the following page a sectional view of this same stove is shown, displaying the coal reservoir, or self-feeder, as it is sometimes called; the damper; the cut-off draft in the upper part of the stove front; the cylinder and anti-clinker grate, which is a notable feature. By opening the doors which surround this part of the stove, all debris can be removed from the grate, and a fresh, bright fire will be secured at once. By this means the fires need not be drawn through an entire season. The fire cannot become choked. It is always clean.

FIRST-CLASS MODERN HEATING-STOVE.

The stove shown here has a sheet-iron top. For the sake of increased orna-mentation, the tops are usually made in cast-iron, with nickel-plated panels and embellishment. It is an open ques-tion which kind of top gives off the more heat. A tea-kettle attachment may be made just above the upper tier of doors if desired. By this contrivance tea may be boiled, and some other mi-nor culinary wants be met. A nickel-plated foot rail may be placed around the base, adding to the beauty of the stove, and also to its utility.

Fireplace heaters are favorites with many communities. Like a low-down grate, they fill the opening of the man-tel, but they are constructed as heat-ers, with drums. They heat the room in which they are

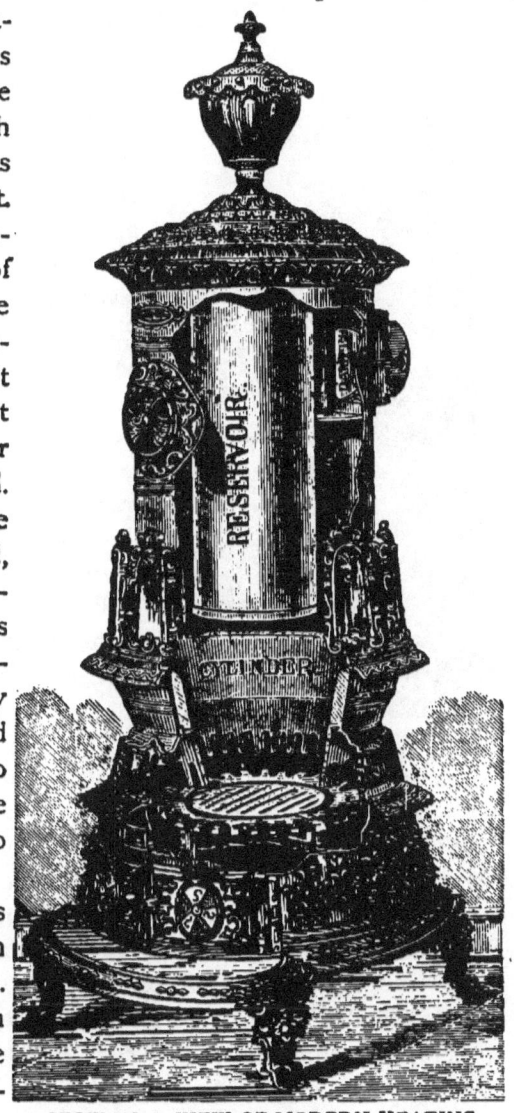

SECTIONAL VIEW OF MODERN HEATING-STOVE.

placed by direct radiation and heated air; and to the room above heated air is supplied abundantly.   These, like other modern stoves, are finished in very ornate styles.

Hot-air furnaces have come into very general use. They combine so many advantages, and are withal so effective, that they well deserve the favor they have met.   To elucidate the subject fully, a sectional view of a portable heater is given. This differs from the permanent or brick-inclosed heater chiefly in the method of inclosure, and in the capacity of the heating-drums.

The time was when but little attention was given to the construction of heaters. Almost anything with an iron cylinder and a casing around it, that would consume coal,

SECTIONAL VIEW OF A PORTA-BLE HEATER.

was considered a sufficient heater.   No matter how much dust and dirt were made in the cellar or basement, and conveyed through the flues to the parlor or rooms above, it was nevertheless supposed to answer for heating purposes. But those days have passed away; careful and scientific study has been applied to the subject.

One valuable point in the heater shown in the cut is that whereby all ashes and clinker can be removed from the fire-pot without dropping the fire. This can be done with less trouble than it takes to rake the old kind of heaters, and a continuous fire be kept always fresh on the grate. By this means the entire surface of the heater can be relied on for heat. In the old heaters, when the grate surface became covered with clinkers, and the cylinder half filled with ashes, only the upper surface afforded heat, which very often resulted in overheating the top and ruining the furnace.

This heater is supplied with a magazine, making it a self-feeder. Another new feature is a radiating drum, and, in place of taking the damp, impure air from the cellar floor, with the dust and ashes, there is a cold air collar at the back of the heater so that a pipe can be attached, and pure, fresh air be brought from the outside of the building.

At the base of the heater, on each side of the cylinder, are placed the water tanks, easy of access, where a sufficient quantity of water can be evaporated without boiling it. It also has a damper at the smoke-pipe.

To all hot-air furnaces there are serious objections. They exhaust the moisture so completely that furniture is dried out and falls apart, and, worse than this, the moisture of the human system is so reduced that parched lips and difficulty of breathing often result. Furnace-heated air is drier than that ever heated in the midst of the Desert of Sahara. Evaporators may be introduced into the heaters and moisture may be restored again to the air, but a new danger arises. The sediment left by the constant evaporation of the water becomes unhealthy. This is demonstrated when, by reason of lowness of water in the evaporator, the sediment begins to stew or to bake, in which case the house soon becomes rank with its offensive odors. The water-pan of the heater must be kept clean. Stewing or simmering animal or vegetable matter cannot be healthy.

The principles to be regarded in determining the size of a heater are these: The greater the heating surface in a heater, the greater is the volume of air it can heat to a given temperature in a given time. A low fire will therefore impart warmth to a room fully equal to that from a hot fire in

a smaller furnace. The one does a large volume of work
deliberately. The other does it with a rush; but in the
rush the air is baked, its moisture is exhausted, it is made
unfit for use. The coal required is more in bulk in the
larger furnaces, but it is not used half so fast. Large fire-
pans are better, therefore, and cheaper—of course within
reasonable bounds. Then, too, the moisture produced at a
low temperature is preferable to that from excessive heat.
The former is a gentle vapor, the later a driving steam.

Hot water and steam are used in various applications for
heating purposes, but not very generally in private houses,
except as they heat air carried through coils containing
steam or hot water.

Among the contrivances applicable to furnaces and
heaters of all kinds are governors or regulators, which can
be set so that when the heat reaches a certain height the
drafts will close automatically. When the heat falls they
will open. Thus an equal temperature is maintained even
in the absence of immediate supervision.

GAS HEATING-STOVES.

After seeing the wonderful adaptations of gas to cooking
purposes, no one will wonder that there are many happy
adaptations of the same to heating purposes. The Goodwin
Gas Stove Company, from whose constructions the illustrations already given were selected, furnishes heating-stoves
also.

The principles upon which these stoves are constructed
are thoroughly scientific, and at the same time so simple
that they require little or no attention. The ventilating
principle is so applied that no injurious products of combustion can escape into the room in which they are placed,
but all are carried off to the flue or out-of-doors by the pipe
seen in the opposite cuts. The stoves have an air passage

through the centre by means of which the air passes up from the floor, and in its passage comes in contact with the sides of the centre tubes and becomes highly heated. The stoves can be made to draw their supply of air from out-of-

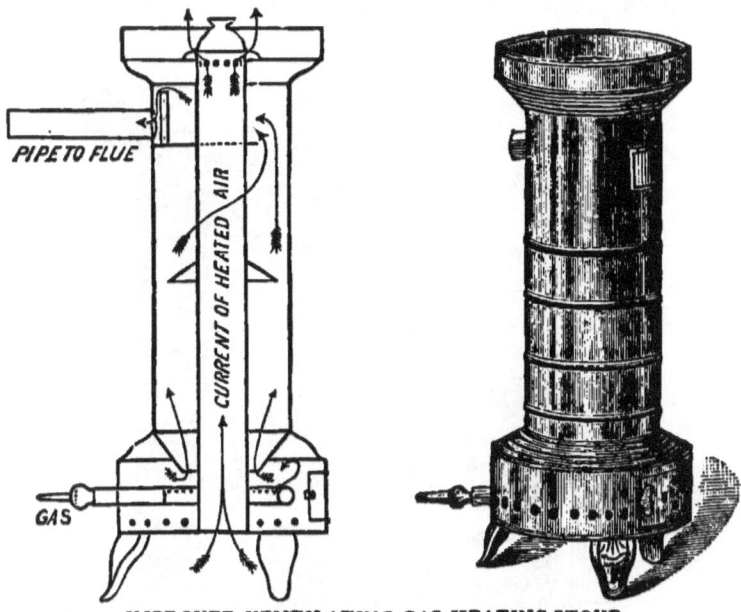

IMPROVED VENTILATING GAS HEATING-STOVE.

doors by means of a tube when so desired. Their consumption of gas is but seven cubic feet per hour. One of them will heat a room containing from eight hundred to one thousand cubic feet of space. They are six inches in diameter and twenty-three inches high.

If the open fire appearance is desired, the stove called the "Cheerful" meets the case.

These stoves are especially designed for use in parlors, libraries, and sitting-rooms. The panels in the front and sides are fitted with porcelain or metal tiles. The frames are nickel-plated, or enameled in black or brown with bronzed chambers. The tops are of marble, and can be varied in color to suit the taste.

They are constructed upon principles so correct scientifically, and at the same time so simple, that they require little or no attention. They, too, may be made to draw their supply of fresh air from out-of-doors, and they carry off the results so perfectly that no injurious products of combus-

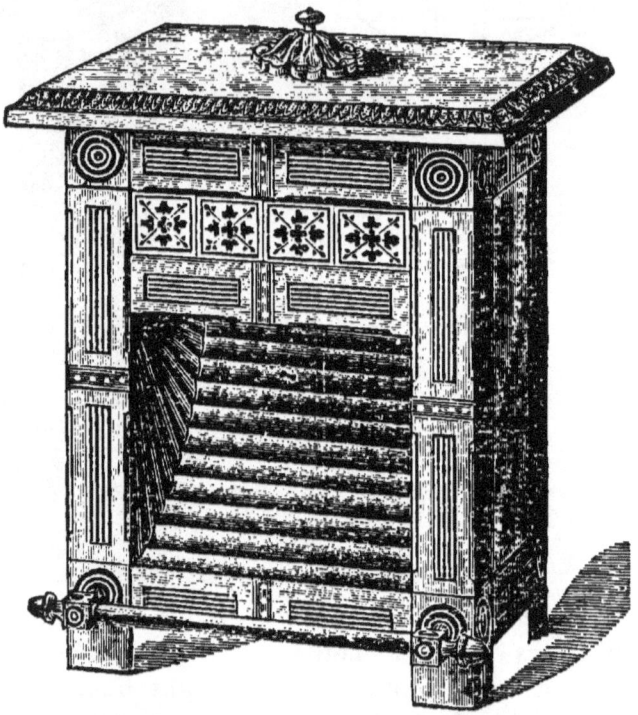

THE "CHEERFUL" GAS HEATING-STOVE.

tion can escape. This stove, in its largest size, is thirty inches high, sixteen inches wide, twelve inches deep.

Smaller stoves are in cast-iron only, but these have a boiling burner at the top. The smallest of this line is eleven inches high, ten and a half inches wide, and nine inches deep. It will warm a small room or take the chill from a large one.

IV.—ILLUMINATION.

CANDLES, lamps, and gas are so familiar that in their ordinary uses they need not be so much as mentioned.

But all these articles have undergone so much of improvement that a few points concerning them may be of value.

Candles are now furnished of very superior illuminating power and also very beautiful in appearance. When used simply for show, as is now very common, they can be had in many colors and very artistically decorated

MODERN BRASS CANDLESTICKS.

with flowers, birds, etc., so as to be highly ornamental.

Finely wrought brass candlesticks, for use or for ornament, are quite popular also, though it seems like a return to the days of our fathers.

The student-lamp (for kerosene oil) has come into very extensive use. It receives the oil into the large vessel at the

BRACKET STUDENT-LAMP.

side, from which the oil is supplied to the wick by the

35

connecting tube, the wick being circular and on the argand principle, so that the largest possible amount of illuminating surface is secured, with the best possible results. In specialties of this character, the Manhattan Brass Company, of New York, has done many good things. The above bracket-lamp is one of theirs, as are the artisan's lamp and others which follow. The adjustable nickel reflector shown in the artisan lamp enables the person using it to concentrate the light just where he wants it. For sewing, reading, or most mechanical operations, this lamp is a very helpful auxiliary.

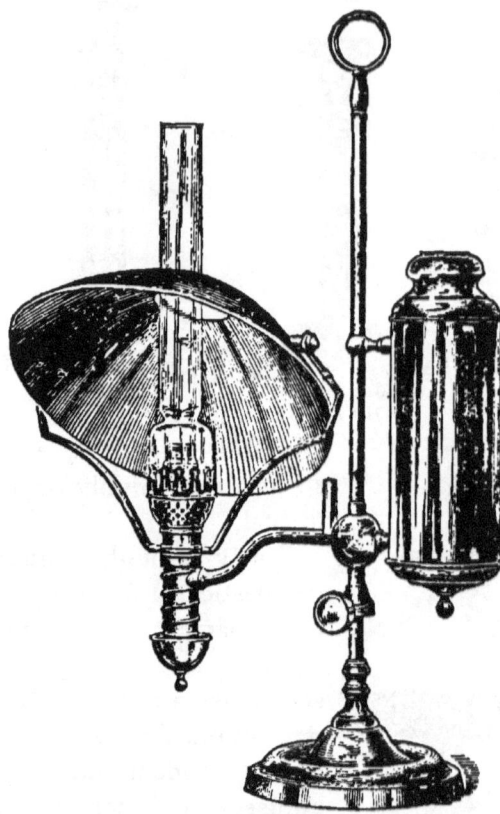

ARTISAN'S LAMP.

But student-lamps are popular in libraries and sitting-rooms. For such uses something more elaborate is desired, and all that can be wished for is found in the Parlor Student-Lamp. For real elegance nothing could be better, and for illuminating power it is rated as equal to thirty-three wax candles, which would make bright a room of great capacity.

Parlor lamps in other patterns of surpassing beauty are numerous, two of them with richly ornamented globes being shown on the following page. All these lamps are made in fine cast or wrought brass and form exquisite decorations.

When gas is introduced into a house, the possibilities afforded in the fixtures are very fine, as will be illustrated farther on under the head of "Home Decoration." The facilities for the home manufacture of gas are many and very satisfactory.

Gas machines are designed especially for the illumination of buildings beyond the reach of public gas works. They can be adapted for large factories and hotels as also for private houses. In the

PARLOR STUDENT-LAMP.

Springfield Gas Machine gas is produced by bringing a current of air in contact with gasoline, the vapors of which combine with the air and produce a clear, white, agreeable gas, which is distributed as common gas by similar fixtures. The apparatus, as will be seen by the engravings which follow, consists of two instruments—an air-pump, operated by a weight being used to produce the air-current, and a gas-generator (a cylinder containing evaporating-pans or chambers, in which the gasoline is kept). The generator is always placed in a vault under ground and removed from

ELEGANT PARLOR-TABLE LAMPS.

the building a safe distance; or it may be buried in the earth, in which case the expense of the arched vault is saved. The air-pump is usually stationed in the cellar of the building to be lighted. Supposing a machine to be set up and connected by pipes, as shown, the generator to be filled with gasoline, and the weight of the pump wound up, the process of gas-making is as follows: The action of the pump draws a supply of air through the induction-pipe from without the building and forces it through the air-pipe leading to the gas-generator. In its passage through the generator it becomes carbureted, thus forming an illuminating gas that is returned by the gas-pipe from the top of the generator to the burners within the building.

GAS-GENERATOR IN VAULT
(Distant from House Fifty Feet or more).

The machine is automatic in its operation. Gas is made only as fast as consumed. When the burners are shut off the pump stops and the manufacture of gas ceases, but immediately commences when they are opened again. The gas-generator is recharged

AIR-PUMP (in Cellar of House).

whenever exhausted—usually once in from three to six

months, varying according to the rapidity of the consumption of gas. Gauges upon the generator show at any time the amount of fluid it contains and when necessary to replenish it. A double-way cock connecting with both the filling and vent-pipes in the vault is used, so that of necessity a free vent is given while filling, thus preventing any backward pressure of gas upon the pump or strain upon the generator. The weight of the pump does not require winding, commonly, oftener than once or twice a week, and this takes but a moment's time.

The pressure of gas in the ordinary gas works is so strong that there is an immense waste at the burners and at every possible crevice for escape. It is wise to turn the gas wholly off during the day, using for this purpose a connection between the meter and the street, so preventing all waste. Even at night the full pressure should not ordinarily be allowed. When the burners are lighted as may be desired for the evening, turn down the valve at the meter until the gas flame just shows the effect. This may cut off nearly half the flow of gas, and yet the light remain ample. A great reduction of gas-bills will be secured in this way. You will get the benefit of all you pay for, as no gas will escape unconsumed.

When light is desired all night in a bedroom, by all means use tapers. A box of these, costing ten cents, can be bought at the apothecaries, and will last many weeks. Each box contains a tiny socket, or circle, of tin with three sharp points holding a bit of cork. Into this socket sets a button-mold a quarter of an inch in diameter, with a hole in the middle, in which is inserted a bit of waxed wicking. The whole affair, not larger in circumference than a walnut, floats on the surface of a cup or tumbler full of lard-oil, and gives a very soft and pleasant light, and is perfectly safe and wholesome.

V.—SANITARY CONDITIONS.

THERE is much sickness in these days which passes as Bilious, Typhoid, or Malarial Fevers. The inciting causes of disease are not easily determined. There are physical conditions which predispose to disease. Often these are wholly independent of the immediate cause under which the patient succumbs. In other cases, the final crash is only an advanced stage of the derangement which has gone forward steadily under continuous inciting causes. This is the case in that class of diseases to which reference has been made.

When a good housewife sees any of her charge losing appetite, vigor, color, and ambition, it is certain that some evil influence is at work, for which thorough search should at once be made. It may be that poisonous gases are creeping up the waste-pipe of the permanent wash-basin. It may be that the bath-room is belching forth death. It may be that the cistern whence the drinking-water comes is receiving pollution from surface drainage or from some hidden flow of vileness. It may be that noxious gases are exuding from the ground itself, " made ground," perhaps, into which filth of all sorts has been dumped. It may be that a drain-pipe is broken or leaking, and that the soil about the house is becoming saturated with waste waters, which ferment and putrefy, and send up deadly vapors, even from beds of flowers. These are a few of the insidious ways in which sewer gas and other poisonous influences do their work.

41

When water is introduced into a house its drainage must be perfect. Every opening from the pipes must be so "trapped" that gases cannot work back into the house. Scientific plumbing alone can secure this point. The best made trap may be so set that the water will syphon out of it, and leave no "water-seal" to stop the ingress of sewer gases. If this be properly arranged gas will not force back through the water except under pressure, as when a heavy rain storm fills the sewers. To meet this liability, every trap should have a ventilating pipe from its arch, or the side away from the opening into the house. This pipe must be carried to the roof, and there left open. All the gases will thus find vent. A still better plan is to carry the soil-pipe directly to the roof, capping it to exclude storm, but not to restrict the outflow of gas. Scrupulous cleanliness and frequent disinfecting of the pipes by copperas, dissolved in hot water, are essential. In a few hours the water of the seal will absorb gases so as to become in itself a source of impurity. What is known as "seat ventilation" is the best remedy for this, or frequent flushing.

Filters will separate material impurities from drinking-water, but the deadliest ingredients are not removable in this way. The only remedy for a well that receives impurity from the depths is to fill it up. If impure from surface drainage, cement and better grading may save it. Chemical analysis alone can detect the subtle poisons which often lurk in water. Some most sparkling and beautiful waters are rank poison. If suspicious of water and unable to provide a sure remedy, use rain water. It lacks the life of good spring water, but it also lacks the death that always lurks in city wells and generally in those of villages and rural settlements.

Cellars are nearer akin to graves than many suspect. Good, hard, impenetrable cement floors and walls are essential in most localities. Noxious influences lurking in the soil and oozing thence can be hermetically sealed down by no other means. An abundance of whitewash is good for a cellar. Frequent sweeping and airing, with the careful removal of decaying vegetables or fruits, must be added.

If suspicious of drainage, dig and see. A leaky pipe, even when several feet under ground, has cost many a life. Allow no marshy places, no pools of stagnant water, no compost heaps, or other foul spots upon your home premises. Do not allow the earth about the kitchen door to be saturated with slops thrown out. Make other disposition of such refuse. Cleanliness is akin to godliness and also to healthfulness.

In a drain for a private house a four-inch pipe is sufficient. It is better than one twice the size, as the flow is more concentrated and powerful. Straight lines and even descents are always desirable. Every deviation presents an obstacle and invites stoppage. The jointing must be very perfect, or it will check solid material, causing stoppage and leakage, with their long train of expense and sickness. To prevent the slow flow of water, which is apt to result in stoppage in drain pipes, flushing tanks have been invented. These operate on a syphon principle, emptying the tank at intervals with a rush of water which sweeps all *debris* before it.

The latest conclusions in scientific drainage require an air-pipe to connect with every trap of the drainage system, on the sewer side of the curve, so that when water goes down the soil-pipe with a rush, it will not syphon the water out of the traps. It usually does this because the rush of water creates a momentary vacuum into which the water of the traps is forced by the atmospheric pressure behind it. This air-pipe, when introduced, supplies air to the vacuum, and so prevents syphoning and its consequent ill effect of a trap without water, which leaves an open passage for sewer gases.

But, after all, it remains true that all the modern systems of interior drainage are liable to imperfection.   There will be some putrefaction, and, consequently, some development of those insidious germs of disease now known so surely to lie at the foundation of all contagion and infection.   To hit the death-blow to these, or indeed to prevent their ever coming to vitality, an apparatus known as the " Germicide " (germ-killer) has been invented, and is strongly indorsed.

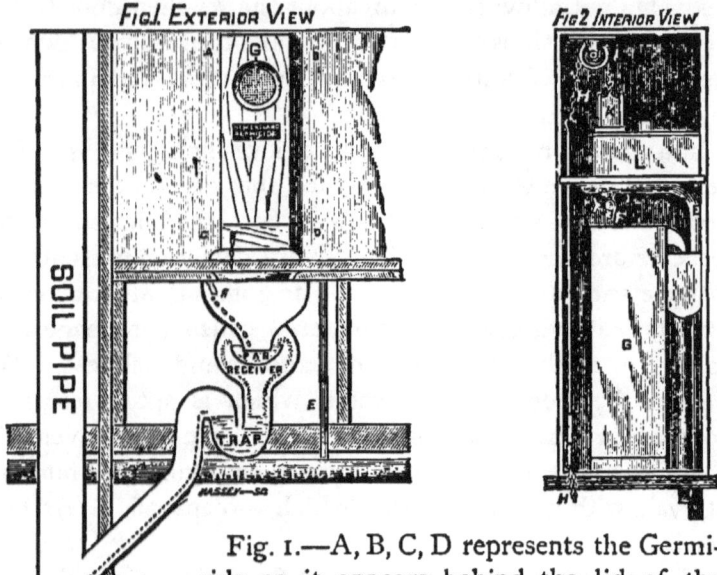

Fig. 1.—A, B, C, D represents the Germicide as it appears behind the lid of the closet, being nearly concealed when the lid is raised.   E is the pipe which carries water from the "water-service pipe" into the appliance where chloride of zinc is gradually dissolved and conducted into the basin, dropping from the pipe F, as indicated by the dotted lines.

Fig. 2 represents the interior of the Germicide.   The pipe E conducts water through the faucet F into the compartment G, which contains chloride of zinc in solid form, and from whence it escapes as a solution, dropping into the basin as indicated. The chain H, attached to the closet-lid, passes over the pulley I, actuates the plunger K, causing it to enter the thymol compartment L whenever the closet-lid is opened and to be withdrawn whenever the lid is closed. The plunger, being clothed with an absorbent, becomes saturated with thymol solution when lowered, and when raised liberates thymol vapor through the circular aperture G.

The Germicide requires no attention whatever from the inmates of the house, as it is always under the supervision of the Company's uniformed, experienced inspectors. The appliance remains always the property of the Company, and is placed for service at such an annual rental for inspection and supply of chemicals as to bring it within the means of the most humble householder. It is neatly encased in black walnut and is attached without interference with the plumbing of a house. Germicide Companies are located in New York, Cincinnati, Chicago, Boston, Philadelphia, etc.

On the need of a disinfecting agent in every drainage system of a house, Professor Joseph C. Richardson, of the University of Pennsylvania, thus speaks :

" The true method of obviating this danger is by sterilizing with slow currents or drippings of solutions of sulphate of iron, corrosive sublimate, arsenic, carbolic acid, etc., the whole interior of our waste-pipes, just as the shores of the Dead Sea and the banks of certain small streams are sterilized by mineral ingredients or poisonous metallic substances from manufacturing refuse, with which their waters are mingled. . . . I am confident that the key to this momentous problem of how to avoid infection from ' sewer gas,' or, more correctly, sewer air, entering our dwellings, is to be found in the principle of so sterilizing the whole interior of all pipes communicating with sewers, and, if possible, of the sewers themselves (by frequently irrigating them with fluids containing metallic compounds poisonous to plant life), that no vegetable organisms can propagate within them."

Cold air driving in at cracks and crevices of a room may not endanger health by introducing germs of disease, but, by creating drafts and reducing temperature, it may promote colds, coughs, pneumonia, and the long train of kindred ills. The plea that an open house promotes ventila-

SPRING BOTTOM-STRIPS FOR OUTSIDE OF DOORS.

tion is valid, without doubt, but out-of-doors is even better ventilated, yet no one greatly prefers to live there. Leakage at cracks is a certain inlet for dust and dirt also.

To rebuild doors and sashes is not practicable or necessary. The protection needed, can be had by neat weatherstripping, prepared in forms to meet all ordinary needs, as llustrated in the samples here shown.

These represent a short piece of each kind, drawn full size. They are neat wood moldings of walnut, oak, and painted pine, with a strip of vulcanized rubber inserted

FOR WINDOWS.

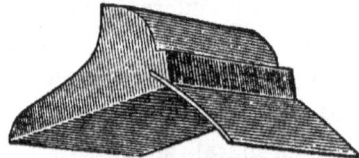

FOR JOINTS OF WINDOWS, ETC.

securely with Diamond Cement in grooves, at such angles as will insure the greatest efficiency. These strips require no additional painting, covering, or expense, as they are already nicely painted white or oiled, and are a permanent and ornamental fixture.

SECOND DEPARTMENT.

HOME FURNISHING.

Nothing worth having is to be had without expense either of time or money, but many of the best things in house decorating and furnishing are those that cost least.

CLARENCE COOK.

HOME FURNISHING.

IT is true that "Home is where the heart is." But some hearts are low in their tendencies, and are satisfied to tarry where others find no rest. There are hearts of refined quality and lofty aspiration. These dwell among life's better and nobler things. The best is none too good for them. They "covet earnestly the best gifts," and as opportunity allows they add one and another of these best things to their personal possessions.

Some have a passion for clothes; some for jewelry; some for books; but the true housewife desires that her home, "be it ever so humble," shall at least be clean, neat, and tasteful. She asks how others live; how the homes of those more favored of fortune are furnished; how her own little abode may be made more home-like, more lovely, more cozy. Such questions deserve answer.

Decoration has more to do with many homes than the furnishing has. It puts the finishing touches on the furnishing. It embellishes the home. But furnishing can lay a good foundation for decoration. It can prepare the way splendidly.

Forms of beauty may be introduced into every part of a house. Standard furniture is everywhere made with this idea in view. Every furniture store of any advancement shows it. The time was when the "Cottage" setsled the market.

49

These were sold at low prices, and they were in many cases really beautiful. The coloring and decoration, as well as the lines of the work, were artistic. They formed a good basis for decoration.

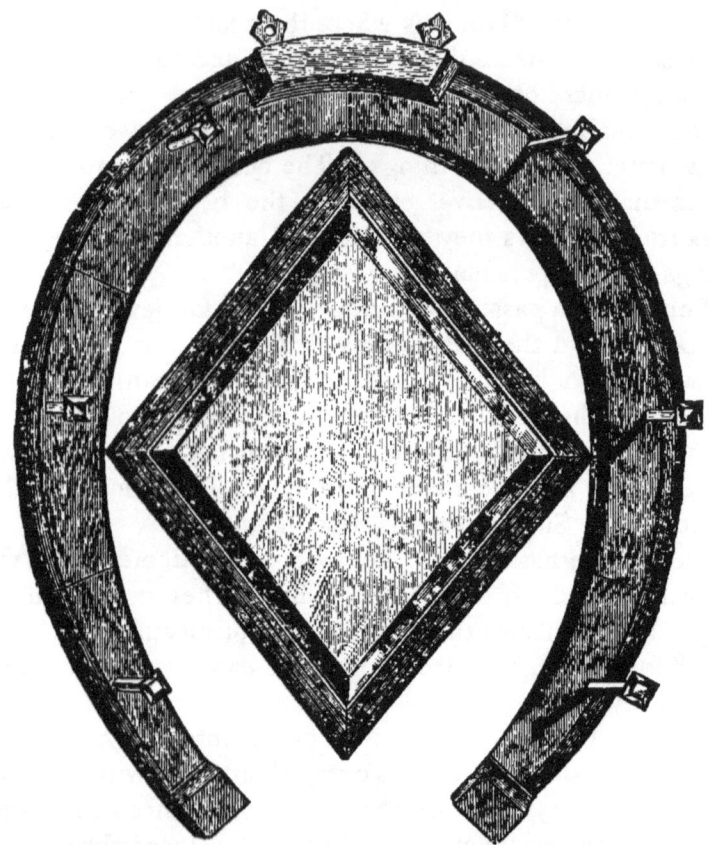

"GOOD LUCK" HAT, CANE, AND WHIP RACK.

Natural woods, finished in their natural colors, are now the style. And who shall say they are not a correct style. Nature's beautiful graining and colors, left in her own woods, are surely not to be buried under paint and imitations of nature.   All hail to the native woods in their own native colorings, therefore! Correct taste bids them welcome in standard and in special furniture.

With special furniture only can these pages deal. The woods most used in standard furniture are ash, chestnut, and walnut. In special furniture, the splendid old mahogany, the rose-wood and satin-wood, with fire-gilt metal, are

"FAN" HAT AND COAT RACK.

now the leading materials. Standard furniture now contains turned work, molded work, and carved work, sometimes running the cost of a bed-room suite to ten, twelve, and fifteen hundred dollars. The special furniture combines all these resources of the art, and adds special taste, artistic study of effects, the combining of the truly beautiful with the really useful.

American art furniture is now manufactured by skilled arti-
sans in all the leading cities. From their choicest supplies the
accompanying illustrations of this subject have been chosen.
How superior to ordinary hall racks are either of the three
shown? Finely finished in mahogany or ebonized woods,
with brass pins and a superior mirror, they are all that the

"GEM" HAT AND COAT RACK.

most elegant hall requires. The largest of them is thirty
inches wide by thirty-seven high.

Corresponding with these glasses and racks are hall tables
to place beneath to receive wraps and hats, while at the ends
are cane and umbrella racks. An ordinary table with a
heavy covering or a plain cloth, if desired, may stand beneath
these racks.

Passing into the house from the hall or entry-way, the parlor naturally receives the first attention. As managed in the average American home, this is the most costly and the least useful of all rooms. The cabinetmaker usually rules here and sways his sceptre with unquestioned supremacy. Whatever works of art or objects of beauty creep into these parlors are ill-assorted, if of value, though they are more frequently both valueless and destitute of beauty. A careful fur-

"CANTERBURY."
A Stand for Music—Mahogany, Walnut, or Ebonized.

nishing of a parlor would, for the sums usually spent there, give honest hard-wood furniture, beautifully fashioned and upholstered, a few choice photographs or steel engravings, and in many cases a good painting or two by a reputable artist. The Rogers Groups and some other inexpensive pieces of statuary are ranked as works of art and are freely admitted where good taste holds sway.

Parlors generally have too little that suggests ease. Window-shades are stiff, square, and mechanical ; while curtains, especially if falling from rings and a rod rather than from an angular cornice, are full of ease and grace. Hard wood is not suggestive of ease in chairs, sofas, etc., nor is cane-seating. We need a liberal share of cushioning on all such articles. This invites to repose and furnishes comfort. It does away with the stiffness which in so many parlors pro-

MUSIC PORTFOLIO IN VARIOUS WOODS.

claims the room to be not meant for use. So furnish this room that its appearance will invite to use. And this use should be of the festal, joyous sort, rather than of the laborious, meditative kind. Here is the place for the piano or organ, for the illustrated books, for a neat cabinet of bric-a-brac, or good curiosities, though neither of these must be overdone. The parlor is neither a library nor a museum, but works of art may be admitted there, and books which charm by their beautiful exteriors as well as by their cuts and their literary contents. Books for this purpose should be choice selections, standard poems, and new and attractive books.

The carpeting of a parlor has much to do with its attractiveness. Of course, the expense involved often becomes the prime consideration. But ingrain carpets present many very beautiful combinations at low figures. Passing upward into the various grades of Brussels and Axminsters, the highest taste

CARVED PEDESTAL.
For Statuary—Walnut, Mahogany, or Ebonized.

may be gratified and the longest purses taxed. But in any case aim at a beautiful result. Do so in the materials and

styles employed in upholstering furniture. It should harmonize and beautify both the wood used and the carpets
laid. Cherry and mahogany furniture is not best set off by
crimson reps or damasks, nor are ebony and black walnut
best shown by dark coverings. Light and bright colored
woods show best with dark and rich colored goods, while
the darkest woods best display
the brightest colorings and
textures.

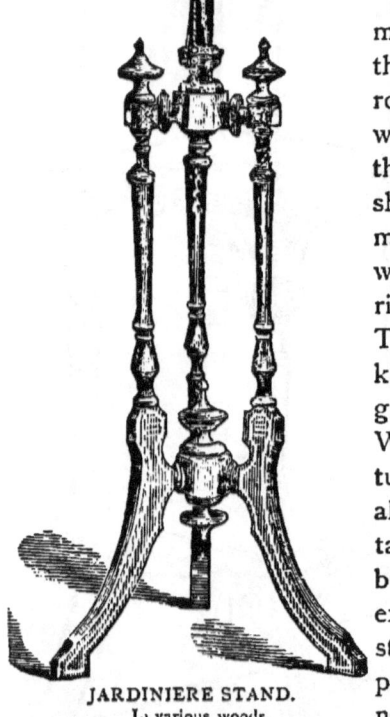

JARDINIERE STAND.
In various woods.

If the walls are papered, it
must be with due regard to
the other appointments of the
room. Such combinations as
will make all the contents of
the room help each other
should be sought out. Where
many paintings adorn the
walls, the papering must be
rich but subdued in colors.
The finest work of art may be
killed by the flashy background on which it is hung.
Where there are but few pictures, or where engravings
alone appear, the paper may
take on rich forms and colors,
but it should never run to
excess. Loud, glaring, flashy
styles may be suitable for
public places, but they are
not for cozy homes. To secure
what is right, consult your best paper-hanger; try samples;
do not decide at once or off-hand; weigh the subject; sleep
over it; thus you will probably reach a decision that will be
a permanent satisfaction.

Now that this company-room, or best living-room as it had better be considered, is carpeted and papered, what furnishing shall it contain? Sofas and chairs? Yes, but not of stiff, uncomfortable, regulation patterns. A neat lounge is preferable to a stiff sofa. Even the old-fashioned wooden settees can be made really comfortable by cushions on the seat, against the back, and on the ends. These should be of brightly colored goods; chintz will do, though reps, cretonnes, or special goods are better. Do not stuff the cushions with cut straw or any other substance that will shift position and leave one sitting on the hard wood directly; but use fine corn husk or some other cheap material, if not disposed to procure hair. Make the cushions square, and tuft them to keep the filling in place; run light braid around the corners for adornment; then tie the cushions in place by strong braid or tape,

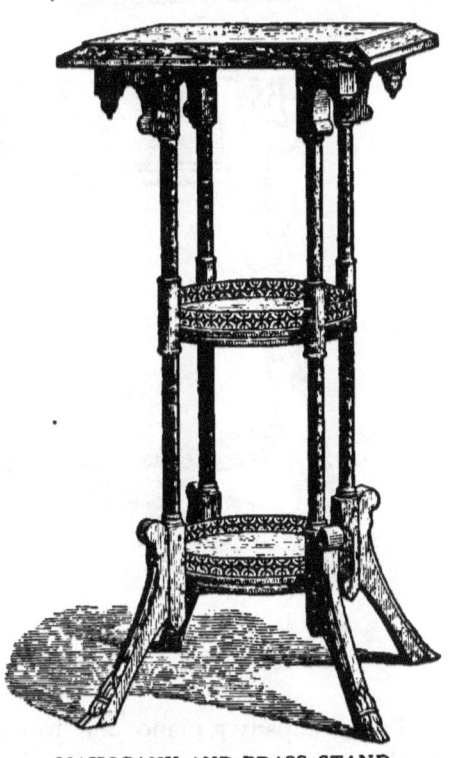

MAHOGANY AND BRASS STAND.

which should be out of sight. In this way an old-style settee can be transformed into a thing of beauty and a minister of comfort.

One of the prettiest tables for a parlor, library, or sitting-room, and one that is highly artistic as well as of historic interest, has been designated the "Shakespeare Table," being

fashioned after one still shown in the former home of the famous old bard. The cut shows the square Shakespeare table,
but it is made oblong also in two sizes, and in mahogany,
ebony, walnut, and ash. For the ornamental covers now so
generally used on tables, this style is specially adapted. It
is entirely free from the top-heavy appearance and unstable
condition of many ornamental tables in general use.

COOPER'S SHAKESPEARE TABLE.

To accompany a piano and to retain music and music-
books in good order a very handsome piece of furniture,
"The Canterbury," shown in a previous cut, is just suited.
It can be had in a variety of styles and in woods finished to
match the ordinary standard pianos. Another contrivance
for similar purposes and very beautiful in construction is
shown on the page following the "Canterbury." It is made

in different woods and is known as the "Music Portfolio."
What a beautifully ornamental piece of furniture it is a
glance at the engraving will show.

We have also shown a highly ornamental carved pedestal,
on the upper stage of which a piece of statuary may be
placed, the tops being varied in size to suit different pieces.
On the lower stages other ornaments may be placed, with
books, flowers, or bric-a-brac, as necessity may require or
as taste may suggest.

Similar in purpose, but of far lighter construction, is the
Jardiniere stand. For floral displays, card receivers, statuettes, and such articles, it is most beautifully adapted. Its
structure is so light and
graceful that it pleases the
eye and gratifies the taste
of every observer.

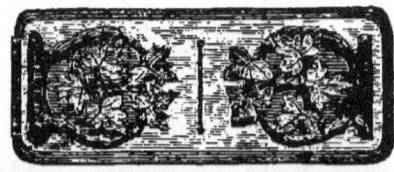

Other forms of beauty ap-
pear in the department of
stands and tables. One constructed in dark wood and
fire-gilt metal is next shown.
It meets all the require-
ments for small stands of this

BOOK-RACKS.

character. The use of brass ornaments is coming more and
more into vogue also, so that this construction is fully up
to the times.

When books are displayed in a parlor or sitting-room,
the large ones may lie upon the table, but the smaller ones
should be placed in book-racks which hold them in position
neatly with their backs upward. Two of these racks are
shown in cuts given above. The ornamental ends of the
racks turn upward upon hinges and are capable of longitu-
dinal extension, so that few books or many, as may be
required, can be held in proper position by this means.
They are entirely in style.

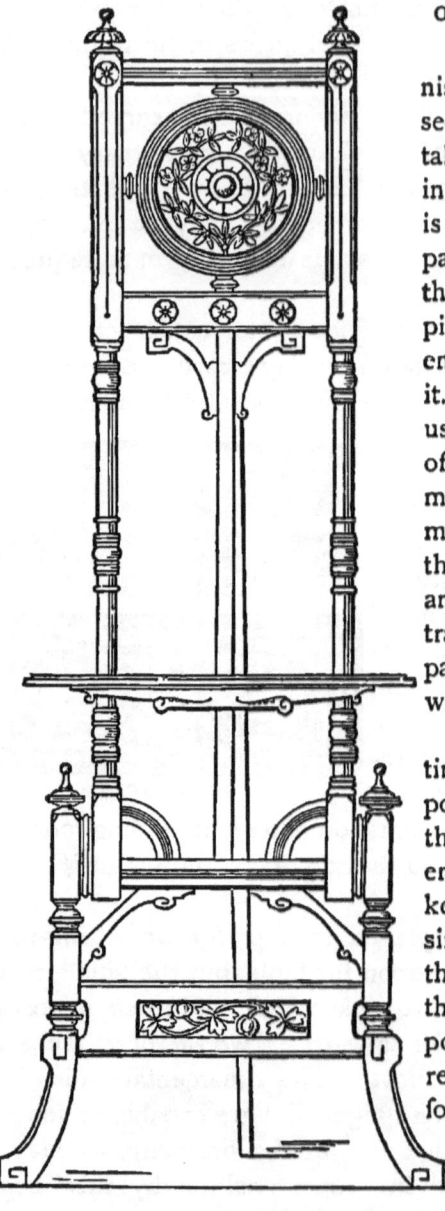

ORNAMENTAL EASEL.

A fine corner-furnishing for a parlor is secured in an ornamental easel, one of which in very beautiful form is shown in the accompanying cut. Of course, the easel implies a picture or handsome engraving to rest upon it. Because of this use, an easel should be of dark wood, ornamented only in the matter of carving, so that it shall not present any dominating or detracting colors in comparison with a picture which may rest upon it.

Easels are sometimes finished with a portfolio or pocket at the lower part in which engravings may be kept. When it is desired to show these, they are placed upon the shelf above the pocket, and afterward returned to the pocket for safe keeping This receptacle presents an ornamental front.

A library or reading-room should be studiously fitted for its purpose. All glaring colors should be avoided as injurious to the eye and tending to divert from work. Green and oak are favorite colors for the library, though dark brown and walnut answer well. Arrangements for light by day or by night must be scrupulously regarded. It should

LADIES' WORKSTAND.
Thirty-three inches high, made in various woods.

never shine in the student's face, but always upon his work in such direction that the shadow of the hand shall not obscure the page in writing.

Doors are little used upon book-cases. The backs of the books do well enough without their protection, and dust

26

may be kept from the upper ends of the books by a strip of fancy colored leather attached to the edge of the shelf, and hanging a little below it, so as to reach the tops of the books. If this be "pinked," as is not unfrequent, it is apt to curl up and fail of its purpose. It is better to use a strip with a plain edge, ornamenting it with gold stamping.

ELABORATE WALL CABINET.
Thirty-seven inches in extreme dimensions. In various woods, with French mirror.

Unless the books are very numerous, let the book-case be low, say five feet only in height, so affording shelf room on their tops where ornaments or heavy books may be disposed, and over which pictures, brackets, wall-pockets, and ornamental articles may be placed. The lowest shelves of the cases are best wrought into a row of drawers, as dust from the floor soils books which are so near it. Whether a table or a desk be preferable depends on the leading purpose for which the room is used. A cylinder desk which may be entirely closed is best where private papers are liable to be disturbed. For most home uses, however, this is not needful.

Carpeting, paper-hanging, curtains, and other accessories of the room should be in keeping with its general purpose and plan. If there is a low-down grate or fireplace, it should be done in tiles. The mantle should be of carved wood to match the furniture, surmounted with light shelving at either end for books and ornaments. A mirror may be placed over the centre. Restful chairs, a comfortable lounge, a student's lamp, and such appliances find appropriate places in this room.

BRIC-A-BRAC SHELF.
In various woods. Beveled mirror.

The library may be combined with the ladies' sitting-room, unless it is needed as a real study. If devoted to the double use, a ladies' workstand, such as has already been shown, is quite in place. This is suitable in any room where it will serve as a convenience. Hanging cabinets or brackets, which are abundantly illustrated in previous pages, are admissible in the library. Their contents are illustrative of beauty and art. They are object lessons on topics which many books in the library are fairly presumed to discuss. The scrap-basket on some of the beautiful patterns illustrated under home decoration is appropriate in the library. Wall pockets and pocket easels are numerous and beautiful, and they, too, naturally belong here. As receptacles of newspapers, letters, etc., they are just in place. But they must not be allowed to degenerate into rubbish holders. They may gather papers for a week, or some such short period, but they must be overhauled frequently, or they will offend good taste, which is always allied to neatness.

HANGING CABINET.
In various woods. Beveled mirror.

A rich wall bracket, or a corner bracket, is admissable in any room, and may be used for many purposes. Our illustrations of these embody the stag's head. Uniformity in the pattern of brackets for a given room may be followed, or, with equal propriety, it may be disregarded. Nor is it important in the incidental decorations of a room that the prevailing wood of the furniture be followed. Variety may be admitted with all readiness, provided that it is not carried to the extent of evident and glaring incongruity.

Concerning the dining-room, a fine writer on domestic affairs speaks thus: " Probably there is no better test of the refinement of a family than the relation of its dining-room to the rest of the house. If the family meal is regarded as a mere feeding, the place where it is taken will plainly show the fact. If the meal be a cheerful household ceremony, where the best qualities of head and heart engage, and to which the most honored friends are gathered, these facts, too, will be indicated by the room."

STAG'S HEAD CORNER BRACKET.

The central object of the dining-room is the table. It should be on the extension principle, and between meals it should be covered with a rich colored cloth. To set the table for the next meal as one is cleared away may save labor, but it savors of untidiness, for the dust must gather upon cloth and dishes in the interval. True, the laid table may be covered to protect it. Dining-room chairs should be covered with leather. A lounge or a rocking-chair is out of place in this room. It is not the place to lounge nor even to sit, except at meal times.

STAG'S HEAD WALL BRACKET.

Ornamental wood floors are much used in dining-rooms. Linen rugs are laid on these to subdue the hardness of the tread. Carpets are not regarded as out of place there, but they are not essential if the floor be of the proper sort. The papering varies with changing styles and differing tastes. More coloring is admitted to the dining-room papers than elsewhere, because high colors in their decorations are not deemed best. Engravings, carvings, statuary, and paintings in some cases, are admitted to elegant dining-apartments. Some disapprove of the introduction of subjects connected with food, such as game, poultry, fruit, etc., in dining-room decorations, but good usage holds to this line, nevertheless, and with eminent fitness.

ORNAMENTAL POCKET EASEL.

In the superb dining-hall of the Lick House, of San Francisco, art has done its best. Columns, carvings, stained glass, and painting combine to make it simply magnificent. Immense pictures of Pacific coast scenery fill the panels around the room between its clustering columns. It is undoubtedly a superb hall, but no guest can appreciate the display as he sits at his own seat, and no refined guest wishes to be craning his neck this way and that, to see all these gems of the painter's art. Nor does a lover of art wish to parade around the room and study the pictures while others are at their meals; nor does he wish so to do while the servants are preparing the room and the tables for the meals. The fact is, that in this sumptuous room art has gone astray. A dining-room is not a picture gallery.

The conspicuous piece of furniture in a dining-room is the sideboard or buffet. Its possibilities are well-nigh illimitable. Ancestral plate, if there be any, may repose here in its venerable dignity. If you have none such, bright china, glassware, lacquer work, and natural fruit or flowers will do full well. It is worth while to study effect in this article of furniture, for it is the one article at which your guests will look. A wooden top to your buffet is safer for the glassware than one of marble. Valuable glass and china will inevitably be chipped and marred if set frequently upon marble.

When a meal is in progress good taste allows the finger bowls to stand ready for use on the buffet. Each should be on a plate with a small doiley under it. Harlequin

ROMAN HANGING-LAMP.
Recovered from Ancient Ruins.

sets of finger bowls, no two being of the same color, but all bright and beautiful, are now in style, and they ornament the buffet very richly. High glass dishes cut into diamond points are also highly ornamental, especially if the buffet be well lighted, which it should be. Natural flowers are a welcome adornment on the buffet as well as upon the table, but they should be very choice and of delicate odor.

The gas-fixtures or lamps of a dining-room go far to beautify it. An unending variety is at command, with all shapes and colors of shades or globes, and untold variety in the fixtures themselves. Be careful even in the choice of a table lamp, for these can be had in forms of exquisite beauty. Terra-cotta lamp stands, beautifully embossed and colored, are now exceedingly popular. Lamp shades are sold in a variety of hues, or white shades are covered with tasty paper covers, so that inexpensive decoration is within the reach of all, even though they shrink from the more costly articles.

Bed-room sets can be had in good wood and in elegant

PLAIN BED-ROOM SET IN NATURAL COLORS OF WOOD.

finish at very low prices. In making selections attend carefully to the mirror on your bureau. Test its clearness by holding a white card beside it and noting whether the reflection is darker than the original. Test the thickness by lightly tapping with the knuckles. A good glass will give back a solid sound; a thin one will be tinny. Be sure the glass does not distort its objects. A poor mirror is a constant annoyance. Marble tops cost more than others. They are liable to injure brittle objects which may be set upon them, and the style now is to entirely cover the top with various lace goods and other materials of fine texture and beautiful color. Wood, hence, is preferable to marble.

Have a good spring bed covered by a mattress of hair. This may cost more at the outset, but it will last long and give constant satisfaction. Considering that about one-third of life is spent in bed, it is worth while to make the bed the best possible. Then, too, our hours of suffering are spent there, and there we expect to die.

In getting up a mattress do not have it in one great mass. Do not have it in two long sections, either, as a joint down the middle never answers well. Make it in two parts—one the square of the bedstead's width, the other to occupy the remaining space. The square part can readily be turned in the bedstead, so that each side of it shall in turn be at the head of the bed. It may then be shifted to the foot and the smaller section come to the head. Each part may be turned over also, so that a new combination may be made each month for a year, and the gullies usually worn in mattresses may be wholly avoided.

Quiet colors are best for the bed-room, both in carpets and on the walls. No object should be admitted there that is not an object of beauty. What the eye catches last at night and first in the morning, what it dwells on continuously in sickness and exhaustion, should be an object inspiring peace, good-will, and placid joy. Heavy curtains or shades are needed at the windows, that light and heat and noise may be excluded when one is sick or needs to sleep in daytime. All that is in the sleeping-room should be neat and beautiful. Beautiful forms are no more costly than those which are homely, and they pay far better, for Keats has truly said:

"A thing of beauty is a joy forever."

Utility may also be happily blended with beauty. What could be more beautiful as an article of furniture than the parlor cabinet here shown. It contains shelves and spaces for ornaments. The carved work is in the highest and most modern style. The finish and workmanship are

PARLOR CABINET.

of the best. This cabinet can be furnished in walnut or in ebony finish with gold lines. The centre panel is fitted with a beveled French mirror twenty inches by thirty-four. All the lines of this cabinet will bear close study. They are lines of beauty.

But now comes the practical side. An irruption of company comes upon you. Or you have not the bedroom you really need, and sickness disarranges the natural order. Or you have a cottage by the sea or elsewhere, and company comes. You go to your cabinet; you set aside the ornaments from the front shelves; you manipulate it skillfully

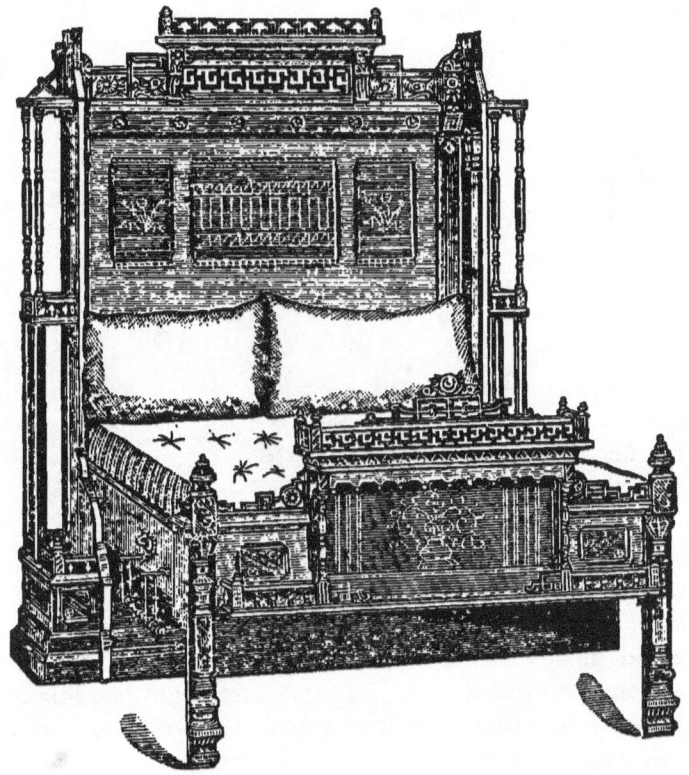

PARLOR CABINET BEDSTEAD.

for a moment, when lo! see the transformation presented by this second cut. You have a perfect, full-sized bedstead, with spring mattress and pillows, all evolved in a moment from the parlor cabinet. By this change the crown of the cabinet becomes an elaborate footboard; the front shelving and mirror drop underneath. A new and beautiful head-board is disclosed, and all is ready for the making up of the bed. The inside measurement of this sumptuous place of rest is fifty-two inches by seventy-six. The outside measure-ment of the closed cabinet is sixty-six inches by ninety-one.

This is the Champion Automatic Bedstead, invented and made in Philadelphia. It is offered in various sizes and styles and at various prices.

But a bedstead does not furnish a bed-room. True, but this beautiful parlor desk, which is shown also, will do for a wash-stand. Throw up its top, and you find a permanent basin and all its proper accom-paniments. Throw open the doors, and you find a portable reservoir into which the waste water drains, with drawers for towels and other convenien-ces. This article can

PARLOR DESK WASHSTAND.

be had in any of the standard woods, and may be finished in ebony and gilt if desired. It is fitted with hand-painted tiles, and is ornate as well as useful. A still more artistic desk washstand is shown on the following page.

In light, ornamental beauty it cannot be excelled. The most inquisitive observer would scarce suspect the extent of its practical value. It would detract nothing from the beauty of any parlor. Both these stands, or similar ones, can be furnished by any good dealer.

What may well be considered a masterpiece, however, is known as the "Telescope Bedstead." When opened out it is as complete as that shown a few pages back. When closed it appears in various forms. The movement in opening this bedstead is simply a turning down of the lower part of the front so that it lies parallel with the floor. The slab or top becomes the foot-board, supported by the side ornaments of the front, which in the act of lowering come

PORTABLE RESERVOIR WASHSTAND.

into position as supporting feet. The part thus formed is then drawn outward to secure the full length, leaving a bedstead of full size, with spring bed, hair mattress, and bolster complete, and of the best quality.

These bedsteads are made in the *Chiffonier*, or bureau style; the desk style, bevel front and cylinder front; the sideboard style, the book-case style, and the ᵥrgan style. The desk style furnishes a very useful desk, with its inkstand so hung that it cannot be overturned by any move-

ment of the bedstead. The book-case style furnishes a good
sized book-case in its upper part, which is not disturbed by
adjusting the bed portion. It also contains a desk. The
sideboard pattern is shown in the first of the illustrations.
Its neat and attractive form commends itself. The height

TELESCOPE FOLDING BEDSTEAD.
Sideboard Pattern.

of this article is seventy-five inches; its width, fifty-nine
inches; its depth from front to back, twenty-six inches. Its
mirror is ten inches by twenty-four. All of these telescopic
bedsteads are made in plain finish, or are richly veneered,

handsomely carved, and embellished with ornaments, beveled mirrors, etc., as taste may demand or cost warrant.

TELESCOPE FOLDING BEDSTEAD.
Cylinder Desk Pattern.

A smaller size is made, furnishing a bed thirty-six inches wide, the larger bed being fifty-two inches in width.

The second illustration of this line is the cylinder desk

style. In dimensions it is about the same as the style just described. It is three inches deeper from front to back on account of the cylinder portion, which also includes a desk.

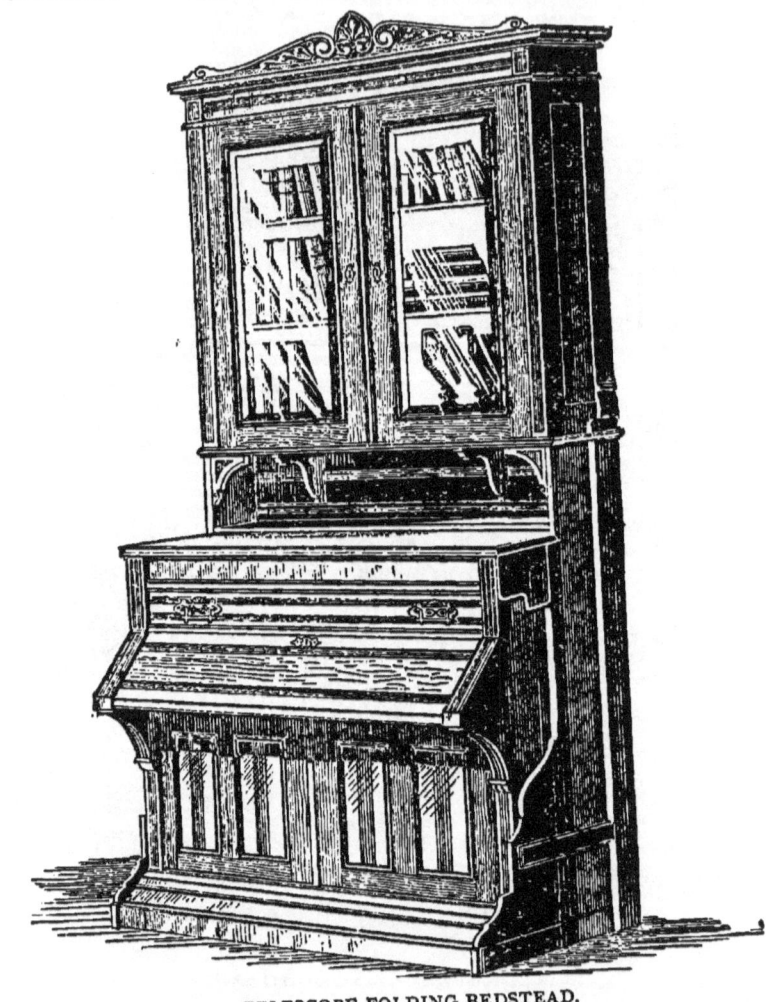

TELESCOPE FOLDING BEDSTEAD.
Book-case Pattern.

The upper portion is fitted with three beveled French mirrors. Other patterns of this style are offered.

The book-case style varies in height from the others, and in several respects combines more advantages than any of the line. Its desk and its book-shelf are both of practical

COMFORT AND BEAUTY COMBINED IN A LOUNGE.

value, and its general appearance is possibly less suggestive of a variety of uses than in the other styles.

The articles last described belong to a class known as " Combination Furniture." There is scarcely a limit to the possibilities of such articles. Tables are made which can be converted into armchairs and writing-desks; children's high chairs are to be transformed into low chairs with table attachments; ottomans can be changed into settees and armchairs; an armchair can be adapted for an invalid couch or a library chair with reading-stand, writing-desk, etc.; and so through unending varieties. The climax in combinations is capped, however, by a New York cabinetmaker,

27

who has exhibited a Secretary, which combines a bedstead, writing-desk, bookcase, washstand, wardrobe, medicine-chest, secret silver-closet, dressing-bureau, jewelry-case, and, as a finial to the whole, a musical and alarm clock. Such a combination would need a machinist to run it. It is overdone.

A nursery, or play-room, is indispensable where there are children in a home. It should have a hard wood floor, with a drugget or rug fastened at its centre. This can be removed easily for shaking or washing. Have no curtains or drapery in the room. Plain, dark shades will be best at the windows, so that light may be excluded wholly or admitted freely, as is desirable. A long, low table, the feet of which can be folded under, allowing the table to be placed out of the way, is just the thing for this room. Toys, books, strings, paper, pencils, and a good clock are needed. Have low chairs for the little ones as well as higher ones for the adults. Hang bright, cheery pictures on the walls. A blackboard and an assortment of colored crayons make lots of fun for children. Furnish one room at least where the little ones may romp at full liberty.

Easy chairs and good, comfortable lounges are in place almost everywhere. Do not be misled into purchasing the stiff, hard, cylindrical affairs on which one can neither sit or lie with comfort. Study the picture of a comfortable lounge, shown on the preceding page, and get one on that principle. The best furniture now shows little or no wood. What you save in fancy woods and polish, you can spend in upholstery. Try it. Make home so bright, so restful, so homelike that no place shall be like home.

Servants' rooms should be light and well ventilated. Good servants will not be satisfied with mean quarters. Iron bedsteads are recommended for these rooms but absolute cleanliness is more important. A bath-room for servants is very desirable. Many of them never knew the luxury of a thorough bath.

THIRD DEPARTMENT.

HOME DECORATION.

To make home what it should be—a cheerful, happy habitation, to which the absent members of a family may look with love, and to which the wanderer will always return with joy—we must have it not only clean, for cleanliness is next to godliness, and wholesome, which is another way of saying holy, but also beautiful. Refinement cannot go with sordidness and ugliness.

W. J. LOFTIE.

HOME DECORATION.

NEVER before was there so general an interest in the decoration of homes as there is to-day. A truer conception of what home should be is everywhere prevailing. It is not a mere barracks, where a family may congregate and sleep and eat, but it is a place of enjoyment and repose. To this end it must be filled with enjoyable and restful things; and the enjoyment and rest must rise to something better than the physical. The best powers of the soul must be delighted as they repose at home. Nothing which offends can be tolerated there. Beauty—which in the old Roman tongue was *decor*—is home's presiding genius. To *decor*-ate home is to bring it under beauty's sway.

Beauty means fitness, because it always rests upon a basis of utility. It is never unmeaning, but can always give a reason for its being. The first consideration, hence, is: What is good for certain persons, places, and seasons? What is beautiful in a palace is not so in a cottage; what is beautiful at a feast is not so at a funeral. Beauty and fitness ever go hand in hand.

Decorations may be fixed, forming part and parcel of the house itself; or they may be portable—capable of change in position or of entire removal. There are internal decorations and those external, and all these need attention.

81

I.—FIXED INTERNAL DECORATIONS.

IN treating of permanent decorations, floors first demand
attention. What shall we do with our floors? Floors
are not merely to walk on. They should please the eye
continually. Carpeting and oil-cloths have been the time-

TESSELLATED PAVEMENT IN WHITE AND BLACK MARBLES.

honored devices for beautifying floors, or, at least, for con-
cealing their unsightliness. But changes have come in
these usages.

ELEGANT FLOORING.

Beginning with the outer vestibule, or main hallway, of a
house, oil-cloth once reigned supreme. But oil-cloth fails.

Its colors arc soon worn off. It becomes puffed into ridges and it shrinks from the surroundings. It is at best only a patch, a sham. Three superior substitutes for it are now offered:

(1) Marble is used either in one uniform piece, or with borderings of other color; or it may be cut into squares, diamonds, etc. Nothing for a hall or vestibule can be superior to marble. The material and its style may be plain and quite inexpensive, or they may be of the richest grades, as shown on page 424, with surroundings of carving and sculpture, which run the cost into tens of thousands of dollars for a single entrance-way. Wainscoting should be in harmony with the flooring. One *motive* should rule each apartment. It should not seem that the

MARBLE STAIRCASE IN THE SULTAN'S NEW PALACE, CONSTANTINOPLE.

builder started with a grand idea, but ran out of funds and finished in a cheap way. The above illustration is not a pattern that many will imitate, but it is a model of harmony. Marble is the one rich material, and elegance breathes in every feature. Wooden balusters and handrail on this marble stairway would be a disgraceful inconsistency. Unity of purpose must prevail.

(2) Tiling and mosaic work take rank with marble, and may surpass it in cost. The most beautiful tiles in the world

are the Minton, manufactured in England, but represented in this country by Sharpless & Watts, Philadelphia. The elegance of this work is well illustrated by fine specimens in almost every grand home. These tiles are glazed, enameled, or plain. They are made in all desirable colors and shapes. Some are embossed, others printed, and the finest are painted by hand. Tiles are suitable for vestibules, hallways, wainscoting, hearths, facing and lining fireplaces and mantels, for bath-room walls and floors, for flower-boxes, panelings of doors, and ornaments in door casings. The choicest of them may be framed richly and serve as superb wall pictures. The decora-

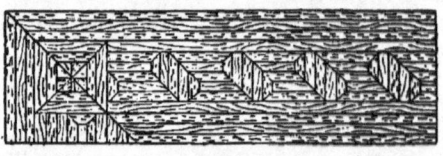

BORDERINGS AND CORNERS FOR INLAID FLOORS.

tive uses to which tiles are put are practically numberless.

Mosaic work differs from tiling in the smallness of its

pieces and the consequent increase of possibilities for artistic effects in their use. Its cost is proportionately greater, of course. There are many grades of tiles and mosaics, but the best will last a lifetime, and are worth all they cost.

(3) Inlaid floors are just the thing for dining-rooms and other much-used and more public rooms of the house. This work may be elaborate and very expensive, or it may be plain and of low price. Three methods of preparing these floors are followed. The first employs the ordinary tongued and grooved boards, laid diagonally or in other patterns; the second kind is made of pieces, usually seven-

FIRE-PLACE TILING IN MAJOR ANDRÉ'S ROOM, BEEKMAN MANSION, NEW YORK.

eighths of an inch thick, cut and fitted together in blocks of any desired patterns, in sections usually twelve or twenty-two inches square; the third method is to make up the design required from lumber one-quarter of an inch thick, glue the edges together, and then glue this pattern to a backing of hard wood. These are called *veneered* floors, and this is the style used in all elaborate designs, as it admits of much greater variety of patterns than either of the other methods. In Europe all such floors are known as Parquetry, or Marquetry, and their use is universal in the better houses.

A much cheaper and very satisfactory substitute for these forms of fancy floor-work is " Wood Carpeting," an invention of Mr. E. C. Hussey, an American architect. Agencies

WOOD-CARPET FILLINGS IN VARIOUS PATTERNS.

for this valuable article can be found in most of our cities. It is not, as many suppose, a temporary floor covering, to be laid down and taken up at pleasure, but a permanent new floor on top of the old one, and is carefully fitted into all the offsets and around all the projections of the room. It is firmly nailed down with small brads, and when finished has

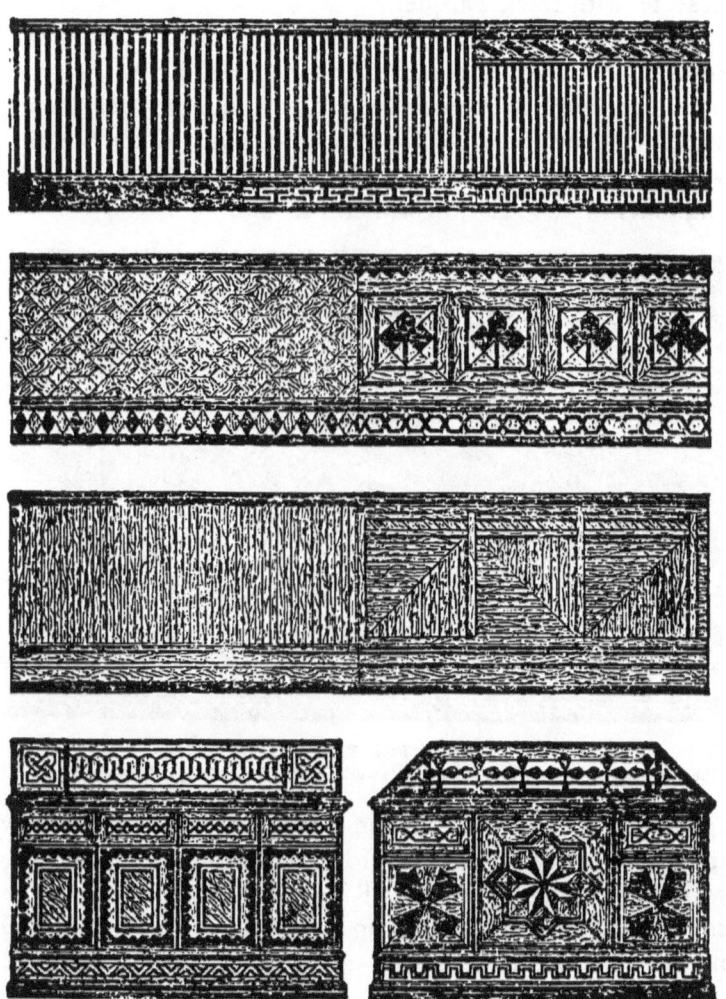

WOOD-CARPET PATTERNS FOR WAINSCOTING.

the effect of a thick European floor. It is made, however, in the same elaborate and beautiful designs by the process of gluing the wood on cloth, instead of to another piece of wood. So it is made at a much less cost, and occupies but one-quarter of an inch, instead of one inch or more in thickness, as with thick Parquet.

The common remark, " A bare floor is so cheerless," comes wholly from the impression given by an ordinary pine floor with its unsightly cracks, and from not having seen the effect of a well-laid Parquet floor, in combination with the furniture and other articles in keeping with the character of the room in which it is laid.

SCINDE RUG FOR FLOOR CENTRES.
[Characterized by borders with angular vine work. Prevailing colors, red, yellow, and blue.]

When rugs are used on the floor of a room—as is now the prevailing fashion—a border of wood only is laid, into which the rug fits exactly. Rug and border are about the same thickness, and so the rug is not liable to be displaced nor an unaccustomed foot to trip over it. There are three ways of finishing these floors.

1st. By giving them a good soaking coat of " Parquet oil." This should be renewed at least once a month. Apply with a rag and wipe off as dry as possible. The best substitute for " Parquet oil " is five parts of good, light mineral oil to one part of good, light Japan.

2d. By putting on two or three coats of best white shellac

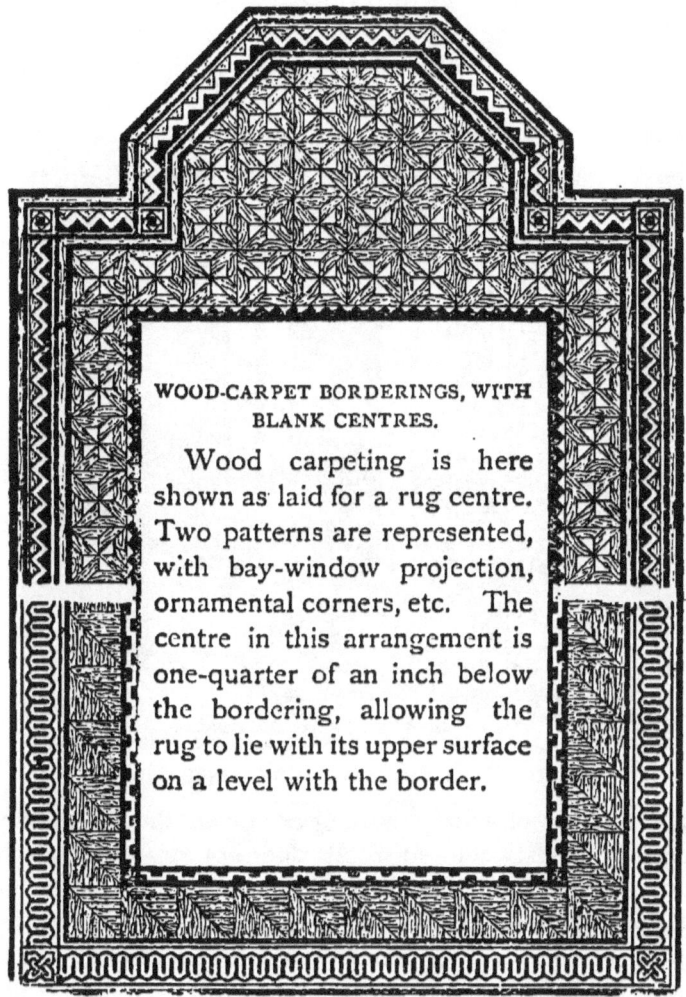

WOOD-CARPET BORDERINGS, WITH BLANK CENTRES.

Wood carpeting is here shown as laid for a rug centre. Two patterns are represented, with bay-window projection, ornamental corners, etc. The centre in this arrangement is one-quarter of an inch below the bordering, allowing the rug to lie with its upper surface on a level with the border.

with a brush. Plane, scrape, sand-paper, punch the nails and putty up in a most thorough manner before shellacing, and sand-paper lightly after each coat but the last.

3d. By waxing. This is the European plan, and if persevered in, as there, is the best known finish for floors. Use pure white beeswax dissolved in best deodorized benzine with gentle heat, or in turpentine. Apply while warm to the floor with a rag, then polish with a heavy waxing brush thoroughly. The brush must be used often and well to get and maintain a good polish and the desired smoothness.

WOOD-CARPET FLOORING AND WAINSCOTING.

Illustrations of wood-carpeting are given, though the fine effect of variously colored woods does not appear in a plain print. These floors should not be used in vestibules and halls, where they are exposed to the weather. Such places require marble or tiles which endure exposure and are in nowise injured thereby.

If these methods of beautifying are too expensive, the floors may be simply stained and polished. A cheap method of securing a neat floor is to cover it tightly with muslin and to cover this with an unobtrusive wall-paper. A border may be run around the edge and a good coat of varnish added. Dancing would mar such a covering; but if rugs be laid in the places of hardest wear, it will serve well and last long. This plan is especially adapted to a music-room, where clear, distinct sounds are desirable.

BEAUTIFUL WALLS.

After the floors, the walls come in for consideration. When papers can be had at prices so low and in styles so elegant as now, bare, cold walls in white-wash or paint are inexcusable. Indeed, they are extravagant — for better results can be had for far less expense. So elaborate have paper-hangings become that they are in great part supplanting the fresco-work formerly so much used in elegant houses. Wall hangings are offered at from eight or ten cents to twenty and twenty-five dollars a roll. Just now the pre-vailing taste is to the quieter forms and col-

ORNAMENTAL FRIEZE PATTERNS.
[Design by Fr. Beck & Co., New York.]

ors. The following illustration of a ceiling decoration in paper is from one of the most artistic establishments of New York. The quiet elegance of its forms are seen at a glance and the color effects would heighten it greatly. The leading producers of paper-hangings are sparing no pains to produce results which shall in all respects be artistic and elegant. One house offered three prizes, respectively of $1,000, $500, and $250, for the best designs. The result was the selection of three offerings, all of them combining an idea from nature, a water idea, a beehive idea, etc., and all of them conspicuous for rich simplicity and artistic effect.

As illustrative of beautiful frieze patterns, two selections from the choicest patterns now offered are shown in cuts above. An elegant Easter Lily pattern, also for frieze work,  is shown in the adjoining engraving. But these are samples only. The variety is wide as the freaks and fancies of genius. Indeed, the genius of the past is laid under contribution also to beautify our 19th-century homes. Antique forms are much in demand, and the very ruins of the

EASTER LILY PATTERN FOR FRIEZE.

world have been scoured to furnish suggestions for modern decoration. The trouble with these strange forms is that it is hard to make them harmonious with the other appointments of the room. If there is an Egyptian or Chinese or Japanese room wherein the peculiarities of these nations are the dominating motive, then you have an harmonious effect. Such a result is artistic. But a Japanese banner, on a Chinese paper, with a French ceiling, a Turkish rug, and American furniture, is too much of a mongrel to be indorsed by good taste.

In fine wall decorations there are many specialties. Em-

CEILING DECORATION IN PAPER.
[Design by Fr. Beck & Co., New York.]

bossed papers are well known, and they are constantly improving in style. New materials have appeared also, chief among which is " Lincrusta Walton "—a preparation of ground cork and linseed oil. This has the tenacity and flexibility of leather. It can be bent around any curve and it will endure the hardest wear. In its preparatory state it is subjected to heavy pressure under molded rollers, whereby its upper surface is brought out in bold relief, while its under

ANCIENT EGYPTIAN WALL DECORATION.

surface remains entirely smooth, so promoting its facility of adhesion to the wall. The relief-effect on this substance may be made very prominent. It also takes coloring beautifully and becomes as enduring as the wall itself. It is the invention of Mr. Frederick Walton, an English architect, and is now made for this country at Stamford, Conn., and is sold by first-class paper-hangers everywhere.

Lincrusta-Walton has been largely used, both abroad and in this country, in palaces, mansions, country houses,

theatres, hospitals, churches, hotels, clubs, and other public
and private buildings; also in yachts, in the vessels of the
British Navy, and of the Cunard, Inman, White Star, British
Indian, and other steamship lines. Wherever the effects of

CHINESE FURNISHING AND WALL DECORATION.

carving are desired, Lincrusta-Walton is in demand. "Nothing less than stern necessity," says a writer on this article,
" should compel an architect to forego, in interiors, the in-
finitely various and charming effects produced by light
glancing on raised, rounded, and re-entering surfaces in

addition to the ordinary methods of pleasing the eye by colors and lines. It is only necessary to see the interiors of grand French buildings, with their admirable moldings, or the Gothic carvings of Belgian town halls and old English cathedral choirs, to appreciate the unapproachable refinement and beauty of work in relief."

The advantages of Lincrusta-Walton have been thus summarized: " For the interior decoration of houses its warm

JAPANESE DINING AND WALL DECORATION.

and comfortable surface makes it peculiarly applicable. It has no glaze to break up and reflect the light with the cold glitter of Dutch tiles, nor does the moisture of the air condense upon its surface, unless water is present in excessive quantities in the atmosphere. It is not warped, cast, eaten by worms, or pulverized like wood. It does not become ice-cold in winter and hot in summer, like stone and terracotta. It does not absorb moisture and give it out again, like uncovered brick and plaster. On the contrary, it offers an impermeable resistance to wet from within or without, and if the air within is so dangerously damp as to communicate moisture to the walls, Lincrusta-Walton does not conceal the effect by absorbing the moisture."

A substance termed " Gerveta" is coming into use for high grades of decoration. Its general effects are like those of Lincrusta, but more bold and prominent, as Gerveta is applied to the walls in a pulpy state and is there worked by molds and tools. It may also be worked separately, though to work it on the wall is deemed preferable, securing more perfect adhesion and bolder effects.

The substances just named have great possibilities in artistic hands. Paneled ceilings and covered walls ; doors and door-jambs inset with these preparations ; wainscoting and heavy furniture, similarly adorned ; fire screens, picture frames, newel posts, and lighter decorations, resplendent with a variety of patterns and colors, are some of the uses of these wares. Inquiry concerning these goods should be made by all parties interested in extensive or even incidental decorations.

Fresco paintings were the dominant mural decorations of the world until a somewhat recent day. The artists of St. Peter's, St. Paul's, and other grand structures are immortalized by that class of work. It is seldom now that homes are frescoed throughout. Ceilings are often finished thus in part, or even entire, for the sake of the freedom and grace thus attainable. The best of papers must, to a great degree, be set and formal ; but in fresco there are no limits, save in the capacity of the artist or the purse of his customer. For home walls, at least, this art has suffered decline. More effective decoration can be had in other ways, especially for private houses.

But the highest style of wall decoration demands something more elegant than either paper or paint. Silks, satins, and laces fill this requirement. Silk or satin decorations

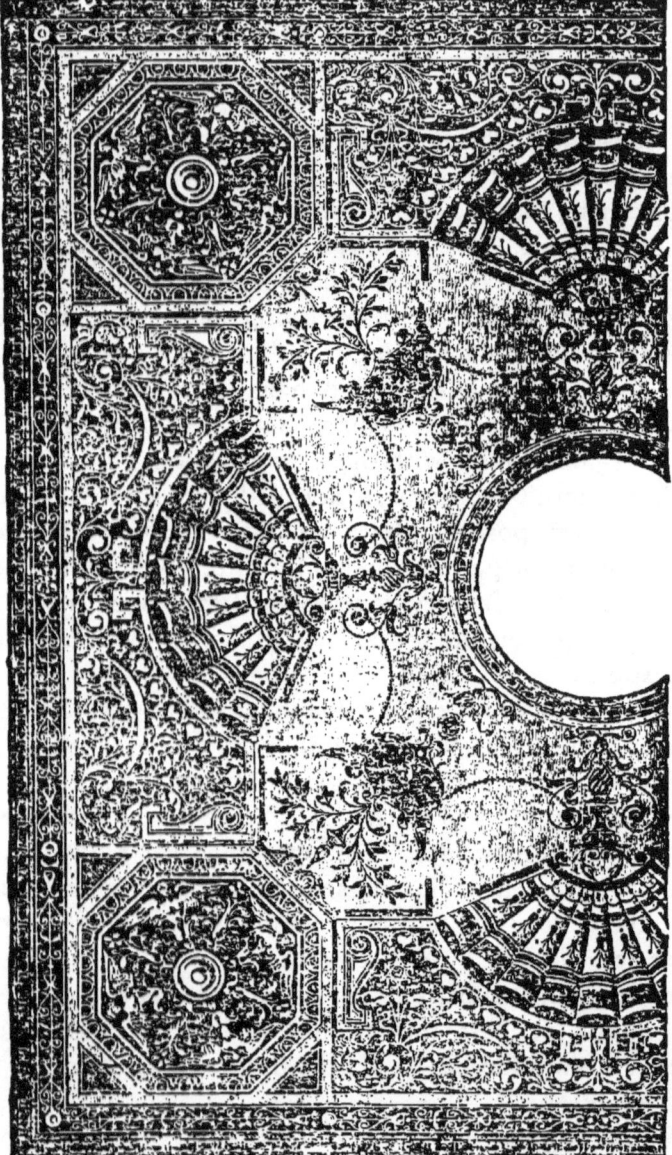

FAC-SIMILE OF AN ELEGANTLY FRESCOED CEILING.

are attached to light frames, over which muslin is stretched as a basis. These frames fit the wall closely from wainscoting to cornice. Silk may be stretched smoothly on these frames, or it may be fluted, or gathered to a central rosette, or worked in any other beautiful design. To pad the silk into a light cushion and tuft it is very elegant. This silk finish may remain uncovered, or, from a rod at the cornice, Gobelin laces or other tapestries may hang to a point a little below the top of the wainscoting. The combinations of material, colors, and graceful forms which may be produced in this style of work are numberless. The silks may be plain, watered, or figured; they may be of one color or of many harmonizing colors in stripes

ORNAMENTAL MOORISH CEILING.

of greater or less width. The laces may be of various qualities and patterns, and may hang free, or be draped apart in sections, or be fluted close to the foundation-silk or satin.

Carving also lends its aid to the decoration of walls, ceilings, doors, door-jambs, window frames, etc. Papier-maché and stucco produce very satisfactory results in this direction; but imitations are not admitted in first-class mansions. Genuine hard woods, carved by hand, are required there. John La Farge, the New York decorator, spent $100,000 on a single room of Cornelius Vanderbilt's mansion.

A hundred thousand dollars can soon be spent on one room where floors are laid in mosaic; where door-jambs are elaborate carvings; where door-heads are networks of exquisite chiseling in the rarest and richest woods; where statuary adorns the corners and the niches; where groined arches spring to centres of carved or of inlaid work studded

ELABORATE CARVING FROM THE BEDCHAMBER OF MARIE ANTOINETTE.

with decorator's jewels ; where windows are of stained glass,
wrought into most delicate forms and adorned with jewels

ROYAL SPLENDOR—THE THRONE ROOM OF WINDSOR CASTLE.

which glow like real gems; and where satin-covered walls are draped with exquisite Gobelin laces.

The centre-piece of the Hon. Samuel J. Tilden's dining-room ceiling in New York city is an elaborate carving representing branches of trees, amid which birds seem to be

BANQUETING-ROOM OF THE MANSION HOUSE, DUBLIN.

flitting, and in which their nests, with eggs and young, are resting. Any amount of money may be spent on such work.

Chandeliers afford fine opportunity for splendor in decoration. The nickel-plated or the glass-covered and prism-

decorated styles are most popular, because of the magnifi-
cence of their illumination. Globes or shades for these
fixtures are t'ited, ground, enameled, figured, highly

ELEGANTLY ORNAMENTED VESTIBULE LAMPS.

colored, or cut—thus affording wide and elegant variety.
They are even more diverse in their forms, so that if elegance is missed in the chandelier and side-lights, it is not
chargeable to lack of assortment from which to choose.

Lamps, too, are wrought into very elegant forms. They may adorn as well as illuminate our homes, and are adapted for halls, parlors, and all other apartments.

Stained-glass windows present one of the richest effects

in ornamentation. They have been in use since the sixth century, and have ever held their supremacy with lovers of the beautiful. Objects presented by stained glass are shown by transmitted light in all the fullness and richness of their colors. Objects presented by reflected light, as when one views pictures and solid ornaments, are to some extent shorn of their rich coloring. The surrounding white light produces somewhat of grayness on all colors. To test this, notice the shade of a delicate leaf when seen only by reflected light; then hold it between the eye and the sunlight so as to see its coloring by means of transmission.

PATTERN FOR STAINED-GLASS WINDOW.

The fine effect of stained-glass windows is heightened by the dark lines of the sash-bars about the several pieces of glass. These serve to intensify the rich colorings, which diffuse through the apartment a warm, genial, brilliant glow.

The glass throughout a house should be made appropriate for its particular position, and so add a greater charm to such beautiful work. In the vestibule-doors, words of greeting; in the dining-room, fruits, flowers, fishes, etc. General pieces may adorn the sitting-rooms, etc., two samples of which, from a series representing the seasons, suitable for any apartment, are given as illustrations of outline merely, the charm of color being absent. Where a single piece of stained-glass work is wanted, nothing could be better than a handsome fire-screen, which in the daytime catches the reflecting lights, and in the evening is lit up by the open fireplace. Such a piece is always handsome and never out of fashion.

The American departure in glass marks a new era, and by the use of new forms of glass, as the "iridescent," "opalescent," "Venetian," "Florentine," and many others, more brilliant and artistic results have been obtained than ever before. To the architect, these glasses furnish the richest of all decorations; to the artist, they present a wide field for sacred, historical, and heraldic illustrations;

PATTERN FOR STAINED-GLASS WINDOW.

to the householder, they offer one of the best means of making home attractive. A judicious expenditure for stained glass will prove the correctness of the old adage, "A thing of beauty is a joy forever."

IMITATION STAINED-GLASS DESIGNS FOR TRANSOMS.

The costliness of stained glass is a great objection to its use. This varies in proportion to the quality of glass used, richness of design, smallness of pieces, numerousness of "jewels," etc. For home uses, what is known as "Imitation Stained Glass" is a very satisfactory substitute. It is made of thin, translucent sheets of richly colored and elegantly designed papers, closely imitating the genuine stained glass. It is durable, inexpensive, and easily applied to any window. It is covered by an American patent, and can be had in the prominent cities of dealers and decorators, who also can apply it if desired. Four outline designs of this preparation are given to illustrate its styles. The transoms show combinations which may readily be worked into other forms. They are composed of borders, grounds, and centres, either of which can be used in an endless variety of ways. The library window shows the combination applied to the entire opening. The emblem of wisdom is appropriate here. In a dining-room window, birds, fruits, or game would suit better. In a parlor, music and flowers, or the Muses, the Graces, etc., would be more at home. The panel pattern shown on the page next following is suitable for any

IMITATION STAINED-GLASS DESIGN FOR LIBRARY WINDOW.

door, being beautiful, but not of decided characteristics.

A French preparation, "Diaphanie," is offered for the same purpose; also, "Glacier," an American patented article. In the Diaphanie French skill appears, and the designs are of great and beautiful pictorial variety, including coats-of-arms, religious subjects, landscapes, fruits, flowers,

IMITATION STAINED GLASS
DESIGN FOR PANEL.

historic and chivalric subjects, etc., etc. The leading papermen and decorators anywhere can refer to agents for Diaphanie. Glacier can be had of paint and glass dealers generally. Probably the best method is to combine these several preparations, selecting from each that which is best suited to the specific work proposed. Great opportunity for the exercise of good taste is afforded in the use of these materials.

With home windows in the ordinary form, a very happy effect is produced by covering the upper half with imitations of stained glass (unless, indeed, the genuine article be used), and then hanging the window shade for the lower half only. This shade should be dense and not brilliant in color, so that all the light of the room shall take its mellowing from the colors above. An upper shade may be used to exclude glare. The excellence of all stained glass effects depends on transmitting all the light. Reflected light always detracts from the beauty of stained glass.

II.—PORTABLE INTERNAL DECORATIONS.

THERE are important decorations in the home which are not part of the house itself. They are personal property, not real estate. They are carried with their owner in his migrations and are adapted to each new resting place he may find. Of these we may discuss, first:

CARVINGS, PICTURES, AND CURTAINS.

RICHLY DECORATED APARTMENT.

In the hallway there may be carvings, statuary, or vases. The stag's head or horns is much used in this situation—

rather too much, indeed. A buffalo's head is too heavy
and beastly for a beautiful home. Armorial carvings are
light and ornamental as wall decorations, but real armor is
better. In a hallway it is suggestive of romance; for as we
leave hats, canes, and riding-whips in the hall, ready for use
as we pass out, so the olden knights left swords, helmets,
and battle-axes there, ready to be used at a moment's
notice. On the same principle, ancient arms or historic
weapons may be there, though the peaceful home-tastes of
most people prefer more quiet emblems. The Alpen-stocks,
now so popular with mountain tourists, may properly rest
with other trophies of travel in the main hallway.

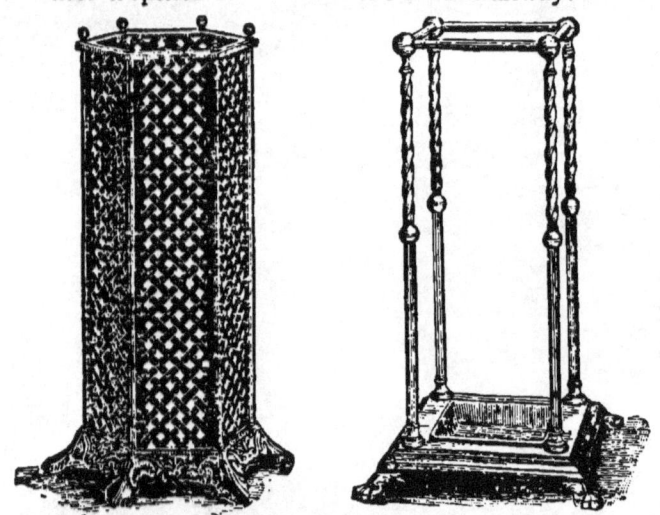

POLISHED BRASS UMBRELLA AND CANE STANDS.

Ideal fitness must rule in all decoration. Because in
conflict with it, pictures are rarely in place in hallways.
You can seldom get a standpoint from which to view them
properly, and it is a farce to locate pictures where their
effect is lost. On this ideal fitness, the old family clock is
properly placed in the hallway, where it may mark the
incomings and the outgoings, and where it will sound out

the passing hours for all in the house. Longfellow, who, more than any of our poets, touched the heart and home-life of our people, had his old clock on the stairs and in his hall the bust of Washington, who once made his head-quarters in that very house. There are pictures in the hallway there and on the landings ; but they are little gems which need close observation, and can be fully seen.

In the dining-room, decorations may be held to the five F's— namely, Fish, Flesh, Fowl, Fruits, Flowers. These may be in carved work or in paintings, either fixed or movable. If mottoes are used on din-ing-room walls, which is by no means to be advised, do seek one different from " Eat, Drink, and be Merry," and other conven-tional platitudes which are so common in the cheap boarding-houses.

In the sitting and sleeping rooms the eternal fitness of things must be observed. Ease and pleasure are desirable

STAIRWAY OF THE LONGFELLOW MANSION.

here, and articles which promote them are always in order. But such articles have their own character, and should be located accordingly. There are articles for the parlor, others for the dining-room, and so throughout the house.

A piano is not for fit the bed-room, though a music-box may be allowed there. Nor are superb paintings for bed-rooms, but for more public places. Where there are many fine paintings, it is worth while to have a picture gallery or apartment where lovers of art may sit undisturbed and enjoy their favorites. Much of a collection of fine paintings is a luxury permitted to but few, as none but millionaires can hold the celebrated pieces. But from these costly works there is a gradually descending scale till the little,

PICTURE GALLERY OF MALMAISON.
[The favorite residence of Josephine.]

inexpensive gems of true art—such as Prang, of Boston, furnishes—are reached. These are artistic and exquisite. They charm and elevate, and one such is worth far more than a roomful of daubs, such as wandering auctioneers and artistic tramps hawk about.

A beautiful illustration of fitness in decoration is afforded in the music-room of a wealthy musical gentleman of Cincinnati. He has there a grand organ, two pianos, a cabinet organ, a harp, and many other musical instruments, together with pictures of the masters and curious musical instruments of other days and lands. In the ground-glass transom of the entrance-door the opening strain of "Home, Sweet Home" is wrought. Over the grand organ the opening strain of the "Hallelujah Chorus" is frescoed in the cove of the cornice, at other points of which snatches of other celebrated compositions are wrought so delicately as to escape casual observation, and yet so beautifully as to charm every artistic eye which catches them.

All living things turn toward the light. The bright side of a room is that most seen. The parts next the windows are those for special effect. A mirror between windows is condemned by some critics. One says: "People of taste . . . sometimes put mirrors in this spot. Philistines always do." But the poorest light of the room is just there. An observer at that point is dazzled with the radiance on either side and cannot see clearly what stands between. A mirror there, however, reflects the illuminated objects of the room, and does so

JARDINIERE STAND.
[Metal, variously finished.]

all the more from receiving no direct light itself. Put a mirror between the windows, therefore. In front of it a piece of statuary will be seen to advantage by direct and reflected views. This may to some extent obscure the mirror, but in a parlor its use is not as a dressing-glass, but to beautify and enlarge the room.

In the front corners of the room, statuary, jardinieres with flowers, or any beautiful objects which are high, but not broad, are appropriate. Statuary should always be shown against a suitable background—very dark for white marble and bright colors for the Rogers' groups or other dark-colored pieces.

When statuettes are used upon brackets or cabinets, this principle must be observed. On ebony a pure, white ornament is splendid. Bronze shows to best advantage on white. Dark walls are best for gold frames and rich-colored paintings.

Do not feel compelled to make each article of an apartment balance with some other article. Irregularity is more natural than regularity. The finest mosaics are purposely made irregular to avoid the "machine-made" appearance. Do not square your chairs with the walls; do not set them at one inevitable angle. Do not keep things forever in one place. Nature is free in her forms and her movements, and the highest art walks lovingly with her.

JARDINIERE STAND.
[Metal, variously finished.]

Changes in arrangement come from various demands. Persons weary of one style. "Variety is the spice of life." Even a less elegant change is preferable for a time to stolid grandeur. The march of improvement, too, demands change. Competition in fabrics of all kinds begets improvement. Better goods come into the markets continuously, crowding out the old and the inferior and making place for the new and the better.

It has become quite popular, and deservedly so on many accounts, to curtain doorways as shown in the cut. Where

CURTAINED DOORWAY.

there are sliding doors they remain to be used when required. Hinged doors are usually removed entirely when curtains are employed. In an arched doorway the curtain should hang from a rod on a level with the spring of the arch; unless, indeed, the opening lead into a cold apartment, from which chilling drafts might come. For such an opening, however, a more solid door seems best. Rods and rings of polished wood are the proper articles for these uses. Metal rings are not now used with curtains.

The material of the curtaining may be as varied as the tastes and purses of parties demand. Curtaining doorways is, however, a movement in the direction of luxury and beauty. It should express itself, therefore, in elegant, if not sumptuous, forms.

Real elegance can assert itself in many ways. The carpetings, the wall papers, the curtains, the substantial

furniture, the shelves and racks for ornaments, the l rd
cagcs, the flowers, everything, can be invested with an air
of refinement, or it can lie inelegant and unattractive.   In

A PEEP AT ELEGANCE.

such surroundings there is a grand inspiration to personal
elegance. Our surroundings and ourselves are part and
parcel of one great whole. It is not we that make our
surroundings merely, but our surroundings in turn make
us. We are molded by the things we mold. The very
act of fashioning beautiful forms forms us into beautiful
fashion. And so the peep at elegance, as given in the cut,
is without any inelegant detractions.

A pen picture of the private apartments of the President
of the United States will be of interest. The sleeping-room

THE POET LONGFELLOW IN HIS LIBRARY.

of His Excellency is a model of tasteful and rich furnishing.
The curtains, carpets, portieres, and paper of this room are
of a pale-blue tint, commonly known as pigeon-egg blue,

and the furniture, with the exception of the bedstead, corresponds with the other appointments.

Adjoining this room is the private study of the President. Surrounded by books of choice engravings, photographs of intimate friends, and articles of vertu indescribable—a cozier nook could not have been selected, and the view on all sides is charming.

Passing out of the study into a large hall, one is impressed by the magnificent surroundings. Several of the best works of Bierstadt adorn the walls, a large painting of the Yellowstone region being the most striking. A unique and handsome cigar-stand, formed of the head of a Texas calf and three steers' horns, highly polished and mounted in silver, is placed near a favorite lounging-place of the President. A large, semi-circular window of French plate, surmounted by jeweled designs in glass, is at the end of this apartment, and the perfume of the choicest flowers in the conservatory beneath scents the air. Easy chairs, lounges, and tete-a-tetes are scattered through the hall and invite delicious rest from the affairs of state.

A large, carved door opens from the hall into the bedroom at the southwest angle of the mansion, in which the late President Garfield suffered. A communicating door opens into the large room used by the doctors in attendance upon the stricken President. The most notable article in this apartment is a handsomely carved mahogany bedstead, bearing in bold relief the coat-of-arms of the United States, the whole surmounted by a heavy red silk canopy. A pair of steps lead up to the bed, upon which are four mattresses, topped off by a feather bed. The furniture of the room is of a heavy, sombre, antique pattern. This furniture is valued at thousands of dollars and is the only thing about the mansion which connects the past with the present.

Another pen-picture, showing some of the elegancies of the house of William H. Vanderbilt—the grandest private mansion of America—will be welcome. The hall is sixty feet deep by twenty wide. In the centre, upon the right side, is the grand staircase, down whose broad flight the daylight streams, mellowed through stained-glass Venetian windows. Opposite the staircase, in the hall, is a splendid fireplace. The andirons are of iron hammered into artistic shape and furnished with chains. Five torches, with wax candles, give brilliancy to the hall by night. The candles are held in bronze branches which spring from bronze columns, up which Cupids climb. The walls are wainscoted with Caen stone, elaborately carved, the panels separated by classic pilasters and decorated with scroll work. A drapery of Oriental silk hangs above the stone-work, embroidered with figures of birds. The mantel-piece of this hall is a wondrous work of art, made of Caen stone and ornamented with superb carving. Looking from this fireplace up the staircase, the eye meets the twelve Cæsars in two stained windows, each on topaz-colored medallions on a ground of ruby red. Between the two windows stand female saints in carved wood, with carved pedestals and arching canopies. The side-wall and the balustrade are of Caen stone, the balusters being of acanthus leaves terminating in dragons' heads.

At the end of the hall is the dining-room, thirty-five feet wide and fifty-four feet long, its ceiling of dark, carved wood thirty-two feet above its floor. In a deep recess at the western end of the room is a stained-glass window of enormous size, representing the meeting of Henry VIII of England with Francis I of France. Four chandeliers hang from the groined ceiling. Here, too, is a huge fireplace of richly carved stone and terra cotta. The walls are covered with Venetian gilt and colored leather. A frieze above the mantel of the fireplace in the dining-room represents sea-nymphs and Cupid sporting in the waters and playing with sea-horses and seals. Above this is a solid work of carved oak.

The drawing-room is thirty-four feet wide by forty feet long. The walls are paneled in cream color, with gilt moldings, and on the doors hang hunting trophies of gilt. The doors once belonged to an old French château. The fireplace is of two marbles, super-ornamented with heavy bronzes. The ceiling is adorned with the fresco work of Baudry, of Paris, representing Olympus and its gods and goddesses. The ceiling is circular in form and the corners are filled with triangular panels, in which are figures of Cupid. A large mirror is set in the paneling above the

ROYAL BED-CHAMBER OF THE EMPRESS JOSEPHINE.

fireplace. Branched candlesticks of brass hold out their lights from the walls and two torches of white marble stand before the entrance.

The Japanese room of this mansion is superb as the boudoir of an Oriental princess. The ceiling shows open rafters; the upper portion of the walls is finished in bamboo, while around the lower portion is cabinet work, tinted in rich red lacquer. On each side of the door a life-size figure in Japanese costume holds aloft a magnificent cluster of lights. One of the grandest features of this sumptuous room is its stained glass window. It represents flowers and birds, the main object being a peacock, the tail of which is pronounced a marvel of splendor and fidelity.

DECORATIONS FROM NATURE.

Home decoration owes an immense debt to flowers. These beautiful adornments are so free, so fragrant, so varied, and such favorites with all, that every true home should be brightened by them. Granting that it be a city home, with no lawn, no trees, no extended flower beds, still, within the house, by a little skill and care, beauty may be made to smile the year through. While snow and sleet reign without, buds and blossoms may reign within.

The cut below is a bright illustration of what may be in any home by careful window gardening.

FLOWERS IN THE HOME.

A window for flowers must be upon the sunny side of the house. Unless the sashes fit unusually tight, a double sash will be needed for the winter, as the winds will almost certainly penetrate the room and nip the tender plants. If the heat of the room fall off during the night, this danger will be greatly increased. And yet an arrangement must be made for an abundance of fresh air. Want of oxygen is as fatal to plants as to people.

The equipment for such a window garden as this cut represents are few, simple, and inexpensive. Hanging-baskets are innumerable in style and price, as will be illustrated in the pages beyond. Wire flower stands are very pretty, substantial, and cheap. Flower-pots may be had in all styles. The old-fashioned earthern pots cost very little. It was once thought they were the only ones which, by virtue of their porous character, would effectually promote plant growth. But that idea was erroneous. You may paint the pots, so beautifying them even while you destroy their porosity; or you may use any of the many forms of glazed and ornamented pots now offered at the stores.

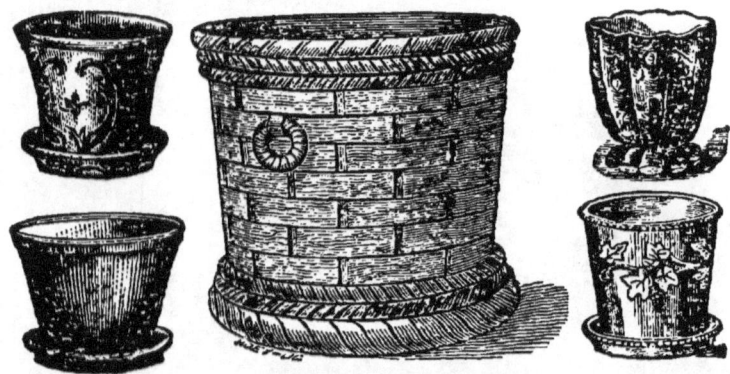

VARIETIES IN FLOWER-POTS.

What actually has been done in Bay-window Gardening is shown in the next cut, which is from a photograph. The floor of this bay-window is finished in hard wood. This is desirable, as it allows free watering of the plants without damage to carpets. An oil-cloth covering, or a floor laid with tile, neither of which need cost much, answer well. It is a good plan to have a hard-wood floor laid upon the

WINDOW GARDENING.

regular floor, thus making the bay-window flooring slightly higher than the main floor. A tenant may make this portable, so as to be easily removed, if need be.

THE BAY-WINDOW GARDEN.

The pots in this window are placed directly on the floor. The corner pots contain ivy vines, which are trained up the wood-work and across the window head with very pretty effect. The strip on the floor, around the pots, is merely to give a good finish to the outline of the room. It may be movable or permanent, as is desired. The plants to be used must be selected by advice of a florist, who knows the exact possibilities of the locality. Houses have peculiarities, also, which must be discovered. The purse, too, needs consultation, for from very inexpensive plants one may rise to those of finest character and highest cost. Birds, vases, hanging-baskets, and other elements of such gardens will be discussed hereafter. One thing must be remembered, however, in this connection, namely: A bay-window garden cannot be used for much else. It cannot be a play-ground, a smoking-room, or a lounging-place, though it makes a beautiful sitting-place for the ladies in their moments of leisure.

No advice as to the care of plants for a window garden will apply everywhere. The best way is to consult local florists who are successful, and to observe carefully your own experiences. Generally speaking, the best flower for the

SQUARE BAY-WINDOW GARDEN.

house is the geranium. It requires but little care, is never troubled with green fly or red spider, stands a dry atmosphere well, and blooms profusely. Heliotropes and begonias are easily grown and are good bloomers. Callas will grow well almost anywhere if they get plenty of water. The ivy is well fitted for use in the house. Fuchsias are exquisite flowers for summer use, but do not bloom well in winter. For fall use nothing is better than the chrysanthemums. After these have blossomed the plants can be put in the cellar. Carnations, abutilons, oleanders, and myrtles are all adapted to culture in the house, and generally give excellent satisfaction. It is always best to confine attention at first to such plants as are not too particular. When you can grow these well, try other kinds. Do not attempt too much, but do your best with what you start. One good plant is a treasure. A dozen poor ones are worse than none at all. They lead a poor, sickly life that is a pleasure to neither the cultivator nor the beholder.

Surprising results may be attained by special care. The adjoining cut shows the appearance of a house-grown lily of the valley which came to the

LILY OF THE VALLEY, FIVE WEEKS OLD.

condition here shown in five weeks. Of course, it had skillful and constant care, but it had no advantage of hot-house or special accessory. Its chief forcing was on the reservoir of a kitchen cook-stove.

On the use of vines in the house an expert says: "There is nothing in the way of home decorations that may be had with so little expense, managed with so little trouble, or will give results so satisfactory, as the ivy. There is no room so

palatial to which it may not add embellishment, and it will
give an air of cheerfulness and refinement to the one room
of the settler's log-cabin.   Of course, we refer to the true
evergreen ivy, *Hedera*, and not to the tender plants known
as ' Parlor,' ' German,' ' Colosseum,' and other ivies   If
one has a sprig of ivy and a pot or a box of earth, wonders
can be accomplished if the owner possesses one other requi-
site—patience.   The growth is slow at first, but it is in-
creasingly rapid, and each year the plant will reward patient

care by becoming more beautiful and
more valuable."

Boxes for window gardens, with
casters for ease of movement, may be
constructed by any person.   One of
the prettiest may be made by covering
the box with pieces of bark nailed upright on its sides, sawed off at the top
and bottom edges, and then making
the supporting stand and overarching
trellis of saplings.   Vine stems may be
trailed over the rustic work and fastened there.   The effect of growing
flowers and vines on such a rustic

HYACINTH BULB IN   stand is very beautiful.
WATER.

Some plants show to best advantage
when separated from others and in positions not favorable
for the display of ordinary plants.   For example : For
brackets the best plants we have are the drooping varieties
of fuchsias, the eupatorium and begonias.   No one knows
what grace there is in the fuchsia unless he has seen it growing on a bracket placed about as high as his head, the
branches being allowed to droop over the pot.   To secure
plenty of branches, the centre of the plant should be pinched
out when it is small.   Where one stalk was there will be
two shoots thrown out.   These, in turn, should be pinched

back, and at least a dozen thrifty stalks should be induced
to grow from the base of the plant. No piece of statuary
can make a more elegant filling for a corner. Eupatorium
Mexicanum blends beautifully with fuchsias on two-pot
brackets, and the effect is more than
doubled if placed in front of a mirror.

One of the most tasty decorations
is a bouquet or basket of flowers, or
even a single beautiful rose, lily, or
hyacinth. Small vases for these can
be had in abundance at all prices.
Miniature gypsy kettles, with flowers
of delicate form and size, are exceedingly beautiful on a mantel or bracket.
Artificial flowers may be used thus,

MINIATURE GYPSY
KETTLE.

but they must be small and exquisite, not large or gaudy.

To "make a bunch of flowers" is no trouble, but to make
a bouquet or tastefully fill a basket of flowers is a high art.
Arranging flowers loosely and naturally in vases, saucers,

and other ornamental receptacles requires
good taste and some knowledge of the
harmony of colors. To fill a basket, first
line it with tin foil, or scatter a little lycopodium or other green material, to form
a lining. Over this put a lining of strong
paper. Then fill the basket with damp
sawdust, rounding it off at the top and covering with damp moss, inserting the stems
of the flowers in the moss. If the natural
VASE FOR FLOWERS. stems are not suitable for this work, the
flowers can be "stemmed," that is, fastened to small pieces
of wood or broom splints. It is well to make the border
of drooping green. Fuchsias border very elegantly.

Few flowers have stems suitable for bouquet work ; so it
is the custom to "stem" all flowers for this purpose. These

stiff steams can be made to hold the flowers in any position desired. To keep the flowers from crowding each other

and to supply moisture, wind damp moss around the stem at its connection with the artificial stem. The central flower, which should be the largest, must have a stiff, strong, straight stem, which really forms the backbone of the bouquet as well also as the handle. Fasten the stems of all the smaller flowers around this main, central flower. After the flowers are all properly attached and the bouquet is well formed, cut off the entire handle to the desired length and cover it with tin-foil, or wind it with white ribbon, leaving a loop, so that the bouquet may be suspended by it if desired.

STEMMED FLOWER. Ornamental papers can be obtained at a very small cost which will cover the handle and bottom of the bouquet and also make a richly ornamental border. These hints apply, of course, to hand bouquets, but larger bouquets are made in the same manner, except that they are more pyramidal in form.

ORNAMENTAL BOUQUET PAPER.

If ferns or flowers for bouquets or other work are laid in water for several hours after being cut and before they are used, they will endure much longer without flagging than if immediately arranged. The more water they absorb after being severed from the plant, the better they will stand.

A new device for the arrangement of flowers consists of a piece of cork about a quarter of an inch thick, circular in form, and perforated with holes, like the rose of a watering-pot. The diameter of the cork is made to correspond to the size of the saucer or shallow dish with which it is to be used. The cork, floating on the top of the water, supports the flowers, whose stems are inserted through the holes. For the display of small flowers and those having short stems this method is well adapted. It may possibly be better than damp sand, as the cork may be preserved and will always be ready, even when sand cannot be had.

The *Ladies' Floral Cabinet* lays down the following rules on bouquet-making: " Never put more than three varieties or colors in the same vase or bouquet, and let those colors be such as perfectly harmonize. Arrange the flowers so that each one can be seen entire." This is good, but exceptions are numerous.

Autumn leaves, which are a deservedly popular decoration, require but little preparation. When fully ripe they contain very little moisture and the colors are quite permanent ; but they contain some moisture, and may curl up if brought into a warm room. To prevent this, place them between papers, giving a light pressure. In a few days take them out and give a light dressing of varnish to brighten the colors. For this purpose, clear, boiled linseed oil is good, using the least possible amount Some prefer balsam fir, cut with alcohol ; others use gum shellac dissolved in alcohol ; others dip each leaf in melted wax and press it a moment with a warm iron.

It is stated that the colors of flowers may be preserved by dipping them occasionally in a boiled solution of eleven grains of salycilic acid in a pint of water and afterward carefully drying them between sheets of blotting paper.

There are several methods of drying flowers so as to preserve their color to some degree. The most common way is to spread them in a pan of dry sand and sift sand upon them, keeping them, when thus covered, in a warm, dry place for several days, until free from moisture ; or they may be dried between thin sheets of wadding placed between two pieces of glass. The pressing will injure the form ; but this is more or less so by any process.

The field for ingenuity and taste here opened is very broad and is well worth diligent cultivation.

Floral or evergreen letterings are often desired. Mark out the letters on strawboard, placing them close together,  as in diagram No. 1. If no expert in lettering is available, determine the height you wish the letters to be, and divide that into six equal parts, marking these on the strawboard. Cross these with other lines at the same distances apart. The proportions so given will answer for most letters, six spaces high by four wide, and will suggest the proportions for others, as in diagram No. 2.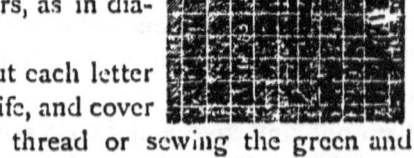

When thus marked, cut each letter clearly with shears or knife, and cover them by tying with dark thread or sewing the green and flowers to the surfaces. Keep the work even and trim its edges when done. Everlasting flowers or bright berries should be mixed with the green to relieve the uniformity. Moss may be tied upon the letters; into this flowers with paste or glue upon their stems may be stuck, and they will  remain fixed, showing a result as in diagram No. 3. Glue will hold some coverings of letters sufficiently.

Immortelles, Pampas plumes, ferns, oats, with many weeds and grasses, are well suited for drying. Vases, baskets, and wall-pockets may be filled with them and serve well as decorations. The unnatural coloring frequently put upon these grasses by dealers is a monstrosity. Better retain the natural conditions when natural objects are used.

Holiday decorations of ivy, laurel, holly, ferns, mosses, and the whole range of evergreens are beautiful if well done. Picture frames, window curtains, doorways, mantel-pieces— indeed, any and every part of a room—may be made cheery and elegant by this means. It consumes time, but it cultivates taste.

A few little floral fancies are worthy of passing mention in closing this subject.

1. To grow a pretty vine from the sweet potato: Put a tuber in pure sand, or sandy loam, in a hanging-basket, and water occasionally. It will throw out tendrils and beautiful leaves, and climb freely over the arms of the basket and upward toward the top of the window.

2. Procure a fine, healthy acorn and crochet around it a little network case after removing the cup. Then hang it, point downward, in a deep glass, having so much water

PAMPAS PLUME.

in it that the point of the acorn just reaches it. Keep it in a dark closet until it has sprouted; then put it in the light. A chestnut thus kept in water will sprout in the same way, and either will be beautiful.

3. Cut off evenly the top of a carrot and place it on the top of a pot full of sand,

BASKET OF FERNS AND GRASSES.

so that the leaves look as if they sprang from it. Moisten

it well and keep it in the dark until it has begun to sprout ; keep it damp, and move it into the light when the leaves appear. If the cultivation is successful, an ornament pretty enough for any room will be the result.

4. Take a sound turnip and clean the outside, taking care not to injure the part from whence the leaves spring. Cut a piece off the bottom and scoop out the inside. Fasten string or wire to it, so that it can be hung up. Fill the cavity, and keep it filled, with water. In a short time the leaves will sprout and curl up toward the ball of the turnip, forming a beautiful miniature hanging-basket.

TRANSPARENCY OF DRIED FLOWERS.

5. Put the stem of a freshly cut tuberose or other white flower into diluted scarlet ink for a short time. The liquid will be drawn up into the veins, coloring them in a very elegant manner. It also shows whether a plant is net-veined or parallel-veined.

6. A transparency of dried flowers may be made as follows : Take two panes of glass of equal size—one of them ground, the other clear. By the use of gum tragicanth attach to the under side of the ground glass about half an inch of the edge of a dark ribbon, which should be over an inch wide. Allow this to dry. On the upper side of this

glass arrange the grasses, attaching them to it by touches of the gum. On the glass, just around its edges, fix a narrow strip of cardboard; on this lay the clear glass, pressing the grasses flat. Bring up the unattached edge of the ribbon and fix it firmly by the mucilage over the upper glass, so imprisoning the grasses in the inclosure.

One of the most beautiful decorations which may be maintained within the home is found in the aquarium. The theory of the aquarium is that it shall so combine animal and vegetable life in such exact proportions that the water shall be kept entirely pure, never needing change. In other words, the vegetable life shall take up the surplus carbon yielded by the animal life, and the animal life shall take up the surplus oxygen yielded by the vegetable life, and so things will remain in *statu quo*. The theory is good, but it cannot be applied under circumstances sufficiently favorable to guarantee success.

In the great aquariums of museums it is found necessary to continually force fresh air through the water, that it may be maintained in a sufficiently oxygenized state; and even then, such is the capacity of water for absorbing gases and odors from the atmosphere, that it must itself be renewed frequently. But the aquarium pays. Aside from the finish of the vessel itself, which is usually artistic, the plant life in water and the activity of the animal life, are unceasingly attractive. A common glass jar is better than nothing as an aquarium, though glass globes

BOX AQUARIUM.

well adapted for small fish may be had at a low price. A better form of aquarium is shown in the accompanying cut. Such boxes may be had of all sizes and with great variety of finish.

But a box is not essential as a beginning for an aquarium. The fact is, that any one having a little ingenuity, and the assistance of a handy tinsmith, can fit up a handsome and attractive affair. A frame-work may be made of tin to hold the glass, and to this frame a zinc bottom should be soldered. A bottom of wood underneath all should be finished nicely with a deep molding. After the glass has been set and well cemented in, the frame may be painted black, or green, or gilded, as taste may decide. The tank should be filled with fresh water every day until it is thoroughly cleansed, before fitting it for occupancy. Then the glass must be polished, the bottom covered with clean pebbles, stones, and small shells. A rockery, of rich brown and pure white stones should be constructed for the centre, surmounted by a large shell or two filled with earth, and Lycopodium growing therein. Cover this earth with pebbles and press them down firmly about the plant. After all this is arranged, put the water in with a dipper, pouring against the glass to avoid a disarrangement of the furniture.

Every morning dip out two or three dippers of water, wipe the glass, and fill with fresh water. Use care not to disturb the water more than is necessary. There is no reason why gold fish will not do well in an aquarium if managed in this way. During very warm weather a lump of ice occasionally is appreciated by the little golden beauties, for they can stand the cold much better than the heat. The fact is, that fish, supplied with clear water and a cool temperature, have scarcely any other want. The omission of all attention to feeding, except in the spring months, is as great a kindness as can be shown them. In moderate latitudes, from the last of February to the first of July, the least crumb of cracker or fish-wafer suffices, and during the rest of the year experienced fish-fanciers say very little need be given; that little, may be a few bread-crumbs or a pinch of plain cake.

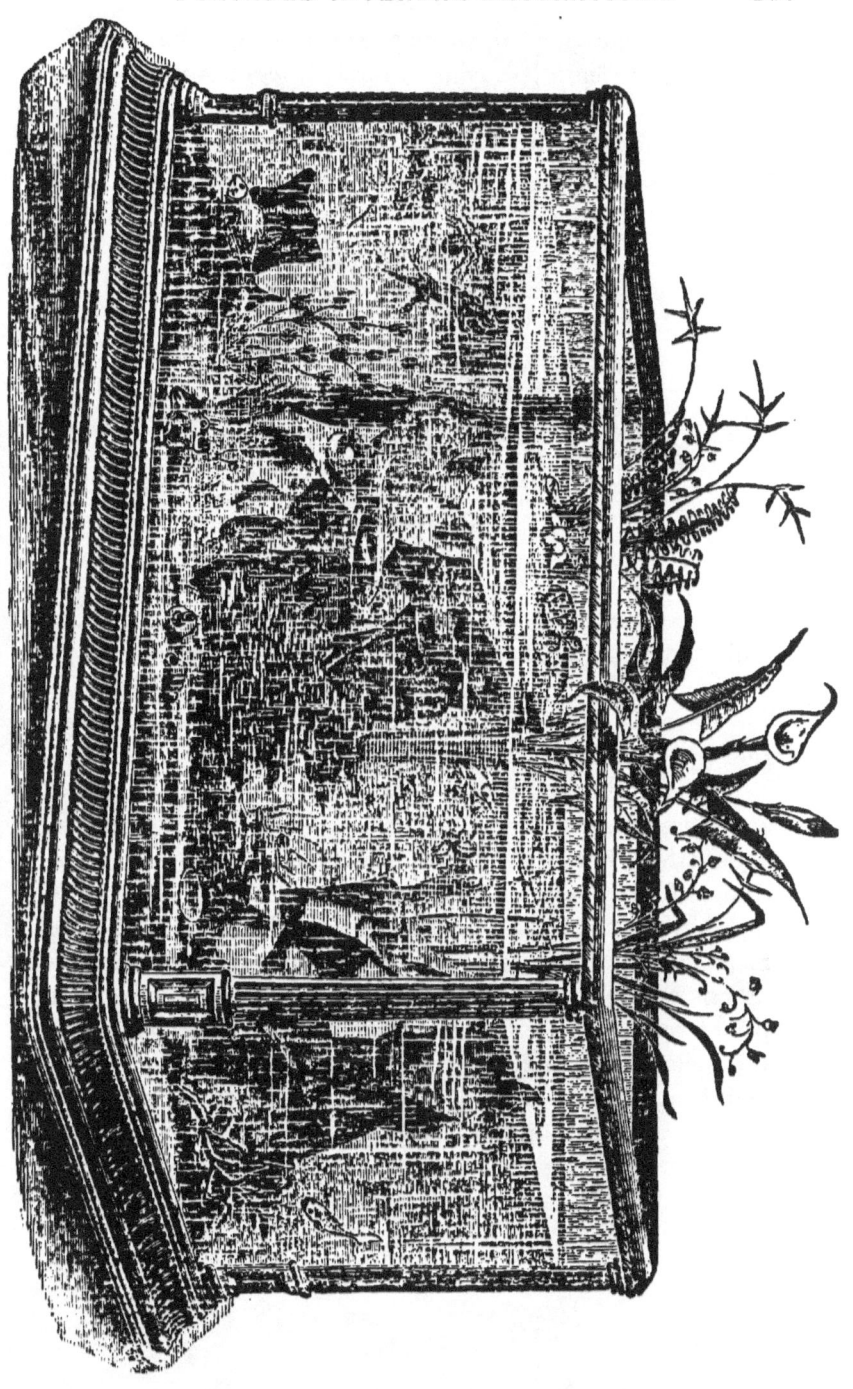

ELABORATE AQUARIUM WITH PLANTS AND FISHES.

While arranging aquariums attention may be paid to parlor rockeries, a less common but no less beautiful home decoration. A small parlor rockery can be made most satisfactorily by combining the aquarium and rockery, somewhat as is shown in the accompanying engraving. In a

PARLOR ROCKERY.

living-room or parlor a good deal of sprinkling of the rocks must be done, or plants placed in the crevices will dry up. This necessitates a basin to catch and retain the drippings. It may be of sufficient depth for gold and other fish. It can be made of any form desired, and with any ornamentation that taste may suggest.

Or it may be shallow, and be bedded with mosses, ferns, and marsh plants, so making a bog-garden. A small faucet should be inserted at an inconspicuous point, by which to draw off any excess of moisture. Excursions to the marshes will furnish an abundance of soil and plants for the basin, while a liberal assortment of plants will suit the conditions of the higher portions. Central to the rockery, a pot of roses, lilies, or other plants may be placed, its upper rim being concealed by the surrounding rocks. Variety and beauty can seldom be secured in one object so freely as is a well-kept parlor rockery.

Ferneries are a well-known parlor decoration. A great variety of styles and sizes of bases and vases can be had.

COMBINED AQUARIUM AND FLOWER-STAND.

They are made of pottery, of rustic work, of tiled work, of iron, and of cabinet ware, and home ingenuity can meet all the requirements, even to the inclosing case of glass. The fernery shown in the cut we give is in imitation of oak, in rustic style, with rustic base. These bases are of different sizes, from eight to twelve inches in diameter, the whole

RUSTIC FERNERY.

height, with glass, being from twelve to eighteen inches. Although these are small, still they serve a good purpose and are easily handled and managed.

A more elaborate style of fernery may be made with a table-like base on four legs and casters. The case proper should be say sixteen inches in width by two and a half feet in length, and twenty-six inches high above the legs. This can be made by any joiner, and can be varied to correspond to any style of furniture. The top should be made to open for access to the interior, and also for ventilation. Within the wooden table-frame is fitted a zinc pan about three inches deep, which contains the soil; this pan has an opening for drainage, and a shallow vessel should be placed in a concealed position underneath to receive any surplus water.

Ferneries require a large amount of moisture. The vase, or case covering, retains this and the warmth, so making perennial spring time for the plants within. All the swamp plants are suitable for fernery culture, but ferns do not like stagnant water. They flourish in low, moist places—but it is where the water is renewed by direct flow, or by subsoil drainage, which fact must not be overlooked in the fernery.

Besides ferns, many kinds of mosses and selaginellas

succeed well in cases; also some species of grasses, caladiums, begonias of the tuberous and the rex varieties, the sundews or droseras, some of the aroids, ficus repens, and others. An interesting variety of plants may, therefore, be secured, but ferns must be the principal feature.

The fern-case, after it is planted, should be placed where it can receive a good light without being too much exposed to direct sunshine. Only sufficient water should be given to keep the soil moist and not saturated. Some ventilation is required, but it need be slight, and yet it should be carefully attended to

FERN-CASE JARDINIERE.

each day, opening the doors of the case just enough to clear the glass of moisture. A little experience will enable one to care properly for a case.

Ferneries are frequently adorned with ornaments carved in cork. A magnificent work of this kind was lately constructed in London on an order from the King of Siam. The entire fernery consisted of five frames, each about ten feet in height and width, most artistically constructed, being covered with cork colored to resemble a true rockery. There is a pool at the base for water lilies and other aquatics, with numerous recesses, in which ferns will be placed. Several jets of water are arranged so that the whole surface will be constantly moist with water dripping from the stalactitic projections at the upper part. Spaces at the back are filled with mirrors, and as these artificial " rockeries " will occupy an alcove and be disposed in one line, the effect will be magnificent, and probably, in its kind, unrivalled.

A careful observer of nature will soon discover how nature fixes herself in her prettiest forms. Observe where ferns grow and how they are surrounded. The grasses, the mosses, the pebbles—all the accompaniments of fern-growth in nature—may be transferred by art into the fernery. But art will surpass nature by eliminating all that is unsightly and retaining only the beautiful.

The best cement to prevent leakage in aquariums, ferneries, etc., is made as follows : Take equal parts of red lead, white lead, and litharge; dry, mix thoroughly, pulverizing all lumps. Then make into a putty by adding boiled linseed oil. Add a little at a time, and only a drop or two when nearly done, or you will get it too soft. As soon as the cement has been applied, fill the aquarium with water.

It is possible to make very happy combinations from the natural world in internal home decoration. The illustrations already given have shown this. They combine flowers, vines, ferns, mosses, fishes, birds, rustic work, rocks, and other natural features of beauty. In the cut which follows a style of aquarium is shown which contains many points of beauty. The aquarium itself shows various forms of animal and vegetable life. The trellis allows a fine opportunity in the selection and training of plants, while the bird-cage at

VINE-COVERED AQUARIUM.

the summit provides additional life, with song added to beauty and fragrance.

Taste, patience, and a little expense are all that are needed to produce a beautiful display on this general plan. Taste and skill find splendid opportunity in the case of diminutive plants and fishes.

Few adornments for the interior of home afford so much opportunity for varied, graceful, and really elegant display as do hanging-baskets. Drapery is always beautiful, because so perfectly natural; but when flowers are pendant, mingled with delicate vines and mosses, then nature is seen in her most lovely forms. Such views of nature are furnished in hanging-baskets. The materials of which they are composed, the forms in which they are wrought, and the flowers with which they may be filled, are without limit. Terra-cotta ware, wire, and rustic work are chiefly employed, but natural objects, such as shells, gourds, etc., form the basis of many attractive displays of this character. A neat hanging-basket is exceeding graceful also, and it is in place everywhere, a welcome " thing of beauty."

Plants in vases and hanging-baskets are peculiarly situated in respect to the moisture in the soil. This is subject to rapid evaporation. Not only is there the ordinary drainage, such as plants in pots have and which is absolutely necessary, since stagnant water at the roots would be fatal, but these plant

TERRA-COTTA HANG-ING-BASKET.

receptacles are usually situated where they are fully exposed to the sun and to drying winds. The great demand of basket and vase plants is water, and attention to this supply is almost the only care necessary.

In a room it is almost impossible to moisten plants fully and properly. It is best, therefore, that baskets be taken to some outer room every day or two for a good soaking, where they may remain until dripping ceases. Where a wire basket is used, or an opening is provided for drainage, dripping continues for some time. An arrangement is shown in the next engraving for catching this drip. It is merely a second basket or earthen vessel suspended under the main one, and planted so as to be both useful and ornamental.

As the number of plants in baskets and vases is usually large for the quantity of soil they contain, it should be rich. What is wanted is a rapid, luxuriant growth, without much regard to the form of individual plants. A good soil for the purpose may be made of about one part of old manure, two parts of rotten sods, and one part of sand. If leaf-mold can be had, an amount of it can be added equal to the sand

HANGING-BASKET WITH SUB-BASKET FOR DRIP.

or manure, if not, the mixture without it will be quite satisfactory. When the plants have been placed in their new quarters and watered, it is necessary to keep them shaded for a short time, and if possible they should have the advantage of a greenhouse or cold-frame until they make new roots and commence to grow freely.

ELEGANT HANGING-BASKET.

Concerning plants suitable for hanging-baskets, James Vick, of Rochester, New York, an authority on the subject, makes the following valuable suggestions:

Erect Plants.—Amaranthus salicifolius, Amaranthus Sun rise, Caladium, Canna, Coleus, Cyperus alternifolius, Dracæna, Fuchsia.

Trailing Plants.—German Ivy, Kenilworth Ivy, Ivy-leaved Geranium, annual varieties of Lobelia, Nolana, Othonna crassifolia, Petunia, Tradescantia, Saxifraga sarmentosa, Vinca major variegata, Vinca Harrisonii.

Twining Plants.—Ipomœa Quamoclit, Madeira Vine, Maurandya, Pilogyne suavis, Thunbergia, Tropæolum maius, Tropæolum Lobbianum.

Handsome Foliage Plants.—Abutilon Mesopotamicum variegatum, Acalypha Macafeeana, Achyranthes, Alternanthera, Anthericum vittatum variegatum, Ornamental-leaved Begonia, Centaurea gymnocarpa, Centaurea Candida, Cineraria maritima, Coleus, Euonymus Japonicus aureus, Euonymus argenteus, Euonymus radicans variegata, Farfugium grande, Variegated-leaved Geranium, Fragrant Geranium, Glaucium corniculatum.

Flowering Plants.—Ageratum Mexicanum and var., Alyssum Colossus, Double White Alyssum, Alyssum variegatum, Alyssum The Gem, Begonia, Cuphea, Fenzlia, Fuchsia, Geranium, Heliotrope, Lantana, Mahernia odorata, Mahernia Hector, Mimulus, Nierembergia, Oxalis floribunda alba, Oxalis floribunda rosea, Petunia, Rivinia, Schizanthus.

A good home-made hanging-basket may be constructed thus: Take coarse, heavy wire for foundation and handle and interlace it with old hoop wire, made pliable by heating. Then take young portulacca plants with a lump of earth attached to each; put the plants outward through the open spaces of the basket until it is full. The plants take kindly to their unnatural position and soon become a mass of beautiful green and brilliant flowers. In each basket place an empty tin box, inserted in a cavity in the top portion of the earth. Fill this with water daily, and in it place fresh flowers, as fancy dictates. The effect is delightful.

Another is shown in the next cut. It is made of a gourd, the top rim being cut into scollops and the bottom end cut off to allow drainage. It should be filled with a light, rich soil, and if planted with Dichorsandra for its centre and Othouna for the droop, its effect will be most beautiful.

Hanging vases of silvered double glass can be had. A false bottom is added to promote drainage, and by means of a tube the gathered water can be drawn off. The effect of foliage is greatly improved by the reflecting surfaces of such a vase.

Birds are charming pets in a home. Their sweet songs add exquisite pleasure to other natural beauties. A talking parrot is hardly to be reckoned as a gem; but a singing canary is a prize. The *trouble* of keep-

GOURD HANGING-BASKET.

ing them is sometimes complained of, but bird-fanciers sum up the whole matter thus:

Keep the cage clean.

Place the cage so that no draft of air can strike the bird, and not too near windows in cold weather.

Give nothing to healthy birds but seed, water, cuttle-fish bone, and gravel on the floor of cage. An occasional lump of pure white sugar may be added.

Occasionally a little water for bathing.

The room should not be overheated.

When moulting (shedding feathers) keep warm and avoid drafts of air.

Give plenty of rape seed.

A little hard-boiled egg grated fine is excellent.

LADIES' HANDIWORK.

Beyond all the professional decorator can do, and all that can be done with natural objects, there is a realm of decorative possibility where the wives and daughters of our homes reign supreme.   Their skillful fingers and exquisite taste work wonders of ornamentation.   The internal fittings and furnishings of a house are but the framework on which those who love and brighten home display their choice embellishments.

To specify all the beautiful things which tasty ladies can make with unpromising material is not possible; much less can these attractions be described.   But the subject may be illustrated, and hints concerning it may be given.

Mantel decorations are very popular and elegant.   They are attached to a board placed on the mantel slab.   This is covered with the chosen material, which also depends from the edge—plain, plaited, scalloped, or draped.   An elegant decoration of this kind, recently exhibited in the Decorative Art Rooms, of New York, was made of deep, wine-colored plush cut in a shallow scallop, the centre being about eighteen inches deep, and caught up carelessly with a handsome cord and pompon tassels one-quarter yard from each end, so that a very graceful, draped effect was given.   Its centre was decorated with a branch design of wild roses, so arranged that its uppermost part will lay over on the mantel.   The blossoms—made of rose-colored velvet—were so folded as to be a perfect representation of real rose petals; stamens and pistils were worked with gold thread; leaves and branches in arrasene.   The bottom was finished with alternate tassels of pink and light and dark shades of olive.

Another design was made of olive macramé twine crocheted in an open pattern and having two-inch wide cardinal satin ribbon interlaced in the openings.   This twine comes in a variety of colors, and to make a lambrequin eighteen inches deep and fringe would require five bunches.

There are imported tapestry designs for valances and chair-backs which are sought after by those who wish to furnish in antique style. They come in quaint designs, usually rural scenes, worked in quarter single stitches, which resemble a woven texture in their fineness, and are to be filled in with whatever solid color may seem adapted. Illustrations of this art will be found among the various cuts of this volume.

An ordinary kitchen table can be transformed into quite an elegant piece of furniture for the library. The top and legs are smoothly covered with green cloth ; the seam neatly sewed, and on the inside, that it may not show. It is then tacked at the top to hold it in place. Cloth is then drawn smoothly over

MINIATURE TABLE FOR FRUIT.

the top and tacked all round the sides. The piece extending round the sides of the table must also be covered. An under shelf made of pine wood covered with cloth is then fitted securely to the legs about eight inches below the top. A heavy cord fringe of green worsted must be fastened round the edge of the top, also round the shelf, with brass-headed nails about an inch and a half apart. A caster fitted into each leg will finish this very handsome table.

A miniature table, to be used as an ornamental fruit-stand, is shown in the preceding cut. It is made of bamboo, rustic branches, or turned legs, painted or gilded, as taste suggests. These are attached at their tops to a wide hoop, into which a deep dish fits firmly. The legs are then tied securely at their point of crossing with a cord and tassel. The outer edge of the hoop is then ornamented with drapery of bright colored cloth or satin with bead work, ornamented with tassels. A painted plaque or handsome dish may be inserted in the table, and so serve as a card-receiver.

A handsome table-cover may be made of sateen with a plush bordering. The centre should be of olive green, the border of a darker shade. On the four sides, just above the plush, the names of the four seasons may be worked in fancy letters with crewels or silks, each

ORNAMENTAL COVER FOR TABLE.

word decorated with flowers or leaves appropriate to the season. Fancy stitches worked in different colored silks may ornament the seam where the plush and sateen join.

Great variety may be secured in standing work-baskets. Stands of great variety in wicker-work are sold. Get one with two shelves, in each of which cut a hole large enough to receive an ordinary straw hat, crown downward. The braid around the edges of the shelves must be gilt, also the rings. The brim of the upper hat must have a full facing of blue satin. A bag of the same is fitted into the crown and drawn together with a satin ribbon at its top. A bunch of artificial roses and leaves is fastened on one side of the brim. The under hat has a full facing of satin, cut large enough to serve as a lining for the crown. A large, gilt ring is fastened to the edge of the upper shelf between each pair of supports, and a broad band of satin ribbon, which may be hand-painted, is run through each ring, then crossed to the lower shelf, where it is fastened to the leg with a double bow and ends. The outside of the hats may be gilded if preferred.

The adjoining cut shows another form of stand. This stand may be bought in rattan, or made of rustic boughs suitably curved. Two hoops are used in this stand, into which painted or ornamental dishes fit securely, their edges being hung with crewel or with bead-work. To make the bead bordering, take a narrow strip of oil-cloth and fit it tightly around the edges of the hoops and plates.

VISITING-CARD STAND.

Measure off equal distances and sew on black jet buttons.

From these, string bronze beads for the first or upper row. Make the second row of gold beads and the third of white. Attach these to the jet buttons.   Make a final row of variously colored beads, twisted together, and fastened to

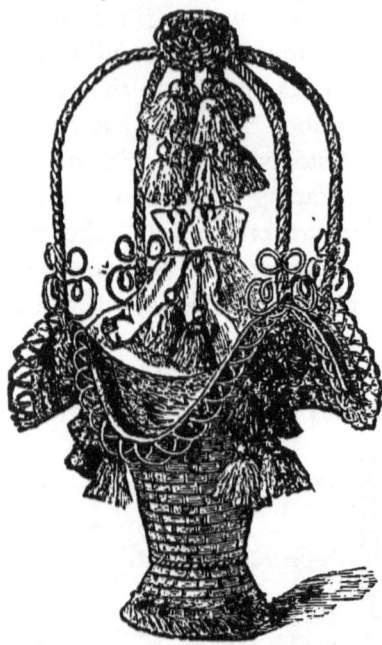

the jet buttons. After these are all in place and gracefully festooned, cut away any of the oil-cloth which shows below the ornaments.

Fancy baskets are capable of very beautiful adornment. Such baskets can be had in the stores in many decidedly attractive forms. The work upon those shown in the illustrations is such as a practiced eye can readily trace.   The blending of colors will afford fine opportunity for a display of taste.   Even the scrap-basket may be so embellished that the container

LADY'S WORK-BASKET.

of refuse becomes a minister of pleasure.   The willow-ware furnished for this purpose is varied so greatly and so elegantly that a good base for operations is easily secured.   The decorations can be attached readily also, which is a point of value.   The result is so light in weight, and withal so beautiful and useful, that scrap-basket decoration becomes specially inviting.

A novelty in scrap-baskets may be made as follows: Select a medium-sized Japanese umbrella with a plain ground and gilt figures.   Glue the knob or point securely into a square or circular block of wood smoothly finished. This block must be heavy enough to serve as a stand for the umbrella and hold it steadily in its upright position. The block is to be painted the color of the umbrella and decorated with gilt figures. To prevent the umbrella from falling open, the points of the ribs must be interlaced with satin ribbon. Several shades of the narrowest ribbons may be turned in and out of the ribs like basket-work, or a wide ribbon may be used. The umbrella should be not quite half open. A piece of gilt paper must be cut to fit the inside of the umbrella and prevent papers and scraps from falling through to the point,

CIRCULAR SCRAP-BASKET.

SQUARE SCRAP-BASKET.

from whence it would be difficult to remove them. If narrow ribbons are used for the lacings, tie a bunch of them round the handle with long loops and ends, and their many colors make a gay trimming. With the wider ribbon use a full bow.

A Japanese umbrella may be utilized as a fire-screen by adorning it with peacock's feathers. Cut off the stems of the feathers to within a few inches of the eyes; then stitch

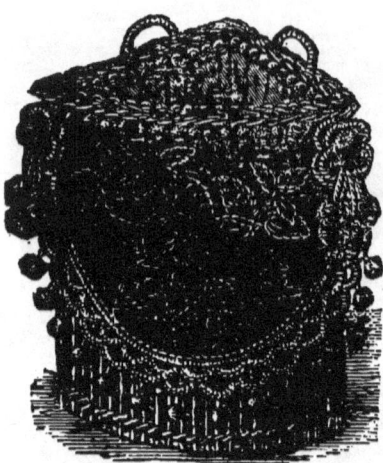

the eyes on in rows around the umbrella, beginning at the outer edge, and have each row to overlap the other till the centre is reached; then finish the centre off with a tuft of small feathers. The umbrella should never be closed, as the shutting would be disastrous to the feathers. When completed, the handle of the umbrella may be set into an upright

CORNER SCRAP-BASKET.   shaft, which is supported

in a base of heavy wood. The umbrella-handle should not exceed six inches in length, the support about two feet high. The base and support should be brightly colored.

A beautifully embroidered fire-screen is shown in the adjoining cut. Frames for these can be purchased in many styles; the taste and skill of home fill out the centre. The materials for this centre are varied and elegant, and if well handled, the result must be delightful. The screens are valuable to

EMBROIDERED FIRE-SCREEN.

shade the glow of a fire or to screen from observation.

An ornamental wall-pocket may be made of cardboard covered with gray linen, embroidered with brown wool. Cut one piece of cardboard to serve for the back and bottom and five pieces for the front. Bind each of these with a strip of gray linen and cover with the same material. Work in brown wool the design selected, stitching through the cardboard. Line the back with linen to conceal the stitches

ORNAMENTAL WALL-POCKET.

and sew the several pieces together. Take five pieces of cane four and a half inches long for the edges of the back; also five more of the same length, five four inches long, and six five inches long, all for the front portion. A half inch from the ends of the canes cut grooves into which the crossing canes may be fitted. Tie them strongly—first with thread, then with brown ribbon—so completing the

cane frame. Into this the cardboard case is fitted and
secured by stitches. For a cover, cut a cardboard double
the shape of the opening in the top of the pocket; cut this
half through across its centre, covering the uncut side with
linen, on which a full pattern is worked, as shown in the

HAND-BAGS FOR LADIES.

illustration. By stitching along this central cut, fasten this
piece to the frame, so that one part of it becomes a back
and the other a cover, to which add a loop and ornamental
bows.

Ladies' hand-bags may be made in styles and of materials

STATIONERY OR NEEDLE BOOK.

innumerable. The cuts suggest enough; taste can supply
the rest. The cut immediately above shows a pretty design
for a stationery or needle book—made of covered cardboard

and neatly embroidered. This book will prove both elegant and useful to its owner.

The wall-cushion illustrated is formed upon basket-work. The upright part is for breastpins, etc., the other for common pins, and a neat jewelry-case may be formed inside.

Pincushions have ever been a delightsome field for artistic effort. In shape, material, filling, etc., they vary indefinitely.

Crewel work, bead work, patch work, ribbon work, lace work, and all other kinds of work, are brought to bear on pincushions, and many are the conquests which have been made in this line. Every home has something in the way of bureau-covers, toilet sets, tidies, sofa-cushions, pillow-shams, pen-wipers, shaving cases, whisp-holders, etc.,

ORNAMENTAL WALL-CUSHION.

etc. In many instances these are but rude attempts, and yet they are not to be despised. Rude attempts always precede success, and sometimes inaugurate it. Welcome, then, every honest attempt at art.

A peep into the best bed-room of a tasty prairie home will be useful. The walls were tinted blue and the paint was white. The carpet was of dyed rags, blue and faint buff the prevailing colors. It covered the centre only, a surrounding strip of bare floor being stained. The bedstead was in cottage style and of a delicate blue. A fancy stool answered also as a coal and wood box. It was a box with a hinged top, which was wadded to form a cushion, the whole covered with suitable cretonne. A sewing-table was made of two circular pieces of wood nailed at the ends of a short, stout pole. On the bottom four casters were fixed. It was then covered with light-blue cambric and tied in the centre of the pole, so as to form the shape of an hour-glass. Upon this was a cover of plain or dotted Swiss, finished with a plaiting of narrow blue ribbon around the top and with small bows. A most comfortable chair

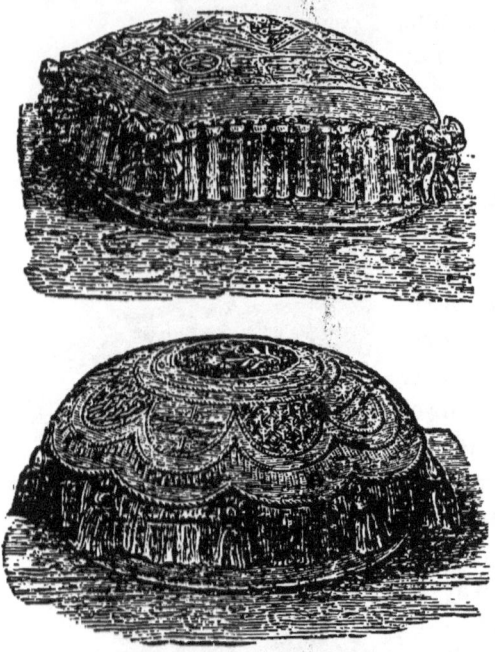

ORNAMENTAL PINCUSHIONS.

was made of a flour barrel. Take a sound barrel and saw off about four inches; then attach casters to the lower end. At the height you wish the seat, saw through five or six staves, as may be necessary to compass the width desired; six or eight inches higher up saw through about four staves on each side, and you have the arms, and the remaining long staves afford the back. At a point a little below the first sawed place, perforate the barrel around its circumference with auger-holes; then with stout twine, interlaced

like a bed-cord, but more closely, weave your seat from side
to side, in alternate holes. In trimming use heavy un-
bleached domestic or ordinary ticking and over this a
covering of cretonne, to harmonize with the carpet. A
cushion may be used and the space left for the arms, and
the back should be padded.

The dressing-table was made of a dry-goods box set on
end, being about two and a half feet high. This was

BEAUTIFUL TOILETS.—MAY BE MADE FROM PACKING-BOXES.

overed with cambric, the same shade as that on the
sewing-table. Over this was a dotted Swiss cover and
around the upper edges a plaiting of narrow blue ribbon.
The mirror was suspended from a nail above the table. To
it was fastened three yards of the Swiss, finished at the ends
with lace about an eighth of an inch wide and caught in the
centre with a piece of blue ribbon tied in a full bow,
which also held it fast to the nail. The ends hung from
each side of the nail down to the front corners of the table,

to which they were attached with ribbon bows and stretched back to the wall.   Upon the table was a pretty toilet set in light blue glass, a set of toilet mats worked upon pale blue Java canvas, and a pincushion to match.   The windows were ornamented with simple Swiss curtains caught back with blue bows.

A few special features of upholstery, which any lady of taste can apply in her own home, may yet be touched.   The opposite cut of an upholstered bedstead is suggestive.   A common bedstead, or one showing hard usage, may be covered on this plan so as to become an object of beauty.

A plain cane-seated sofa, or an antiquated wooden settee, may be similarly decorated, and be far more comfortable and elegant for

SHEARATON SOFA—IN POLISHED WOOD AND LEATHER CUSHIONS.

the work.   To illustrate this method of procedure, the Shearaton sofa is shown above.   Its make is more elaborate, but its covering is on the same general plan as is suggested for the plainer furniture.

In doing any of this upholstered and cushioned work, the best way is to make and fit all the parts with cushions made of ticking or other substantial material.   When the fit is assured, cover with cretonne, leather, or other goods, and finish as desired.   On the top an ornamental tuft or suitable button should show, the cord being drawn tightly and tied on the under side.   The cushions should be firmly attached to the settee.

UPHOLSTERED AND CANOPIED BEDSTEAD.

As a masterpiece of upholstery, intended more to suggest than to be copied, a sofa by Henri Fourdinois, of Paris, in

ELABORATE SOFA.—STYLE OF LOUIS XVI.

the style of Louis XVI, is inserted. It is in all respects a study worthy of profound attention. Its carvings may be too elaborate, but its elegant drapery may readily be copied.

More as a curiosity than as a pattern worthy of imitation, an old style canopied and curtained bedstead is shown below. Excluded thus from fresh air, the only wonder is that royal and wealthy personages managed to live at all. Uncovered bedsteads in well-ventilated rooms are immensely more conducive to health and longevity.

CANOPIED AND CURTAINED BEDSTEAD.—STYLE OF LOUIS XIV.

Embroidery and painting are very popular and elegant employments for ladies. Both these arts may rise very high. The famous Bayeux tapestry contains 1,512 figures, of which sixty-five are dogs, 202 horses, 505 other quadrupeds, birds, or sphinxes; 623 are men, twenty-seven buildings, forty-one boats, and forty-nine trees. It is divided into fifty-eight parts, each representing a scene in the career of William the Conqueror, and each having an inscription in Latin. This tapestry is of linen, two hundred feet long by twenty inches wide. Worsteds in seven colors are used in it. It is preserved in the town hall of Bayeux, France, and is regarded as the work of Queen Matilda, in the twelfth century.

From this pinnacle of art there are gradations, almost imperceptible, downward to the simplest work of school-girls and little children. Knitting and crochet work also are varied beyond the power of adequate description, and so are many other forms of useful and ornamental needlework.

Decorative painting has a scope equally broad. In home work it employs all grades and hues of coloring material and exercises itself upon woods, china, glass, shells, silks, satins, velvets, and almost every other attainable fabric. A thousand or more dollars is not a sum unusual for a hand-painted porcelain vase

PAINTED VASE.

PAINTED VASE.

of no great size. Fifty dollars is a common price for a single high-grade hand-painted plate, and as much for an ornamental wall plaque. But these are the extravagances of decoration. A few such articles tone up the taste of a community, but they cannot be generally indulged in. Some gems of art are, however, within the reach of all. One who has not looked into the facts of this subject will be amazed at the variety and elegance of small wares which are strictly artistic. In wood, china, metal, pottery, and woven fabrics they are found in charming forms, and at low prices.

Among the less expensive and yet very beautiful materials which invite home effort in the art of coloring are certain forms of pottery, prepared expressly for this purpose. The Albertine ware, for instance, produced at the ancient pottery at North Cambridge, Mass., is made of a very fine clay, which, when burnt, is of a rich dark red or genuine terra-cotta color. Even without painting these goods are much used as cabinet ornaments. They are specially adapted to oil colors,

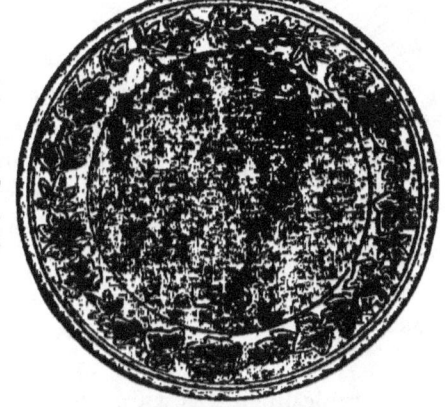

PLAQUE WITH OPEN CENTRE FOR PICTURE, MIRROR, ETC.

which need no " firing," as do the mineral colors. This process avoids much of expense and much of uncertainty as to results of firing, which often surprise the amateur.

Careful attention has been paid in fashioning this ware that beautiful and artistic styles shall be secured in every piece. Forms have been evoked from the ruins of the past. Cups, vases, pitchers, and other vessels — some of

PLAQUE WITH FLOWERS IN BOLD RELIEF.

them dug up at ancient Troy by Dr. Schliemann—have been reproduced with exact conformity in shape and size. High relief is a characteristic of this ware. Flowers, leaves, stems,

and other forms stand boldly out and afford a most inviting field for the artistic hand. The accompanying illustrations show the general appearance of these goods, which vary in sizes from eight to eighteen inches in diameter, or in height.

On this matter of painting and ornamentation a word of warning may be raised. Things are ornamented which are better plain. Every article of mer-

VASE.—FLOWERS IN RELIEF.

chandise has its ornament stamped or attached in some way. Clothing, bed-linen, table-linen, tinware, woodenware, silverware—all sorts of ware—are covered with monograms, coats-of-arms, meaningless emblems, and intricate convolutions, the fundamental idea of which neither owner nor maker can tell. Better leave some articles for unadorned utility.

And some proper subjects for decoration are improperly decorated. Imagine the "Author Dinner Plates!"—An excellent portrait of the honored Longfellow is smothered in gravy; potatoes are piled upon the beard of Bryant, while fish-bones mingle with the curls of Tenny-

VASE.—FLOWERS IN RELIEF.

son. Good taste revolts at such a position for portraits, even though they be elegantly painted. A china set of "Insect Breakfast Plates" is owned by a family of general good taste, but the little girl of the household shrinks with horror from a certain garden-worm whenever her food happens to accompany that decoration. The law is this: Decorate none but proper articles, and decorate them properly.

Clarence Cook, writing on over-decoration, delivers himself in the following forceful words: " The architects cannot design a house or a church, but they must carve every stone; cover the walls with cold, discordant tiles; break up every straight line with cuts and chamfers; plow every edge into moldings; crest every roof-ridge and dormer-window with painted and gilded iron, and refuse to give us a square foot of wall

PITCHER.—FLOWERS IN BOLD RELIEF.

on which to rest the tired eye. Within, the furniture follows in the same rampant lawlessness. The beauty of simplicity in form; the pleasure to be had from lines well thought out; the agreeableness of unbroken surfaces where there is no gain in breaking them; harmony in color, and, on the whole, the ministering to the satisfaction we all have in not seeing the whole of everything at once,—these considerations the makers of our furniture, ' fashionable' and ' Canal Street' alike, have utterly ignored, and the strife has long been: Who shall make the loudest chairs and sofas and give us the most glare and glitter for our money ?"

PYRAMIDAL VASE.

III.—EXTERIOR DECORATIONS.

A RTISTIC architecture is doing wonders in the external decoration of homes. Even where long rows of city houses stand in serried ranks, the present tendency is to break up monotony, to secure beautiful variety. This is done by introducing diversity of forms and colors. Bay-windows, mansard-roofs, Swiss projections, permanent window-gardens, variously colored bricks, slates, tiles, stones, etc., and the splendid decorations in terra cotta, make fine variety possible. Where stone is used ornamentation is limited only by the genius of the architect and the purse of the owner.

In cathedrals and grand public buildings, statuary plays an important part in decoration, but for private use this is unsuitable, except the house be very large and ornate. In private grounds, statuary and vases are allowable if in harmony with their surroundings. Mercury should not be the conspicuous piece in a camp-meeting ground, nor should St. Peter or St. Paul be the chief feature in a commercial exchange.

The choice materials for statuary are marble and bronze. For outside positions, the stress of weather is damaging, however, and the general effect is none the less happy if baser materials be employed. Such ornaments are a specialty with various artistic workers in metal, whose elegant reproductions of the best works of statuary and vases are prepared in iron and zinc, and of all desirable sizes. A few ornaments of this character will greatly improve any grounds. Their location should be artistic, and with an eye for the effect. It is not the vase alone that should be displayed, but its display should beautify the surroundings.

166

The question of color arises here. On a dark background

POPLAR-LEAF VASE ON CRANE PEDESTAL.
[Iron-Bronzed, 41 inches high.]

white shows best; on an open background the bronzes are preferable.

In rural homes, or those where city lots are large, the architecture of the house is of no great consequence, for trees and vines can be so disposed as to make it seem magnificent. And yet a splendid house has greater possibilities. The lawn is a most attractive feature, if nicely graded, well grassed, and closely cropped by a lawn-mower. Trees and smaller shrubbery must be placed with reference to their effect. In the great parks " dummies " resembling trees are used, so that the exact effect of certain locations can

BERLIN VASE
[Iron-Bronzed.]

be determined. These can be shifted from place to place, so helping to correct conclusions. Any other feature, as in landscape gardening, must be located by similar means. Effect is sought, and this must be the best possible, as viewed from the most important point. Nothing in a garden should be at hap-hazard.

BERLIN VASE.
[Zinc-Bronzed.]

Egyptian vases for garden uses are beautiful, but the strong coloring of the ancients must be shunned, especially in the upper part, where they mingle with the flowers. In the accompanying cut of an Egyptian vase the base (B) is constructed of wood, and is painted bright blue, red, and yellow, or merely tinted a light or porcelain blue and red toned to a brownish cast. The flower-pot, or upper part (A), is to be made of red clay or terra cotta, the ornaments in relief to be colored a greenish blue, *eau de Nile*. The pot with its contents should be removed to the greenhouse when the cold weather comes on, the pedestal remaining as a permanent winter decoration.

EGYPTIAN VASE.

Home-made vases may be constructed of cast-off boxes of small size, half-kegs, etc. These are readily covered with rustic strips, made of bark or of pieces of sapling cut in half longitudinally. Holes must be bored in the bottoms, and the whole be mounted on an upright post two or three feet in height. With standing plants in the centre, and trailing plants at the edges, very beautiful display may be secured by this simple and inexpensive means. Of course, the covering strips of bark should be up and down, or else at an angle for beauty's sake.

ANTIQUE FLORAL VASE.

Indeed, the scope for taste to play in these little contrivances is unlimited.

A garden vase which any mechanic can construct, with a
base which any woodman may provide, is shown below to
dispel the notion that objects of beauty cannot be made at
home.   The spaces must be closed with sheets of tenacious

IRON VASE ON A RUSTIC BASE.

moss, the interior filled with rich earth, planted with rapid
growers and abundant bloomers.   Abundant water must be
given so that the whole may remain in bloom.

It has become customary in the most beautiful rural cities and villages to discard fences. A stone curbing marks the street line, while the dividing line of neighbors is not visible, but the open lawn, kept by mutual arrangement, runs on unbroken. Hedges may be employed as necessary fencing, or to conceal unsightly objects which cannot be removed. A good hedge requires a good soil, so that its growth may be vigorous. The plants,

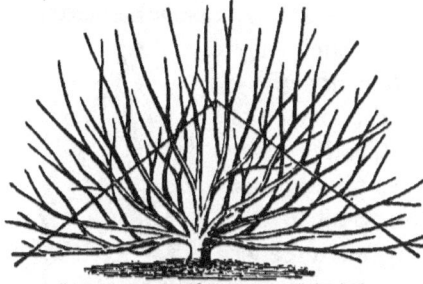

FORM OF PRUNING A HEDGE.

when set out, should be of equal size and set in a single line. The Japan quince can be planted six inches apart, and the honey locust and Osage orange at nine inches.

Different styles of planting have been practiced, such as setting the plants in double or triple rows, setting them very closely, as within three or four inches of each other, and also at distances as great as eighteen inches or two feet. Experience has shown that the plants when close to each other grow thin and feebly; that with sufficient care a better hedge can be made with wide than with narrow planting. In the spring of the

FORM OF FULL-GROWN HEDGE.

second year the soil about the hedge must be well worked. The main shoot must be cut back to within one joint of its starting point, the side shoots remaining a little longer.

In the third spring, trim in a pyramidal form, as in the first cut. This secures light and air at the centre of the plant. A later cutting may bring the branches back almost to the first outline. Four or five years will secure a hedge five feet high and six feet thick, through which neither man nor beast can pass. Its form may be trimmed at last into that shown in the second cut.

Rustic seats always adorn grounds of reasonable extent. Single chairs or extended benches may be made, and stumps or other unsightly objects may be pressed into the service of beauty and utility. Over rustic seats vines should clamber, or trees should cast their shade. No one wishes to sit in the glare of the sun. A Virginia creeper will speedily form a dense covering for such a place. A little care will train it as an arch, an umbrella, an awning, a tent, or almost any desired object.

RUSTIC CHAIR.

For outdoor flower-holders many devices have been worked out. There are terra-cotta pots fashioned to resemble stumps and rustic boxes. Rightly

RUSTIC BENCH.

placed, these heighten the artistic effect of a garden. For all plants in vases, or similar vessels, special attention is needed or they will dry out. If sufficient water is given there is no danger from the heat of the sun—perhaps it is an advantage. Instead of watering with a pitcher, give a pailful at a time, gently and slowly showered upon the plants. After the trailing plants in a vase fall over the sides, they afford a shade; but if anything like proper care is used, plants will thrive as well in vases as in any other location.

The Gypsy Kettle is a pretty decoration for a garden. The error of making it gaudy should be avoided. Its colors should not rival those of its contents. When a crown-

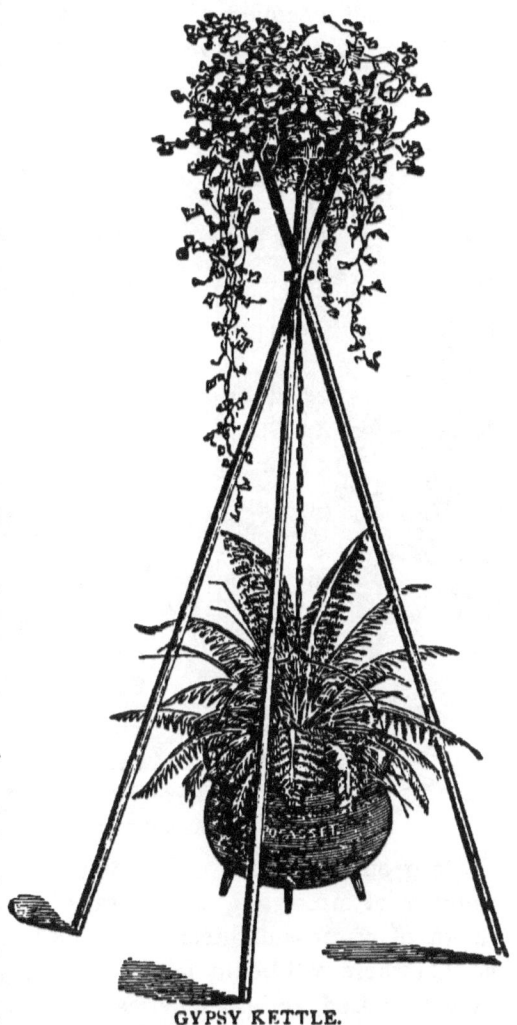

ing flower-pot is used on the stand, allow it the trailing plants, while the erect occupy the larger receptacle. Holes must be made in these vessels or excessive moisture will result, to the serious damage of all the plants. The same plants as suit hanging-baskets suit these kettles, and the same care prescribed for those and for vases will answer exactly for the gypsy article. The adoption of kettle decoration has been sternly condemned as savoring too much of the kitchen, but the romance of the gypsy feature suf-

GYPSY KETTLE.

fices to conceal the homeliness of the "potato-pot." Then, too, it might be presumed that not all who see a thing in itself beautiful, would cling to its commonest suggestions.

Birds may add to the charms of a garden. Aviaries, which can be removed to a warm apartment in winter, may decorate the grounds in summer. They should be elevated, to keep out enemies of the birds, unless the inclosing meshes be so fine as to render this precaution useless.

PORTABLE AVIARY.

On ground which is quite moist, but not submerged, a number of interesting plants may be raised. When the depth of water is eighteen inches and over, and the supply so that there will be no failure in a dry time, water lilies may be raised, and pontederias, or pickerel weed, heteranthera, eel grass, white water crowfoot, water target, and the handsome foreigner, the Cape pond-weed.

For the margin, in shallow water, there is a numerous class of plants, such as the different species of rush, the cattail hair, the water plantain, the loosestrife, or lythrum, nesæa, Dutch moss, or anacharis, and the handsome water pitchers.

Here, too, we may have the mosses, which Ruskin thus describes: "Meek creatures! the first mercy of the earth, veiling with hushed softness its dintless rock; creatures full of pity, covering with strange and tender honor the scarred

GARDEN OF THE SULTAN'S PALACE, CONSTANTINOPLE.

disgrace of ruin, laying quiet fingers on the trembling stones to teach them rest. No words that I know will say what these mosses are. None are delicate enough, none perfect enough, none rich enough. They will not be gathered, like the flowers, for chaplet or love token; but of these the wild bird will make its nest, and the wearied child his pillow. And as they are the earth's first mercy, so they are its last gifts to us; when all other service is vain from plant and tree, the soft mosses and gray lichen take up their watch by the head-stone. The woods, the blossoms, the gift-bearing grasses have done their parts for a time, but these do service forever."

One of the prettiest freaks of nature is that which buries a house in vines. For the most satisfactory results the vines must be favorably rooted in the earth. Balcony gardening and exterior window gardening may go on beautifully by means of pots and boxes, but such work is, necessarily, of limited extent. One of the most striking instances of vine decoration is shown in the engraving here given. It is an actual drawing from a French home. A vine-loving visitor thus described it in one of our floral monthlies: "From the flag sidewalk grew a large grape-vine, with a stem possibly five inches in thickness, without a branch or leaf until it reached the second story. It was then trained over the balcony, making a most beautiful arbor, and ascended still higher. Being the latter part of the summer, the vine was well loaded with white grapes. Some of the bunches

VINE COVERED FRENCH DWELLING.

were grown in thin glass bottles, or vessels of some kind.

somewhat after the manner in which English gardeners sometimes grow cucumbers. I have never seen another balcony that seemed to me so charming."

The Canary Flower is a beautiful vine, but little used, and yet well adapted to our climate. Its leaves are a beautiful, light green, and its flowers of a bright lemon yellow color. The flowers grow in rich masses and make a splendid appearance when in luxuriant growth. The appended cut shows a bay-window shaded by this lovely creeper. On the cool side of a

CANARY VINE.

porch or summer-house the Canary Flower is charming.

In England the scarlet and dwarf Tropæolums are depended upon mainly for heavy masses of bright color. It is a pretty plan to grow Nasturtiums on trellises and single poles, and sometimes

PYRAMID OF NASTURTIUM AND MORNING GLORIES.

make a kind of pyramid by placing six or eight poles in a

circle some four feet in diameter, fastening them together at
the top like an Indian tent, while with these Morning Glories may be blended, so producing a rapid shade, which is
very beautiful to behold.   Shady places are more favorable
to Nasturtiums than those more exposed, but loosening the
soil and watering freely will work wonders for them even
in the dryest times.

CALADIUM PLANTS.

And now, while on the shady places, it may as well be
said that it is by no means easy to obtain flowers without
some sunshine.   Two hours of sunshine a day will, however, give life enough to many plants to insure flowers.   In
shady places we can have ferns, of course, and Caladiums,
Cannas, and other foliage plants, but it is not best to try
flowers.

Where there are two hours of sunshine we can have Fuchias, Pansies, Lily of the Valley, Perennial Phloxes, For-get-me-nots, and many other things that succeed better in partial shade than in the full sunshine. For such places the Japan and California Lilies are pre-eminently valuable.

The Caladium has become a great favorite in this country, as it well deserves to be, because its leaves are so large and handsome, and also because it never disappoints. It is very rare for a bulb to fail to grow and give satisfaction. The preceding engraving is from a photograph of a plant of one season only. Leaves of the Caladium have grown to be by actual measurement three feet and seven inches in length, thirty inches in width, and ten feet three inches in circumference. Another leaf has been reported which reached the enormous length of forty-one inches, and was twenty-eight inches wide. While so gigantic, they are also beautiful in texture, and strikingly so from their splendid size.

Other splendid leaf plants are numerous and inexpensive. The Ricinus, or castor-oil plant, is a king in its way. Rich and luxuriant in appearance and quick to grow, it is justly a great favorite. The Maranta, or Calathea, is a splendidly striped leaf plant. The leaves grow from one to two feet in length, are purple underneath, and beautifully ribbed with velvet on top. This is also a splendid in-door plant.

Everybody knows the value of roses and other flowering plants. The superb catalogues of the leading florists of the country furnish all needed information concerning them, so that the only duty here is to point out these ample sources of information and supply, and commend the public to try the best of them.

A glimpse at French gardening is given in the following view of the garden of Fontainebleau, the pride of the Parisian heart. The very trees are trimmed into perfect order. Indeed, this garden is excessive in its regularity. There are too many right lines. Landscape gardening, with its unending variety, commands more general favor in this country.

GARDENS OF FONTAINEBLEAU.

The same objection lies against the style shown in the following cut, which is a view from the grounds of an Italian nobleman.

Clearly, in this case, the master mind was of a strictly mathematical turn. There are flower-beds, plenty of them, laid out on the square ; plenty of shrubbery, every alternate piece being clipped to a uniform cylinder. There is a liberal display of statuary, all standing just so high and at a uniform

SCENE IN AN ITALIAN GARDEN.

distance apart, the whole ground evidently having been laid out with compass and square to a mathematical point.

A few gardens of this character are pleasing ; or a portion of any garden so laid out secures variety, but such regularity must be occasional only. The distinctly marked figures in the heavens are very few, and we of the earth may take a lesson therefrom. But some right lines and sharply marked figures are admissible.

The ribbon beds, now so popular for parks, lawns, and gardens, are beautiful illustrations of regularity. This system of bedding, it is claimed, is artificial, and not in good taste, which possibly is true; but tastes differ and change constantly. It is now thought in good taste to imitate and admire the productions of Japanese art by those who, a few years ago, ridiculed the poor, benighted Japs. So taste changes in flower beds.

Ribbon beds may be of flowering or variegated leaf-plants, or of both in combination. The principal consideration in making such beds is to procure plants of nearly uniform height, and flowering, that will keep in bloom during the whole season, for a failure in either respect will mar, if not ruin, the bed. The plants must be set so close together, that when they have attained their growth, the whole bed will be

RIBBON BED.

covered without a break. The tops must be pinched off judiciously so that there will be no excessive growth, but that they all will show evenly.

One of the finest displays of variegated flower beds can

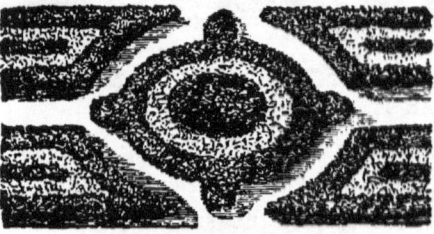

be made with the bulbous plants of the early spring. Crocuses, Hyacinths, and Tulips may all adorn the gardens, and if carefully selected and arranged splendid effects will be

PLAN OF RIBBON BEDS.

secured as the reward of the gardener's taste and skill.

There is really no limit to the styles which may be introduced in these beds, both in their component parts and in their forms. From the diminutive growth of the lowest-growing plants to the most stately of them, all find a place and a use in ribbon beds.

Dwarf trees are a specialty with the Chinese. Pines and oaks a half century old are seen in their flower-pots. The secret of the dwarfing is in weakening the seat of vigor all that is possible without destroying life. Take, for example, a young cedar two or three inches high and cut off its tap root, resetting that on a stone in a shallow pan with a clay

PAMFILI DORIA, A SUPERB ROMAN VILLA.

soil. Water and light enough to keep the plant alive are allowed, but no more. The shape is controlled by pegs and strings, and is often very odd. The Japanese carry this dwarfing to such a ridiculous degree that a Dutch merchant was shown a box three inches deep and with a square inch of surface, in which a bamboo, a fir, and a plum tree—the latter in full bloom—were growing and thriving. The price asked for this botanical curiosity was three hundred dollars.

Tastefully made rockeries are good adornments. They need not be built into arches and beacons, as is done sometimes with questionable taste, but they should be sufficiently large to deserve their title. The rocks must be so separated as to allow deep pockets of rich earth to be con-

structed. Many charming native plants will flourish in such places, but will not succeed in more open and exposed beds. The trailing arbutus, the partridge-berry, the dog's-tooth violet, blood

CIRCULAR ROCKERY,

root, Gentians, and Pyrolas, may be placed on a rock-work such as this. For early blossoms, crocus, snowdrops, the

 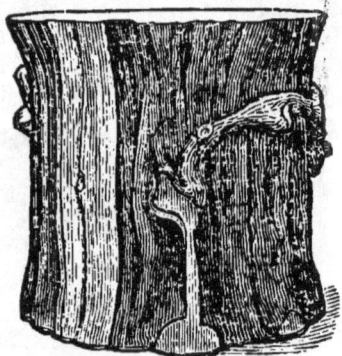

RUSTIC FLOWER STANDS.

smaller Narcissus, and tulips may be planted, and ferns, and even mosses from the woods, will here find a suitable habitation.

POLITE DEPORTMENT.

How sweet and gracious, even in common speech,
Is that fine sense which men call courtesy!
Wholesome as air and genial as the light—
Welcome in every clime as breath of flowers;
It transmutes aliens into trusting friends
And gives its owner passport round the globe.

JAMES T. FIELD.

POLITE DEPORTMENT.

SOME one has said that "a man's manners are his fortune," meaning that the way to position and easy competence in life is often found through gentleness and good breeding, which lead first to genuine respect, then to esteem and confidence. Many a young man has failed to secure a coveted place by reason of his boorish ways or awkward movements at a first interview, and foolishly charged his loss to "ill luck," when the fault was wholly with himself. Many another has moved right up to a well-deserved eminence in his calling more by his genteel and polite bearing than by reason of some superior mental capacity.

WHERE TO LOOK FOR MODELS.

True gentlemen and ladies may be found in the humblest walks of life, among both young and old. The marks that prove them such are not wholly external, though the internal conditions are evidenced by the external. There is a sham politeness which bows and smirks and is obeisant in public, but is detestably wanting in common civility in private. Such as indulge in this kind wear their manners as one wears an outer garment, which is put on when leaving home and left on the hall rack at the door when returning home. Some of these are the over-nice people, who pretend to hide their faces and try to affect blushes at the mere mention of some very natural and proper subjects. Others are known as the Exquisite, the Dandy, the Fop, the Dude, whose brains are generally less than their surface manners.

187

It is evident that as the principles of a language are ̄rived from the usage of the best writers and speakers, so ̤ne principles of polite deportment are derived from the usage of the truest and best people. The rules in the one case are not more definite than in those of the other. The highest point of culture to which any one may attain in either is purely a matter of choice. The beginning must be in one's-self, but with an assurance that the largest success is not only practicable, but a duty to self and to society.

THE REAL GENTLEMAN AND LADY.

A recent writer thus well describes the true gentleman and lady: "To formulate the definition in negatives would be easy. As, for instance, we may say that a true gentleman does not soil his conscience with falsehood, does not waste his time upon sensual indulgence, does not endeavor to make the worse appear the better reason, does not ridicule sacred subjects, does not willfully give cause of offense to any, does not seek to overreach his neighbor, does not forget the respect due to womanhood or to old age, the feeble or the poor. And so, too, the true lady does not condescend to scandal or gossip, does not profane her lips with 'slang' words, does not yield to outbursts of temper, does not sacrifice modesty to fashion, does not turn a deaf ear to the voice of distress. But, to speak affirmatively: A gentleman is one whose aims are generous, whose trust is constant, whose word is never broken, whose honor is never stained, who is as brave as gentle and as honest as wise, who wrongs no one by word or deed, and devotes and embellishes life by nobility of thought, depth of feeling, and grace of manner. As for the true lady—she will be, of necessity, the counterpart of the true gentleman: Pure, refined, generous, sweet of temper, gentle of speech, truthful to her heart's core, shunning the very appearance of evil, and instant in well-doing."

PERSONAL HABITS.

We are now ready to consider personal habits in their relation to polite deportment. Every person owes certain well-defined obligations to society, not only in the line of what is said and done in the presence of others, but in the appearance and habits, which in an important degree affect the comfort and pleasure of others. It has been well said that " cleanliness, neatness, and tidiness represent the triple incentive to the maintenance of any and every system of etiquette." An untidy person of either sex gives evidence either of ignorance or willful disregard of the commonest principles of politeness.

Other things being equal, the person who enjoys good health will be the best-mannered, and no one has any right to live in disregard of those practices and conditions which produce or promote health. The daily bath, proper cleansing of the teeth and mouth, scrupulous care as to the finger-nails, and careful dressing of the hair—without oils, pomades, or perfumes—are essential duties. Over-eating, with its train of headaches, foul breath, and indigestion ; and the use of tobacco in any form, with disgusting expectoration, are not the practices which mark the best-bred persons. " If one must chew, let him be particular where he expectorates. He should not discharge tobacco-juice in public vehicles, on the sidewalk, nor in any place where it will be offensive. The English rule is for him to spit in his handkerchief; but this is not a pleasant alternative. On some occasions no other may offer." Whether smoking is good or bad, wholesome or injurious, the excess of smoking is, at all events, as noxious to the smoker as it is disagreeable to his neighbors. If you must have your pipe or your weed, retire to some apartment kept exclusively as a smoking-room. Do not smoke in a lady's presence ; not even if her good nature prompt her to yield assent. You have no right to impregnate her garments with pot-house odor.

Toilet offices of all kinds should be in private. Cleansing the nose or the ears, or cleaning and trimming the finger nails in public, is an offense against decency, and never should be indulged in. Biting the nails, fingering the beard, drumming on the table with your fingers, crossing your legs and shaking your free foot, loud breathing, yawning, snuffling, and going about with hands thrust in the pockets, are not marks of politeness and good breeding. A quiet and self-possessed manner and quiet movements of the person are always better than restless and disturbing habits, which are sure to be obtrusive as well as disagreeable.

HABITS OF SPEECH.

One's habits of speech will betray the inward character. Truly polite people do not use other than polite language, which is but a plain, simple, and unaffected expression of one's thoughts. Coarse and vulgar words, slang phrases, and profanity should never have place. Some people swear because of an idea that it is manly; some from habit, without thinking of what they say; some are only profane when excited with anger; some from choice, neither fearing God nor regarding man, and in defiance of the divine command, "Swear not at all." A lady was once annoyed by the frequent oaths of a young student sitting near her in a railroad car. She kindly addressed him with a question whether he had studied the languages. "I have mastered them thoroughly," he replied. "Do you speak Hebrew?" she asked. "I do," was the answer. "Then will you do me the favor to do your swearing in Hebrew?" she asked. The rebuke was effectual.

With regard to the use of slang words by a lady, we are reminded of the grisly fairy story of a beautiful young woman from whose mouth, when she opened it, dropped frogs and toads. The practice of slang is as unworthy of a gentleman as it is of a lady.

Civility in speech is due to every person, and on all occasions. Employers would do well to remember that civil words, with kind and thoughtful actions, make friends of workmen or servants. Their use tends to bind more closely those who are already friends. Arrogance of speech and manner toward inferiors is on a par with servility toward superiors. True dignity and self-respect will lead to a correct deportment in dealing with either. There is a possibility of being over-civil. Promptly pick up anything that a lady lets fall, but do not rush to wait upon even a friend, lest you become servile in your attentions to the embarrassment of both yourself and your friend. You will not, however, fail in proper attention to elderly people. A nice sense of respect for the aged and kind attentions to them show a good heart.

General fussiness ought to be carefully avoided. Whether well or sick, it is needless, and entails a great deal of trouble and annoyance upon our friends. "There is nothing more fatal to comfort, as well as to decorum of behavior, than fuss."

AFFECTATION.

Affectation of any kind is ridiculous in any one. It may be termed "posing for effect." An article in *Harper's Bazar Book* paints some specimens: "The delicate young lady with the languid air, the listless step, or die-away posture! The literary young lady with the studiously neglected toilette, the carefully exposed breadth of forehead, and the ever-present but seldom-read book! The abstemious young lady, who surreptitiously feeds on chops at private lunch and starves on a pea at the public dinner! The humane young lady, who pulls Tom's ears and otherwise tortures brother and sister in the nursery and does her utmost to fall into convulsions before company at the sight of a dead fly! and the fastidious young lady, who faints—should there be an audience to behold the scene—at the sight of roast goose, but whose robust appetite vindicates itself by devouring all that is left of the unclean animal when a private opportunity will allow. Such affectations are not only absurd—for they are perfectly transparent—but ill-bred, as shams of all kinds essentially are."

Sidney Smith says: "All affectation proceeds from the supposition of possessing something better than the rest of the world possesses. Nobody is vain of possessing two legs and two arms, because that is the precise quantity of either sort of limb which everybody possesses." The affected individual is always full of self-consciousness, and this is simple vulgarity. A truly polite person is too busy in considering the comfort and welfare of others to devote much time to thoughts of a purely selfish character.

DRESS.

Closely related to personal habits is the question of dress. It has been well said that "the result of the finest toilet should be an elegant woman, not an elegantly dressed woman." Chesterfield's advice to his son was sensible, and applies well to our own times: " Dress yourself fine where others are fine, and plain where others are plain ; but take care always that your clothes are well made and fit you, for otherwise they will give you a very awkward air. When you are once well dressed for the day, think no more of it afterward, and without any stiffness for fear of discomposing that dress, let all your motions be easy and natural, as if you had no clothes on at all."

The objects of dress may be considered as threefold: To secure personal comfort and health, to preserve modesty, and to please the taste. Of men's clothing there is not much to say, except that it should be of quiet colors and well fitting. There is little opportunity for either contrasts or harmonious combinations of colors. But with the dress of women it is different. The most costly materials will fail to produce an agreeable impression unless their colors are carefully blended and the dressing forms a pleasing harmony in its general effect.

Ladies of a medium size may, perhaps, wear a dress with large figures, plaids, or stripes, if the prevailing fashions allow it; but either large or small ladies would scarcely be in taste to wear either. Much drapery is not becoming to a short and stout person, while one who is slender may be improved in appearance by drapery. Then, as to tints: it is well known that fair complexions require delicate tints, while brunettes require rich, dark shades.

Dresses should be carefully fitted to the form, yet not so that the natural functions of the body be impeded. Give nature room to move and breathe, and many a painful experience in bodily suffering will be prevented. By all means avoid tight belts about the waist. The dress should be becoming, and it will then be in taste. It should not be so noticeable that special attention would be attracted to it. To be entirely out of fashion is to be eccentric, yet a true independence will not lead to a servile following of every fashionable folly in dress that may appear. To be indifferent to one's proper appearance is a sign of indolence and . slovenliness

There should be consistency in dress. That is, there should be regard to one's circumstances in life, so that what cannot be afforded without pecuniary embarrassment never should be worn. The dress should be in harmony with the occasion. A ball-dress at a funeral would not be more out of place than the rich toilette of the drawing-room is found to be when chosen for a walking-suit.

But if there is one place more than another where great elegance and showiness of dress are out of taste, it is in the

House of God, where all should meet in equal humility before Him in whose sight outward adornment passes for nothing. Paley says, "If ever the poor man holds up his head, it is at church; if ever the rich man views him with respect, it is there, and both will be the better, and the public profited, the oftener they meet in a situation in which the consciousness of dignity in the one is tempered and mitigated, and the spirit of the other erected and confirmed."

Regard should also be had to one's pursuits and surroundings. A business attire should be neat and not showy; its material serviceable and of a sober color. A traveling attire should be such as will furnish comfort and protection from dust and dirt; soft neutral tints and smooth surface are best. Anything which would attract special attention from fellow-travelers should be scrupulously avoided.

MOURNING ATTIRE.

Where persons wear mourning for style rather than feeling, they will consult the fashion of the day. Deep mourning requires the heaviest black material with crape collar and cuffs. Ruffles, bows, and flounces are inadmissible. The bonnet must be of black crape; the veil of crape or barege with heavy border; black gloves and black-bordered handkerchiefs; jet pins and buckles; no jewels. A widow wears mourning for two years; for a parent or child, mourning is worn for one year; for a grandparent, mourning is worn for six months; the same for a brother or sister; for an uncle or aunt, nephew or niece, three months. There are some good people, however, who from principle never on any occasion allow themselves to wear mourning habiliments, believing the practice to be contrary to a Christian faith. Aside from this exception ladies should always wear black dresses at funerals, and in this exceptional case plain dresses are always worn.

PERFUMES.

It may be that some will think a perfume of some sort is essential to complete the toilet. " The most refined people, however, avoid personal perfumes, and hold that the absence of all odor is the best savor of human communion. Those of nice taste eschew all perfumes but those that are evanescent, such as cologne and the like." A strong perfume of any kind is not desirable, if, indeed, it be not actually vulgar. There is always a suggestion that it conceals some foulness.

POLITENESS AT HOME.

We come now to consider Polite Deportment in the domain of home, which ought to be to us the most sacred and beautiful place on earth. It may be said in general that it is the duty of every member of a family to do all that is possible to promote the happiness of the other members. It is necessary, therefore, to bear and forbear; to make mutual concessions; to keep down selfishness; to cultivate a love of justice and honor; to get rid of our petty likes and dislikes; to conquer and control our temper. Much may be done by a nice attention to the requirements of etiquette, by an observance of those laws which govern the decencies and proprieties of life. There is no reason why a husband should not treat his wife with exquisite politeness; why a wife should not remember that her husband has a claim to be treated like a gentleman; why the finest manners should not be observed by brothers and sisters. This mutual courtesy, inspired by mutual love, would purify the atmosphere of home, and invest with a new dignity our domestic relations.

A DOMESTIC PICTURE.

Suppose we present a single day in such a home as might exist anywhere. It is early morning. An understood signal indicates the time for breakfast to be reasonably near. Plans carefully made require that the family come together at the morning meal promptly, that the happiness of each may be conserved. Sufficient time is taken to become suitably attired to meet the household, and to so arrange the sleeping-room that no one need hesitate to enter lest sense and taste may be offended. Everything is left in good order. The washstand or basin is emptied; the towels properly hung up; the bed-clothing turned over the foot-board; articles of wearing apparel not in use, put away. Without haste or perturbation the family meet in the dining-room and sit down together; grace is said; hot and savory food is brought on; cheerful conversation seasons the hour; respect is shown to parents and superiors; the servants are treated with kind consideration; sufficient time is secured for the purposes of the meal by planning for it, hence there is no bolting of food and rushing off in disorder to meet a train or to get to business in due season.

Either at the end or the centre sits father, perhaps carving the steak, but certainly making himself useful, as well as ornamental. Opposite is the serene-faced mother, justly proud of her honorable position. On one side perhaps the aged grandmother, giving her meed of sunshine to the board. The prattle of children's voices mingles occasionally in conversation. In honor each prefers the other, and all contribute to the peace and glory of the home.

The personal habits, of which so full mention has already been made, now show their effects. The politeness which begins in personal conditions is now working outwardly. There are no slovens here— there could not be. Gentleness and civility rule the hour. Why should they not be more marked at home than anywhere else? There is not a word of slander or defamation. Peace toward each other; charity toward all. Hans Christian Andersen's story of the cobweb cloth, so finely woven that it was invisible, and specially made for the King's garment, stands perhaps for the sweet manners which are the fine and kingly clothing of royal souls.

Domestic duties for the day follow the morning repast. Father is away at business, the children at school, and the elder ones of the household fully occupied. There is found time for healthful reading, for the good wife has early learned that she must not fall behind her husband or children in personal and religious culture. Both, in their dealing with the world of people and the world of books, are constantly growing. She must keep up with them or lose their genuine respect. Moreover, she must be able to direct the tastes of her family in reading, that they may be fitted for cultivated society, and be enabled thereby to do well their parts in life. The best literature of the day has place upon table or shelf, and is read with pleasure and profit.

Perhaps one of the family is ill. The soft tread and gentle care show that politeness is not wanting in extremity and in bodily suffering. There is no slamming of doors; no boisterous talking; no disregard of a single thing which relates to the comfort of the invalid. A due regard for the sufferer leads to a gentle tap at the door before entering; the ignoring of little things which are not agreeable in the sick one's surroundings or condition; and patience in the rendering of such attentions as may be needed; with an affectionate interest born of a really good heart.

The shadows are creeping on apace as the day draws to its close, and the family is now gathered for dinner. It is thought worth their while for each to be in becoming attire, to dress for each other quite as neatly as if the outside world were looking on. There is true grace and beautiful simplicity. The "shop" is left behind. Markets, bonds, stocks, worry and fret, are not brought home at the close of the business day. Conversation does not lag. There is room for each to have part, and what some might think the trivial things in children's experience receive their meed of attention and honor. There is no slang; no impolite language; no "street talk;" no reference to disgusting subjects. The family sit naturally erect, without lounging or appearing to be tired. Elbows are not planted on the table; napkins are not adjusted under the chin like bibs; no one appears to be greedy for food, neither is there any daintiness that is unsuitable. There is no effort to talk while the mouth is full. There is no coughing, or sneezing, or other disgusting noises with nose or mouth. The knife is only used to cut the food, while the fork and spoon are used to convey food to the mouth. Great care is taken that the tablecloth be not soiled. The carving is done neatly, expeditiously, and courteously. There is neither a niggardly supply nor an overloading of plates. It seems as if carving were no trouble, and that it gave pleasure to supply whatever is desired by any one at the table.

If any little accident happens, no notice is taken of it— no frowns, no muttering of reproof. The servants share in the politeness. "Please" is not omitted when a request is made. A "thank you" is not infrequent. The quietness of the meal is not broken by noises made by mastication, or smacking the lips, or gulping of liquids. When the meal is concluded, the whole family rise from the table, and now the "children's hour" is in order.

The children have learned that there is a time to play and a time when not to play, as well as how to play without interfering with the enjoyment of others. There is kindness, good temper, and politeness. There are no rude and offensive practical jokes perpetrated. There is universal mirth and cheerfulness; there is gayety and life. When the proper hour arrives for the children to retire there is neither teasing nor sulks. A beautiful night closes upon a beautiful day for them in the home and the good-night kiss blesses each in order. If friends call, they are made welcome, and the evening is spent no less pleasantly than the day was begun. It is all the result of good nature and good management, combined with good sense and religious principle.

An eminent authority in household etiquette says : " Let no one suppose that because a good wife lives in a small house and dines on homely fare the general principles of polite deportment do not apply to her. A small house is more easily kept clean than a palace. Taste may be quite as well displayed in the arrangement of dishes on a pine table as in grouping the silver and china of the rich. Skill in cooking is as readily shown in a baked potato or johnny-cake as in a canvas-back duck. The charm of good house-keeping lies in a nice attention to little things, not in a superabundance. A dirty kitchen and bad cooking have driven many a husband and son, and many a daughter, too, from a home that should have been a refuge from temptation. Bad dinners go hand in hand with total depravity, while a properly fed man is already half saved."

AWAY FROM HOME.

If people are well bred at home, their deportment when away from home, in ordinary social intercourse, will be such as befits the true gentleman or lady. They will then reflect the home life. But, being in the homes of others, there will be certain formalities and restraints which are essential to the comfort or rights of those whom they may meet. These should always be recognized and regarded. A careful observance of them will also promote your own comfort and well-being.

INTRODUCTIONS.

Introductions, more or less formal, are necessary. They may form the basis of enjoyment for a brief period, or of a lasting friendship. It is usually the way by which parties become acquainted. Sometimes persons are obliged to introduce themselves, and in such cases, unless well known by reputation, there may be some risk in forming an acquaintance. No one will presume on an acquaintance so formed unless it is accepted in the most unmistakable manner.

It is not necessary to introduce a friend to every one you meet, without regard to time or place. This must, however, depend upon the good sense of the parties concerned. It might be very rude not to introduce a friend, even though the parties so introduced might never meet again. As a rule, we should always be sure that an introduction would be mutually desirable; hence, one should never introduce a gentleman to a lady, for instance, without first obtaining her consent. An introduction of any kind implies an indorsement of character. It is right sometimes to decline giving an introduction where there is the least doubt of the propriety of so doing.

Gentlemen, whatever their rank, should be presented to ladies; young men to elderly men; young women to elderly women; those of lower rank to persons of higher rank. When a gentleman is introduced to another gentleman, each offers a hand; when a gentleman is introduced to a lady, he should wait for her to offer her hand. If she does not do so, he must be content with a bow.

At dinner-parties general introductions are unnecessary; though it is to be assumed that you would not seat at the same table persons whom you would not wish to know each other. In sending your guests down to dinner you must, of course, introduce the lady to her destined partner, if they happen to be unacquainted. In this case you do not ask the lady's permission. At morning calls, if the callers arrive at the same time the hostess will introduce them to each other, unless she has good grounds for believing that the introduction would be disagreeable or unsuitable. At "five-o'clock teas" and similar receptions the hostess must introduce her principal guests to each other; but in doing so she must exercise a due discretion and assort her guests with all possible discrimination.

Between gentlemen the form of introduction may be very simple, as: "Mr. A., my friend, Mr. B.," where the parties are of equal station in life and about the same age. Otherwise, it is better to say: "Mr. A., allow me to introduce my friend, Mr. B." As a means of starting conversation and so placing both parties at their ease, a remark should be added, explaining the business, or residence, or any other item which may be considered of interest, especially if the party introduced is on a trip for business or pleasure.

An introduction to a lady should always be more formal. The usual way is to bow to the lady, or slightly wave the hand, and say: "Mrs. B., permit me to introduce my friend, Mr. D.;" or, in case an introduction has been sought: "Mrs. B., I take pleasure in presenting my friend, Mr. D." The precise form is immaterial, so that the proper order be observed. The introduction should be recognized by each bowing to the other and each repeating the other's name. The gentleman should say: "I am glad to have the pleasure of meeting you," or something of similar import.

It is hardly necessary to say that the names of the parties should always be uttered distinctly. If either party fails to understand the name of the other, it is proper to say: "I beg your pardon; I did not understand the name;" whereupon it should be repeated.

When several are to be introduced to one person, the name of the latter should be distinctly spoken, and then the names of the parties introduced should be mentioned in succession, with a slight bow as each name is called. Where relatives are introduced, care should be taken to give both the degree of kinship and the name. For instance: "My father, Mr. C.;" or, "My son, Mr. C." One's wife is simply designated as "Mrs. A."

It is proper always to recognize the title of one who is introduced—as, " Rev. Mr. A. ;" or, " Rev. Dr. B. ;" or, " Honorable Mr. C.," if the party is a Congressman ; or, " Senator J.," and so on. Sometimes a complimentary remark may be well—as, " Mr. Jones, whose recent work on esthetics has given us so much pleasure."

An adherence to etiquette is a mark of respect. If a man be worth knowing, he is surely worth the trouble of approaching properly. It will likewise relieve you from the awkwardness of being acquainted with people of whom you might at times be ashamed, or be obliged under any circumstances to " cut." Take care not to know anybody whom you will be obliged to " cut." " Cutting " is simply declining to recognize a person to whom you have previously been introduced. It may be done direct by a cold look, as if to an entire stranger ; or indirectly, by averting the face on passing and not returning, by word or manner, an offered salutation.

SALUTATIONS AND GREETINGS.

Salutations and greetings are very simple among Americans. The most common phrases are " Good morning," " Good afternoon," " Good evening," " How are you ?" and " How do you do ?" Some people simply say " Howdy ?" or " How d'ye ?" but the latter never should be indulged in except between intimate friends ; it is perhaps not in taste at any time. A pleasant smile and slight bow is desirable as an accompaniment to the words spoken. The most affectionate form of salution is the kiss, which is only proper among near relatives and dear friends. The practice of women kissing each other in public is held to be decidedly vulgar, and had better be avoided. A due respect to childhood ought to prevent the liberty so often taken of kissing young girls who, though mortified, dare not resent it. There is no more propriety in kissing a child without its consent than there is of kissing a grown woman under the same circumstances.

HAND-SHAKING.

With regard to hand-shaking, a few suggestions may cover the points that are worthy of remembrance. It is not well to offer to shake hands with every one in a drawing-room; if the host or hostess offers a hand, take it; a bow will do for the rest. Hand-shaking is not admissible in a formal party or ball-room. The initiative, in hand-shaking, must always come from the lady, from the elder to the younger, and from the one higher in rank. But in no case let there be the "mutilated courtesy," as Goldsmith calls it, in which by the touch of one or two fingers in a pretended hand-shaking a mere mockery of civility is rendered in place of true courtesy.

Remember that there is a right and a wrong way of hand-shaking. It is horrible when your unoffending digits are seized in the sharp compress of a kind of vise, and wrung and squeezed until you feel as if they were reduced to jelly. It is not less horrible when you find them lying in a limp, nerveless clasp, which makes no response to your hearty greeting, but chills you like a lump of ice. Shake hands as if you meant it. swiftly, strenuously, and courteously, neither using an undue pressure nor falling wholly supine.

UNDUE FAMILIARITY.

"Familiarity breeds contempt." Some forms of familiarity are positively odious, such as slapping your friend on the back or nudging him in the side. Such practices should never be indulged in or permitted. Indeed, there need be no occasion, as a rule, to touch people at all when you have occasion to address them. Again, some persons behave in a drawing-room as if they were the only guests, and the remainder of the company had been assembled to admire— at a distance—their intimacy with the hostess. This is an assumption of familiarity and a token of ill breeding. The same may be said of retaining upon the head one's hat in a strictly private office, which is no more justifiable than it would be to wear it in a drawing-room.

Closely related to this latter is the loud and boisterous laugh, which is decidedly vulgar. A hearty laugh is pleasing, but a loud guffaw is never necessary in order to show heartiness, any more than a loud tone in talking is agreeable to the listener.

There are many other acts which may be classed as vulgar. Among these are humming and whistling; standing with arms a-kimbo; lounging and yawning; addressing acquaintances by their Christian names; playing practical jokes, and whispering in the presence of others. Yet there should not be diffidence and embarrassment in associating with either equals or superiors. For instance, there is a great art in entering a room. Some persons stride in with a shamefaced air, as if they thought they had no business across the threshold; others swagger in defiantly, with head erect and chest expanded, like a professional athlete making his appearance before his "patrons;" others, again, steal in noiselessly, as if deprecating the slightest attention, and priding themselves on their humility. Enter a room as if you felt yourself entitled to a welcome, but wished to take no undue advantage of it.

Having entered the room, one need not be in great haste to get into a chair. It may be as graceful, easy, and proper to stand for a while, and converse easily while in that attitude, yet a chair should be accepted when offered.

CONVERSATION.

The art of conversation is one which boasts of a sacred charter: "Iron sharpeneth iron; so a man sharpeneth the countenance of his friend;" "As in water face answereth to face, so the heart of man to man." (Proverbs xxvii, 17, 19.)

It is not possible to teach the art of conversation. On the other hand, it is not difficult to lay down certain general rules, the observance of which must be held as indispensable to the comfort of the company in which one finds himself.

For example, elaborate discussions of political and religious subjects must be avoided. Our differences on these points go very deep, and any debate which forces them on our consideration cannot fail to awaken permanent feelings of irritation and dislike.

However much in the right, yield with a good grace when you perceive that persistence in ventilating your opinions will result in open variance. The true spirit of conversation consists less in displaying one's own cleverness than in bringing out the cleverness of other people. Conversation is the pasture-ground of the many, therefore it should keep to the levels. There are very few who can ascend the heights, and none ought to sink into the depths.

Gesticulate as little as you can while speaking. Some people spread out their fingers like fans; others point them at you menacingly, like so many darts; this man emphasizes his speech by bringing down one unfortunate hand into the palm of the other; that man nods his head like a child's toy figure, and carries his arm up and down like a pump-handle.

When any one is speaking do not yawn, nor hum an air, nor pick the teeth, nor drum with the fingers on a piece of furniture, nor whisper in a neighbor's ear, nor take a letter out of the pocket and read it, nor look at your watch.

There is no flattery so exquisite as " the flattery of listening." It may be doubted whether the greatest mind is ever proof against it. Socrates may have loved Plato best of all his disciples because he listened best. To listen well is almost as indispensable as to talk well, and it is by the skill with which he listens that the man of *bon ton* and of good society is known. If you wish people to listen to you, you must listen to them. Let not your patience give way when elderly people are garrulous. Respect old age, even when it twaddles; you yourself may live to require the indulgence which you are now recommended to exercise.

There are social Munchausens whose narratives make tremendous demands on your credulity. Do not express your belief in what you disbelieve, for that would be to utter a falsehood; do not express an open dissent, for that would be to commit a rudeness. Take refuge in a courteous silence, and—change the subject.

Be careful how you exercise your wit. If curses, like chickens, come home to roost, so do epigrams. Do not applaud the wit which is leveled at your friend; it may next be directed against yourself. Do not give another, even if it be a better, version of a story already told by one of your companions. Be careful how you distribute praise or blame to your neighbors—some of those present will have their prejudices or partialities, which you will be sure to offend— and on no account interrupt or contradict a person who may be speaking.

Speak of yourself as little as possible. If you speak in praise, you expose yourself to ridicule; if you blame yourself, nobody will think you in earnest, and it will be assumed that you are seeking for compliments, or that you are merely affecting humility; or if your vanity be excused, it will be at the expense of your intelligence—if you are not vain, you must be stupid.

Do not "talk shop," that is, unless specially requested; do not talk of your professional occupation, your private studies, or your personal belongings, neither of your house, nor your wife, nor your servant, nor your property.

Do not pay compliments unless you can do so with grace, and in such a manner that, though the person on whom the sweet flattery is bestowed recognize it as undeserved, he or she may still believe that on your part it is perfectly sincere. Dean Swift says pithily: "Nothing is so great an instance of ill-manners as flattery. If you flatter all the company you please none; if you flatter only one or two you affront the rest." But an elegant compliment at an opportune moment, and spoken with an air of frankness, carries with it an irresistible charm.

To be a good talker requires much general information, which may be acquired by observation, reading and study, and listening to others. To this must be added a good memory, which can be cultivated by proper effort; a right knowledge and use of language, and clear enunciation. The use of such vulgarisms as " awfully nice," " abominably horrid," " dreadfully stupid," and the like, are always to be avoided. It is a bad habit which is very close to untruthfulness. Very few people would utter a willful lie, yet many become untrustworthy because of their habit of exaggeration and false coloring.

FORMAL CALLS.

The formal call is a mere device for keeping up acquaintance. Once or twice a year is regarded as sufficiently often to meet fashionable requirements. Simply sending cards sometimes takes the place of a call. A " morning call " means generally any call made in the daytime, and is a mere matter of ceremony. It should not be made in the forenoon, nor just previous to the usual hour of luncheon, nor later than five in the afternoon. Local customs govern the matter of special days for receiving calls.

When a lady for any reason prefers not to see callers, the servant is usually instructed to say that she is engaged, or " not at home." As the latter is not strictly correct, a regard to truthfulness should prevent the statement. A polite mention that the lady could not receive callers ought to be sufficient. To insist on seeing a person after such a message is the height of ill-manners on the part of the caller.

In making a morning call a gentleman should take hat and gloves with him into the parlor, but not his umbrella or his overshoes, and he should not remove his overcoat. In an evening call, all wraps, etc., should be left in the hall. While waiting for the person on whom you have called it is not right to walk about, examining pictures and other articles. A morning call should always be short, and one should not enter upon a subject of conversation which may terrify the hostess with the apprehension that you intend to remain until you have exhausted it.

In calling on a newly married couple, do not congratulate the lady upon her marriage, but the bridegroom. He, of course, is fortunate in having found any one to accept him ; her good luck may be more problematical. A visit to a newly married couple is not a visit of condolence. Be brisk in your manner, therefore ; wear a smile ; and if there be a feeling of pity at your heart, do your utmost to prevent its outward manifestation.

When ready to leave, arise and go. Do not linger and talk and act as if you wished you had not started. Make your adieus and depart at once—yet not in haste. If there are other callers, bow to them collectively.

After a party or dinner at a friend's house you should call within a week thereafter.

VISITING.

Visiting is a privilege that is often abused. Only firm friendship can justify it. One should not be too fast to accept an invitation—certainly not a mere " come and see us some time." Be sure that you are really wanted, and do not prolong your stay until your welcome is clean worn out. During a visit one should conform very strictly to the usual habits of the house, always being on hand and ready at the usual times for meals, and never keep the family up after their usual time for retiring. If unpleasant matters appear they should not be noticed, and in general one's presence ought to be the least possible occasion of trouble. Upon returning home, the family should receive a pleasant letter, renewing expressions of pleasure given when about to take leave of the hostess.

VISITING-CARDS.

As cards have so important a place in etiquette, it will be well to consult a reliable stationer as to styles in order to avoid mistakes. The neat round-hand and angular script has of late taken the place of old English type on cards. Only the name should be on a card. A business card never should be used for a friendly call. A physician may put " Dr." or " M. D." in addition to his name, and an Army or Navy officer his rank and branch of service.

In case a card is left in person when making a call, one corner should be turned down if for the lady of the house ; if folded in the middle, it will indicate that the call is on several members of the family. A card should be left for each guest of the family.

" P. P. C." (*Pour prendre congé*) should be written in one corner of a card left at a farewell visit, before a protracted absence. Such cards may be sent by mail. Ladies about to be married sometimes send them in place of making a call.

An expert in the science of good manners has recently spoken thus on visiting-cards : " Care should be taken to conform with present usage and to avoid anything considered to be in questionable taste, for a card is the representative of one's-self. To the unrefined or underbred person the visiting-card is but a trifling and insignificant piece of paper ; but to the cultured disciple of social law it conveys a subtle and unmistakable intelligence. Its texture, style of engraving, and even the hour of leaving it, combine to place the stranger whose name it bears in a pleasant or a disagreeable attitude—even before his manners, conversation, and face have been able to explain his social position. The higher the civilization of a community, the more careful it is to preserve the elegance of its social forms. It is quite as easy to express a perfect breeding in the fashionable formalities of cards as by any other method, and perhaps, indeed, it is the safest herald of an invitation for a stranger. Its texture should be fine, its engraving a plain script, its size neither too small, so that its recipients shall say to themselves, ' A whimsical person,' nor too large, to suggest ostentation. Refinement seldom touches extremes in anything."

RECEPTIONS.

Receptions usually occur from four to seven in the afternoon, when light refreshments are served. Invitations to them are usually informal. If " R. S. V. P." is on a corner of such invitation it is proper to send answer. Otherwise, no answer is required. All who are invited are expected to call soon afterward—within two weeks at most. Invitations are generally issued in the name of the lady of the house, and are usually engraved in the lower left-hand corner of her visiting-card—thus :

MRS. JOHN THOMASSON.

Thursday, February third.

TEA AT FOUR O'CLOCK. 10 TRAFALGAR PLACE.

If assisted by a daughter or a friend, the name of such assistant is engraved below her own on the card. Sometimes the cards are larger and in the following form:

MR. AND MRS. THOMAS JACKSON,
AT HOME,

Thursday, December sixth,
FROM THREE UNTIL SEVEN O'CLOCK.   150 TREMONT AVE.

These cards, now used in square form, should be inclosed in two envelopes when sent by mail. If delivered by messenger, one inclosure is sufficient.

DINNERS.

The Etiquette of Dinners is worthy of more space than we can give to it. When an invited guest, be sure not to be late. It would be a wrong to your host, to other guests, and to the dinner. Persons invited should be of the same standing in society, though not necessarily acquaintances. Invitations should be in the name of the gentleman and lady of the house, and should be issued at least a week in advance. They should be answered immediately, in order that the hosts may know who are to be their guests. When an engagement has been made it should be kept, if at all possible. It is not proper to invite a gentleman without his wife, or vice versa, unless it be an occasion when gentlemen alone are to be present. The usual time for dinners is from five to eight o'clock.

A dinner-table is said to be laid for so many "covers."

A " cover " comprises : Two large knives ; three large forks ; silver knife and fork for fish; tablespoon for soup; wine-glass for sherry ; wine-glass for hock ; wine-glass for champagne. Where wines are not used, of course the glasses are omitted. In the centre, between the knives and forks, is placed the dinner-bread wrapped up in a serviette. The dessertspoons and small forks are placed before the guests on an empty plate before the sweets are passed around, and extra knives and forks are supplied as they are required.

In the main things of a dinner, the fillet and roast, there is little change, but in minor things the caterer rules. To begin with oysters, five, not six, is now the fashionable number for the half shells. At formal dinners it is the invariable rule that ladies and gentlemen should be seated alternately, never allowing two ladies or two gentlemen to sit together. At dinners of eight, twelve, or sixteen persons, this can be managed only by putting gentlemen at both ends of the table. Hostesses generally have a prejudice against giving up their customary seat, forgetting the old saying : " Where the Douglas sits, there is the head of the table," and avoid the awkward number.

When there are more ladies than gentlemen at the din-ner-party, the hostess should go down alone, and leave the gentleman of highest rank to take down the lady of second rank ; in this case the gentleman will place himself at table on the right of the hostess. In passing from the drawing-room to the dining-room, remember that it is the lady who takes precedence, not the gentleman.

A gentleman must help the lady whom he has escorted to the table, but it is not proper to offer his help to other ladies who have escorts. If the guests pass the dishes, always help yourself before handing to the next. If at dinner you are requested to help any one to sauce, do not pour it over the meat or vegetables, but on one side. It you should have to carve and help a joint, do not load a person's plate—it is vulgar; also, in serving soup, one ladleful to each plate is sufficient.

Conversation at the table should be participated in by all, and should include only such subjects as will be agreeable to all. It is rudeness for one or two to monopolize the talking, and centre upon themselves a general attention.

When the guests have finished, the hostess can indicate, by rising, the time for departure from the table, when the return to the drawing-room can be in the order in which they are seated without regard to preference.

AFTER DINNER.

An hour or more of social intercourse will follow. It will be well if some of the company are musicians. In case one is invited to sing or play there should be graceful compliance, but it is not well to sing or play more than one piece unless specially urged. It is better not to risk boring the company with your performance, however good it may be. When people are singing, do them the courtesy of listening, or pretending to listen. If you do not like music yourself, remember that others may. Besides, when a person is endeavoring to entertain you, the least you can do is to show your gratitude for the intention.

Upon taking leave, express pleasure to the host and hostess, but do not offer thanks in any case. A call should be made soon afterward.

Dinner cards are so useful that they will not soon go out of fashion. The shops are full of them, and beautiful ones are coming over from Paris. Of a dozen recently used the owner said: "They cost almost as much as a dress." Each fan was painted and signed by a well-known artist, and bore the name of a guest. They suggested the lavishness of Lucullus in ancient times, and in modern that famous bonanza banquet in San Francisco, where every lady's dinner card was a point lace handkerchief.

MARRIAGE ANNIVERSARIES.

Marriage anniversaries are popularly designated as follows :

First Anniversary, ...	Paper Wedding.
Second "	Cotton "
Third "	Leather "
Fifth "	Wooden "
Tenth "	Tin "
Fifteenth "	Crystal "
Twentieth "	Floral "
Twenty-fifth "	Silver "
Thirtieth "	Pearl "
Thirty-fifth "	China "
Fortieth "	Coral "
Forty-fifth "	Bronze "
Fiftieth "	Golden "
Sixtieth "	Diamond "

It is proper to say that some of these, in the preceding list, are not often celebrated. Cards of wood, tin, etc., are no longer used, the invitations being issued on square white cards or note sheets, in plain, neat script. The words " No Gifts," are often engraved in the lower left-hand corner of the invitation. The ceremonies on such occasions are somewhat according to the taste and desire of the parties and the length of time they may have been married. The earlier occasions afford opportunities for merriment; the later ones, for the deeper emotions, mingled with pleasure and satisfaction.

COURTSHIP.

With regard to courtship, it may briefly be said that its freedom should not be abused by license, and that the parties ought to regard each other sacredly if their troth is plighted.

Upon engagement, the gentleman presents the lady with a ring, to be worn on the third finger of the right hand. While engaged, neither party should be occupied in flirtations with the opposite sex, yet both should reasonably mingle in society. The gentleman is always thereafter the legitimate escort of the lady and should not devote himself in any marked manner to any other lady.

Society wisely discourages all conspicuous manifestations of personal feeling. Lovers are not expected to " make love " in public, nor married couples to afford extravagant evidence of conjugal tenderness ; and the sincerity of the affection may reasonably be doubted which parades itself in public. When our hearts are deeply moved we do not take the world into our confidence. On the other hand, constant bickering and bantering between husband and wife in public is equally objectionable, even though it be only " in fun."

WEDDINGS.

The etiquette of weddings varies greatly according to circumstances. After invitations are issued the lady does not appear in public. The invitations should be handsomely engraved. Any reputable stationer will be able to suggest the proper forms and styles. The invitations are engraved in the name of the father and mother of the bride, or if neither are living, then in the name of her guardian or nearest relation.

The forms and ceremonies of weddings are generally in accordance with the wishes of the bride. But, whether the wedding ceremonies be at home or in church, a beautiful simplicity is certainly more pleasing than an ostentatious display.

PUBLIC PLACES.

Proper regard is necessary to the rules of polite deportment in public places. Let your walk in life be distinguished by unassuming grace. Look from your window and observe the gait of the passers-by.   You will see at once " what to avoid "—the tread of the grenadier, the clumsy shuffle, the dancing-master's trip, the heel-and-toe movement, the pretentious slide.   But it is easier to know what to avoid than what to imitate.   Perhaps imitation is not advisable, and the chief thing to remember is that you should walk as if your body had a soul in it.   Virgil tells us of Juno that you saw the goddess in her gait, and " grace in her steps " is one of the characteristics of Milton's " Eve."

Observation, which, " with extensive view, surveys mankind from China to Peru," shows that in the country gentlemen do not offer their arm to ladies, but in large towns this should be done as a measure of protection and a token of respect.

When you meet a friend in the street it must depend on your degree of intimacy whether you walk with him or not; but with a lady you must not walk, unless she directly or indirectly invite you.

Gentlemen do not take off their hats to one another; this is a courtesy reserved for the ladies.   Gentlemen generally recognize each other with a nod.   If you pass an acquaintance with a lady on his arm, do not nod; take off your hat, so that your salute may seem to embrace both your friend and the lady.   In bowing to a lady in the street, lift your hat right off your head.   Don't allow her to suppose that you wear a wig and are afraid to disarrange it.   If you pass a friend with a lady whom you do not know, you must lift your hat to him and not nod.

Should you tread upon or stumble against any one, do not fail to make immediate apology.   Of course, you will not stare at nor point to people, nor carry umbrella or cane horizontally under your arm.   Neither will you stop a lady on the street to talk with her.   Turn and walk with her, rather, and lift your hat to her when you have finished the conversation and are about to leave her.

It is very rude to rush for a seat in a car or at a public entertainment. Better lose some comfort than be guilty of impoliteness. It is equally wrong to occupy more space than you are entitled to in a public conveyance; and when at a place of amusement to disturb others by your conversation or remarks while the performance is going on is gross ill-breeding. A polite person will always have regard for the comfort of those who are near.

In public halls a gentleman should precede the lady whose escort he is, unless there is an usher preceding them. He should give her the inner seat and remain by her side. He is under no obligation to give up his seat to another lady and should avoid everything that might attract notice to himself or his companion.

In church there should always be deference and respect to the worshipers, whether or not you agree with them. Stay away if you cannot be respectful and attentive to the services. It is not right to go late, to the possible disturbance of the worship. It is rude to turn around and gaze at any one, to watch people coming in with critical glances, to talk or laugh, and so disturb others, or to leave until the dismission.

TRAVELING.

In our country almost every one travels, and a few hints will be serviceable to those who may not have traveled a great deal. Always keep your head and arms inside the car window. Remember that it is not necessary to be intrusive in order to be polite. Take your time in getting on or off the cars; nothing is gained by haste. Avoid being boisterous and do not try to make yourself conspicuous. Never disclose your business to the stranger in whose company you may happen to be.

Bear in mind that the comfort of others should be taken into consideration when you travel. Your open window may be a source of great annoyance and discomfort to your

neighbors. Do not litter the seat you occupy with boxes
and bundles to exclude other passengers from sharing with
you the accommodation it affords. Respectfully decline
any and all invitations extended by strangers with whom
you are brought in contact to indulge in social games of
cards. Do not ask the conductor foolish questions about
the route; remember that he is not familiar with the run-
ning-time of all the roads in the United States. Do not
address a lady who is unknown to you, unless she invite it.
You may offer her your newspaper with a silent bow. An
" unprotected " lady ought to call forth a gentleman's finest
chivalry.

If you have made some slight acquaintance with a lady
in a railway carriage, you must not presume upon that to
bow or speak to her at any accidental rencontre, unless she
makes the first advances.

Discretion should be used in forming acquaintances while
traveling. Ladies may accept small and proper attentions,
but any attempt at familiarity should be checked at once.
A true gentleman will not offer any familiarity. The flirt-
ing and freedom often indulged in by young people in public
conveyances is unworthy of them—if, indeed, it does not
indicate low breeding, and often leads to evil consequences.
Whether at home or abroad, the same rules of good behavior should prevail.

CORRESPONDENCE.

Correspondence is the medium by which people communicate with each other when, for any reason, they cannot
readily speak face to face. It should be characterized by
the same politeness that marks the gentleman or lady in any
relation of life. It will generally indicate character with
considerable precision, unless there is studied concealment
for a purpose. " It is as great a violation of propriety to
send a carelessly prepared and badly written letter as it is to

appear in the company of refined people with swaggering gait, soiled linen, and unkempt hair." It is at least a questionable compliment to a friend to send a letter written with very pale ink, or with lines crossed and indistinct, or with other evidences of disregard of the objects which you are supposed to have had in mind when writing—namely, to communicate information in a pleasant way. It is not in taste for you to use postal cards, except on mere matters of business. When used, there is no need of any address, except upon the address side. You may omit the usual formalities of salutation in your communication, giving the post office and date at the top, and simply sign your name at the bottom. Postal cards never should be used for any matters that are in the least degree confidential.

Private and personal letters should never be written on foolscap paper. What is known as "Commercial Note" is generally used by gentlemen, and a smaller size by ladies. Either ruled or plain paper is allowable, but the latter is deemed more in style. Envelopes should correspond with the paper used, and should always be of a light color, when ladies are addressed. Business letters are almost uniformly written on half-sheets, but for a social letter a whole sheet should always be used, though only a portion be occupied. The writing should be plain, without flourishes, and be continuous to the close without skipping a page. The inside address, following the date, should be such as the party named is entitled to receive, and the salutation such as is justified by the personal relations of the writer. Business letters generally begin with *Sir, Dear Sir, Sirs*, or *Gentlemen*. Do not use "Gents" for gentlemen, nor "Dr." for dear. For a letter addressed to a married woman, or a single woman not young, the proper salutation is *Madam, Dear Madam*, or *My dear Madam*. Business letters to a young unmarried lady do not require any salutation, the name alone being regarded as sufficient.

When your letter is written, it requires a respectful or affectionate conclusion and the signature. Business letters are generally closed with *Yours, Yours truly,* or *Yours respectfully.* Social letters admit of a great variety of forms, according to the taste and feelings of the writer. Whatever else may be wanting in clearness, the signature should be plain, so that there may not be any chance for mistake in replying. It is proper and desirable that " Miss " or " Mrs." be prefixed to your signature when writing to strangers, that there may not be any doubt as to the manner of addressing a reply.

When completed, your letter should be neatly and carefully folded, so that the edges will be exactly even, and inclosed in the envelope prepared for it by a proper outside address or superscription. The proper place for the postage stamp is the upper right-hand corner, and the stamp should be affixed squarely and head up. Postage should be fully paid.

A letter should always have prompt reply. It is real incivility not to do so, especially if there be anything which specially calls for answer, and in beginning a reply the reception of the letter should be acknowledged, as a rule, in the first sentence. If for any reason a further correspondence is not desired, care should be taken to so write that there will not be anything calling for answer. It is well always to remember that your letter may sometime get into print without your knowledge or consent, therefore do not write a word that would bring a blush to your face if read by the world.

NOTES.

Notes may be considered as differing from letters in being more formal, in being generally written in the third person, and being without signature. They are used for announcements, invitations, anniversaries, acceptances, regrets, and the like. For weddings, receptions, and other ceremonious occasions, your stationer will tell you the prevailing style. For acceptances and regrets, which should always be promptly made, the following models will suffice. They may be varied to suit the occasion and the relations of the parties :

ACCEPTANCE.

Mr. and Mrs. Carleton take pleasure in accepting the kind invitation of Mrs. Bowles to her reception on Thursday evening, November 21st.

Friday, November 15th.

REGRET.

Mr. and Mrs. Carleton extremely regret that a previous engagement prevents their acceptance of Mrs. Sparkle's polite invitation for Thursday evening, November 21st.

Saturday, November 16th.

NOTES OF INTRODUCTION.

Notes of introduction should be brief, and contain the full name and address of the person introduced. For business purposes they are often used, but the receiver is not required to entertain the bearer as a friend unless entirely agreeable. The obligation ceases with the transaction of the business in hand. A business introduction is delivered in person. The envelope containing it should not be sealed, and on its left-hand lower corner should be written the words, " Introducing Mr.————," that its character may command immediate attention. No pecuniary obligation is incurred by such an introduction, unless particularly mentioned. The conventional form is more or less as follows :

New York, Jan'y 18th, 1883.

Messrs. Applegarth & Co.

Gentlemen :—I have the pleasure of presenting to your acquaintance Mr. James Spellman, of Murray & Spellman, Montreal, Canada, whom I commend to your kind attentions.

Respectfully yours,

Samuel Smith.

Introductions should only be given when there is perfect confidence felt in the party introduced. It is right to refuse such a favor, if thought best, merely on the ground of unwillingness to take the liberty of presenting any one to the person or firm to whom introduction is asked.

A social introduction should be given with great caution. The writer should be well acquainted with both parties. Be specially careful in making introductions to ladies. It is an insult to the whole sex if you present to a lady any person of doubtful reputation. Never give letters of introduction, unless you are prepared to be responsible for the persons to whom they are given. Why should you thrust upon the society of a friend those whom you would not admit to your own? Or why ask his good services for individuals whom you know do not deserve them?

In all such letters candor should prevail. Say what you mean. Do not use ambiguous terms which leave a pleasant impression on the reader, but awaken a measure of confidence and generous purpose beyond what you intended. Whatever object is proposed in giving the letter should be distinctly stated, even though it be that you give it simply to rid yourself of a bore. If you know nothing of a party, but desire to get him employment, or some such favor, state the facts, though you defeat the purpose.

The holder of a social letter of introduction should not take it in person, but should send it with his card of address. The receiver, if he be a gentleman, will call upon you without delay. At all events, you are bound to give him an option; whereas, by taking your letter in person you force yourself upon him, whether he will or not. Should the letter introduce a gentleman to a lady, she may, at her option, answer by a note of invitation—appointing a time for him to call.

All polite deportment is based upon common sense. It is not the prerogative of the privileged and favored few, but it is the right and the duty of all. Not one of its requirements is useless if the comfort and welfare of our friends and associates be properly considered. The springs of politeness must be within. If one has learned to correct personal faults, to control self, and to be regardful of others, he has gone a long way toward that refinement of nature which will make him everywhere a welcome and honored guest.

If in the sanctity of home he lives in obedience to these principles, he will not be likely to ignore them when in the society of others ; and when in public places or engaged in correspondence, it will be as natural for him to be well-mannered and self-poised as it is for the thriving plant to drink in the morning dew. If it is worth while to have keen enjoyment of life—to win and to retain friends, and to make society better by our correct life in the midst of it—then it is no loss of time, but a gain in every direction, to understand and practice all that is included in POLITE DEPORTMENT.

CARE OF CHILDREN.

O child! O new-born denizen
  Of life's great city! on thy head
  The glory of the morn is shed
Like a celestial benizon!
Here at the portal thou dost stand,
  And with thy little hand
  Thou openest the mysterious gate
Into the future's undiscovered land.

LONGFELLOW

CARE OF CHILDREN.

By W. B. Atkinson, M. D., Lecturer on Diseases of
Children, Jefferson Medical College, Phila.

FROM the moment of birth it should be remembered that the infant is a being of feeble powers; that while it possesses a wonderful vitality, yet that vitality is readily extinguished or impaired. Such impairment often remains through life, rendering it a delicate, or perhaps deformed, creature, liable to succumb to the most trivial attacks of disease.

HEREDITARY INFLUENCES.

Whereas the child born of healthy parents, and that has been reared under proper surroundings, is prepared to resist the usual diseases of child-life, and if it is attacked, rarely fails to have a mild form, from which it recovers perfectly. For instance, the child of scrofulous, or otherwise diseased parents, when exposed to scarlet fever usually has a bad form of the disease and recovers imperfectly, being left with running from the ears, or even deafness, or other of the common results of this disease. Even where the parentage of a child is tainted much may be done to make it better in health and less liable to continue the taint in its own person, and subsequently to transmit it in time to its offspring.

227

FIRST CARE OF A CHILD.

At the outset let it be understood that the so-called hardening of an infant by exposure, by cold bathing, by a prescribed diet, and other such plans is not only a failure, but frequently itself is the cause of the beginning of disease in an otherwise healthy infant. A new-born child, coming as it does from a position in which the temperature has been never less than that of the human body internally (98.5°F.), is extremely liable, especially in cold weather, to lose its vital heat. Hence, it should not be washed in cold water, or, in fact, for the first twenty-four or forty-eight hours, in water at all. The best method is to cleanse its surface by rubbing the skin with pure, fresh lard or sweet oil. This unites readily with the cheesy matter usually found to a greater or less extent on the skin of a new-born child; then, with a dry, soft cotton cloth the whole surface is readily cleansed. Where blood or other stain still adheres, the cloth may be moistened with warm water, and thus the surface is thoroughly cleansed. The use of water, and particularly of soap, is objectionable for several reasons.

Soap—as often found in the sick-room—is made of impure fats, which often have a poisonous effect, or it may have an excess of alkali, either of which conditions is injurious to the delicate cutaneous surface of the child. Again, the soapy water usually gets into the child's eyes, resulting in more or less inflammation of these delicate organs. Washing, unless when performed in a gentle manner, removes more or less thoroughly the natural oil of the skin, causing chafing, and also giving rise to many forms of eruption so often seen in the young infant. At all times the surface should be cleansed with care and gentleness. When soap becomes absolutely necessary in order to remove dirt, it should be of the best quality and used sparingly. The temperature of the water should be about that of the blood —say 95°—and the child not too long exposed in cool weather, lest its surface be chilled and a congestion of some of the internal organs occur. Bathing is always valuable, not only for the purposes of cleanliness, but also to keep the numerous pores of the skin in a condition to do their work. The water should be sufficiently warm to prevent the child suffering a chill, and the bath must be given in a situation not exposed to a draught, the whole surface to be rubbed dry with a soft towel.

SUITABLE CLOTHING.

The clothing for the very young child should be loose—tied rather than pinned—and in cold weather should completely cover its body up well around the neck, the arms to the wrists, and the legs and feet. Much damage is done by the foolish habit of exposing children in cool or cold weather—even in the house—with short sleeves, low-necked dress, and legs bare above the knees. It must be borne in mind that the blood in the extremities is readily chilled, and by this means cholera-infantum and dysentery in summer, and the colds and other affections of winter, are brought on. In hot weather a young child may usually be allowed to lie on a blanket or comfortable on the floor, unencumbered with much clothing, a light, soft slip being all that is required, and the only care being to avoid a draught. Here it can roll in every direction and move every muscle without hindrance.

While upon the subject of the child's clothing we may properly urge the importance of keeping the child outside the bonds imposed by fashion as long as it is possible. Have everything to fit easily and loosely; give it free scope for every movement, that motion may be a pleasure, not a pain. Especially see that the foot—usually so perfect and handsome at birth—is not confined, cramped in a shoe too narrow, and, almost invariably, too short for it. This point is one of the greatest value, as children grow so rapidly that frequently we find a shoe but little worn has already become too short. Here economy urges many to do a great wrong, for the use of a shoe too short for the foot compels nature, in its efforts to find room for the lengthening toes, to bend them over each other, and thus is produced that hideous and laming deformity—a foot with enlarged joints, with bunions, and with overlapping toes. Such a foot becomes a constant source of misery to its owner who is compelled to walk much. Even in hot weather it is safer for a child to wear next to its skin a soft merino shirt. The infant should wear its flannel band, covering its body from the armpits to the groins, until it is able to run about. This needs to be applied neatly and carefully, or it becomes a mere girdle about the middle of the child. In warm weather this band should be made of soft, light flannel, which may be made somewhat heavier as the cool weather of fall approaches.

The special value of this band is that it prevents chilling of the bowels, almost always the cause of cholera-infantum and other bowel affections. As the child becomes older— particularly in girls—must we urge the necessity of the avoidance of tight bands around the waist by which the skirts are supported, dragging constantly on the hips, compressing the abdomen, and thus forcing the internal organs out of their places. The wonderful prevalence of backache, sense of weariness after the shortest walk, and a host of ills in our female patients, may undoubtedly be traced to this as the commencement—aided, subsequently, by immense loads of skirts, late hours, neglect of the proper care, and the usual habits incident to fashionable life. Nor must we forget the support of the stockings. Garters are a constant injury, as they are generally worn. They compress the entire limb and markedly interfere with the circulation of the blood. Many cases of varicose veins are wholly due to this habit.

SUITABLE FOOD.

The food of the child from the outset must be either that provided by nature, the mother's milk, or something as nearly approaching it as may be. The young mother, the nurse—all, should be cautioned never to feed the child with anything at birth. It should be well understood that this is best for several reasons. All such trash as sugar or molasses and water, or any of the many abominations usually given to the new-born child with the erroneous belief that it must be hungry, and hence requires food, tends to cause indigestion, and produces wind in the stomach and bowels. This induces the child to cry with pain, and it is either fed with more of the stuff, under the belief that it is still hungry, or, worse, it is dosed with "soothing drops" to relieve its pain, and a new source of injury is added. Let me say here that no drops, cordials, sirups, or anything in the shape of drugs should be given, especially to a young child, without the advice of a physician. On this subject we shall speak more fully subsequently.

Let us suppose, for the sake of illustration, that the mother has a good flow of milk and the child nurses well. It is necessary that she should endeavor to so form its habits that it shall at first take the breast about once in every two hours, or a little longer, during the day, and about once in four to six hours at night. The child is greatly the creature of habit, and where the mother begins to put it to the breast at every cry, or whenever it rouses, it speedily acquires the custom of demanding the breast constantly. Indeed, some mothers will lie at night with the infant on the arm, so that it virtually sleeps with the nipple in its mouth. In such cases the child refuses to submit to any other plan and becomes a constant annoyance until it is weaned. As it becomes older, the interval between the nursings should be lengthened, so that it is suckled once in four to six hours and at night generally will go without till the hour for rising has come. The food should be wholly the breast-milk or its equivalent until the child has advanced so far with its teeth as to be fully able to chew the food thoroughly. Nor even then need much change be made; for long after weaning the best food is that into which milk largely enters. Too much of a variety is hurtful to a young child. As children grow, or should grow, rapidly, and require frequent supplies to make up for the wear of, as well as the increase in, the body, they should always be supplied with good, nourishing food whenever they express a feeling of hunger. It is not well to endeavor to restrict such to the exact number and hours for meals, as in adult life.

VALUE OF SUNSHINE.

Not less important is an abundance of sunlight and fresh air. The effects upon plant life of the absence of sunlight is shown by the plant growing thin, pale, delicate; in fact, this is made use of by gardeners to procure tender white stalks, as of celery, etc. Abundance of illustrations will readily occur to the thoughtful of the vicious effects of a want of sunlight. This is one of the most valuable results accruing by the transfer of an invalid to the sea-shore, the mountains, or to the country farm. We may contrast the pale, delicate appearance of those members of an otherwise healthy family who are compelled to remain all day long, and day after day, in the small house shut in from the sun's rays by its overshadowing neighbors, with those whose occupation compels them to be abroad.

Of course, the author would not be understood as advising exposure to the direct, fierce rays of the sun in midsummer. It is its light, rather than its excess of heat, that does the good, that increases the vitality of the little one. That this does not seem by a great number of people to be regarded as of value is shown by their utter neglect of it, in permitting windows to be blocked up by furniture, old hats, clothing, and even dirt. Here cleanliness acts in more ways than might at first be anticipated. Therefore, make the nursery a light, cheerful room. Use only sufficient curtains to prevent the direct rays from being an annoyance. Curtains should be such as can readily bé removed, and so disposed as to afford the smallest opportunity for the accumulation of dust; for where such accumulation occurs is most likely to be the nest for a deposit of disease germs.

GOOD VENTILATION.

Full and free ventilation must always form a part of the means by which we prevent disease, as well as fight it after it has entered. Like sunlight, fresh air is a most valùable factor in health, and its deprivation equally one in disease. The air of every part of a house should be thoroughly changed so soon as the inmates rise in the morning and throw open the dwelling. The bed-room windows, save in extremely cold or wet weather, should be widely opened, and so remain till near nightfall. The living, or work-rooms, should equally be cared for. In the sick-room or nursery the air can be readily changed from time to time by protecting the inmates from the draught. Cover the child, head and all, in cold weather, and open the doors and windows to their fullest extent for a few minutes. Where the air does not enter freely and drive out that which is vitiated, thorough ventilation may be obtained by swinging the door to and fro, shaking the curtains, or some similar plan. Fortunately, we find the fresh air from the unlimited reservoir without is ready to enter and drive out the disease-laden air of the room. At the same time, it must be understood that cold air is not always pure air. The fire may be maintained while this is going on, so that the temperature is not lowered beyond the degree of comfort. Now that thermometers of a good quality can be obtained so cheaply, every sick-room at least should have one as an indispensable article of furniture. By its readings, the temperature should be carefully observed, so that a moderate and even degree of heat can be secured.

While we enforce the importance of pure air to children, it becomes an imperative duty to allude strongly to the vitiation of the air. While in the streets of a large city, and even in other localities, circumstances often greatly interfere with our efforts in this behalf, yet we constantly see an unnecessary, even criminal, carelessness in such matters. The dejections of all kinds are frequently permitted to remain in the rooms during the greater part of the day. When possible, especially in cases of contagious diseases, these should not only be removed at once, but disinfectants should be mixed with them, thus aiding greatly in preventing the spread of disease. A great cause of impure air is the constant use of tobacco in the house. To all whose sensibility of smell is not blunted by their habits, the stale fumes of tobacco adhering to the clothes, the curtains, the furniture, are disagreeable. We may be regarded as speaking strongly on this point, but during an experience, largely among children, for over thirty years, we can recall numerous cases of the use of tobacco by the bedside, and actually in the faces, of sick and dying children; of many instances of sudden illness in infants brought on by the inhalation of tobacco smoke. A little care and thoughtfulness aids greatly in keeping the air of a house pure. Thus, never let a poultice, a mustard, or other application remain in the room. Air the rooms well after cooking, after meals, after the exit of a filthy person. In short, when one enters a room from the outer fresh air and detects a strange odor there, such a room should be thoroughly ventilated as soon as possible. Warmth, not only by clothing, but by heat, as from a fire, is imperatively demanded for children in cold and damp weather. The child that expresses a sense of chilliness, that shivers, is sick or on the verge of sickness.

TREATMENT OF AILINGS.

When the child appears in any way to be " out of sorts," do not rush at once to drugs. Remember, that in many instances a calm, refreshing sleep, a few hours of rest, will find an apparently very sick child again playing with its toys and as happy as though nothing had occurred. All are too much in the habit of accepting the gratuitous advice of those around them—advice from those who possess not the slightest knowledge of medicine. Let it be a fixed rule never to give any medicine without the advice of a skilled physician. See what can be done by sanitary regulations, by removing the causes of disease, by change of locality. Constantly are young children made ill by bad air, bad or deficient food, and bad drinks. In this connection, for the sake of the over-anxious parents who often wildly abandon hope at the slightest sign of disease, and regard the child as doomed to die at the outset, we would say that the strong power constantly shown in a child by which it throws off an attack of disease and recuperates its exhausted powers, often seems as though the result of miraculous intervention. Hence, when sickness appears, no matter how terrible its form, however doubtful may appear the result, preserve to the end courage and cheerfulness. These aid constantly in obtaining the wished-for relief. The nursing is performed faithfully, the child is not dispirited—in short, you thus avoid that injurious condition where, hope being banished from the outset, it would seem as though the first sign of illness were equivalent to a funeral notice and only the forms had to be complied with. A woman who is nursing a child should always remember that her milk is extremely liable to be rendered injurious to her infant by what might seem to her to be but trifling matters. She gives way to her temper, her grief; she exhausts herself by labor; she indulges in improper food, and the next act of suckling is sure to be followed by disorder in some way of the child's system.

The author has seen in his own practice several marked instances of convulsions in the infant to follow immediately after it had begun to draw the milk from the breast of its mother who had just been having a scolding match with a neighbor.   In one instance, the mother had been engaged in washing clothing for several hours, during which time the infant had not been allowed any nourishment.   Finally, having completed her task, she sat down, greatly wearied, to nurse the child.   Almost as soon as the first of the milk had entered its stomach, it fell into a profound stupor, from which it was with great difficulty aroused.   There are other points in connection with the matter of nursing of equal, perhaps greater, importance, but their consideration does not belong to a volume like this.

BAD HABITS.

From the earliest hours the mother should esteem it a privilege as well as a duty to guard her child by the utmost vigilance from the acquiring of bad habits.   Any habit in the child becomes so rooted—so much a part of its existence—that in after years it is virtually impossible to abolish it.   We need not specify such habits, for many, if not all, are well known to parents, and often much deplored.   It behooves the parent, however, not to err, and punish a child for the symptoms of disease under the belief that it is a bad habit.   One such matter, in particular, requires our special attention.   This, while a subject of peculiar delicacy, yet is of so great importance that we feel we will readily be excused for intruding it in a work of this kind.   It is the incontinence of urine, especially at night.   Constantly do we find children punished for this occurrence under the belief that it is a carelessness—a bad habit into which they have fallen.   On the contrary, almost invariably the child

is a double sufferer, and very unjustly so. It suffers from
the punishment and suffers from the act, which causes a
most unpleasant condition until its clothing is changed.

Again : by many people who recognize that this is really a
diseased condition it is regarded as incurable, and hence
nothing is done for its relief. When a child is afflicted in
this way, the parent should at once consult a physician and
persevere until the child is permanently cured. I say permanently, because in so many of these troubles of childhood
improvement is temporary and requires persistent treatment.
When, after such improvement, a relapse occurs, the parents
are too apt to abandon all effort, with the belief that the
disease is incurable. We often find that children who are
troubled with this affliction are in the habit of screaming
out at night, springing from the bed as if in great fear, or
burying the head in the clothing, as though to protect themselves from danger. This is an affection known as " Night
Terrors," and, as in the previous one, the child is constantly
punished for so doing. Such treatment is not only very
unjust, but extremely injudicious. When a child presents
such symptoms it is out of health and imperatively demands
medical care. An additional reason may be given in the
fact that such a condition is very apt to be but the forerunner
or premonitory symptom of loss of mind. Now that we
know so well that insanity in many of its forms is but the
expression of a disease which is constantly greatly relieved,
and often permanently cured, it is well to be warned in time,
and by early treatment prevent the full access of such
disease.

HORRIBLE STORIES.

Scrupulously guard the child against the silly and horrible stories so frequently told them by nurses and others.
In all children, especially those of a nervous temperament,
who are awakened at night, the recollection of these things
comes to them with terrible force amid the darkness and

the loneliness, and it is enough to drive the child into a temporary, if not lasting, insanity. When such an attack occurs, always soothe the little one by every endearment, keep the light burning, and remain with it until it has been composed again to sleep. It is safer in such cases to have a light constantly burning, and when possible an attendant should be near, that, when aroused, it may at once feel a sense of protection.

To prevent a return of these terrors, the general health should be cared for. See that the child has an abundance of out-door exercise. Exercise itself is a valuable means conducive of sleep in children. The child that has played in the open air all day long goes to sleep wearied, but with a sense of happiness as it falls into a sound, refreshing slumber, and, unless disturbed, usually sleeps the entire night and wakes refreshed for a new day's work. A special point in this connection is that every care should be observed not to disturb the sleep of a child. Much harm is constantly being done by carelessness in this respect. Another cause of harm is overwork of the brain, on which point we will speak hereafter. In addition, a child may suffer from such attacks as the result of indigestion, or of being indulged in too much food just before retiring. In all such cases it behooves the parent to remove all causes which may be supposed to incite to an attack, and should they continue, at once to consult a careful physician.

SOOTHING SIRUPS.

In a previous paragraph we alluded to " soothing sirups " and articles of a like nature, of which the name is legion. All such are useless and dangerous. It is safest and best to give no medicine to a child without the advice of a physician. When, however, it would appear necessary to resort to such means, no article should be used of which the component parts are not fully known. Despite the assurances so freely given that this or that remedy contains nothing that is hurtful, we are constantly being deceived. The most hurtful and powerful drugs are usually the basis of all these nostrums, and which educated physicians would hesitate to employ for infants, except under great necessity and with the utmost precaution. The effect is generally to lull the symptoms for the time, while the cause is insidiously undermining the child's health, and finally the little one gets beyond the reach of the aid which, too late, is summoned to it. Again, the child speedily becomes accustomed to such articles, and requires their continuance and in increased doses. The least evil result is indigestion, followed by constipation, stunted growth, enfeebled intellect, and generally producing such a condition of impairment of vitality that the child readily yields to the most ordinary attack of disease, and death ends the lesson.

TEETHING.

The period for the appearance of the second or permanent set of teeth is rarely one when there need be any fear of disease. But it is very important that the parents should observe carefully that these teeth are cut regularly and are not interfered with by the temporary ones. Should they show signs of irregularity or of a tendency to decay, do not delay, but at once consult a skilled physician or dentist, that the trouble may be known and obviated.

EARLY SCHOOLING.

The question of the education of a child should always be one demanding careful consideration. While we are met on every hand by infant prodigies—children of wonderful precocity—yet it should be borne in mind that this is not according to the dictates of nature or of common sense. The hours of infancy and early childhood should be devoted to the accumulation of a fund of health, which in due time will enable its possessor to master, not only attacks of disease, but at the proper time to master the most difficult problems. These hours should be the happiest of life—free from cares or tasks, and particularly free from that irksome confinement to the hard benches of a school-room. " Seven years a baby." This is always true, and never more so than in regard to education. It is time enough after a child has reached and passed that era for it to commence the serious business of attending school. We would urge that, except in the most easy and pleasant manner possible, no positive efforts should be made in the line of what is known as education.

Certainly, a healthy child is always learning, and little by little, with proper care, with scarcely an effort it acquires a valuable fund of knowledge during these early years. But there should be as few set tasks as possible, no memorizing of dates, or of long strings of verses or questions. Rather, in these days, the beautiful, the happy method of the Kindergarten. Especially during the bright, warm days of summer should all confinement to the house be avoided. The school must be in the open air, wherever it can best be obtained, learning from nature's ever-open book. In this connection the evil results of overwork of the brain must constantly be borne in mind. Thus are often planted the seeds of disease, which too soon yield an abundant crop and a harvest of consumption, insanity, and the like. Chorea, or St. Vitus' dance, as it is commonly called, is frequently brought on by overwork of the brain, and even cases are known where an intellect exceptionally brilliant at the outset has in a few years been clouded by idiocy.

A common belief with many is that all our meals should be partaken of in silence, and though not hastily, yet without undue loitering over them. This is a grave error. The table hour at all times should be a social one. Parents and children should, when convenient, enjoy their meals together and enlivened with pleasant chat. This prevents the bolting of food half chewed, and other bad habits, and while the younger ones should not be permitted to monopolize, or even largely share in, the conversation, yet they should be encouraged to habits of attention and respect on these occasions that will enable them to profit in the future.

PHYSICAL DEVELOPMENT.

As a child increases in years it should increase in strength. Here we gain by open-air exercise. In the very young their very exuberance of spirits prompts, even compels, them to romp and frolic. They are like young animals of all kinds, which we see wildly rushing back and forth in the fields, as if utterly unable to keep still. But as a child gets older it is too apt (especially is this seen in young girls) to be content with quiet play. Here comes in the value of light gymnastics. When not carried so far as to become a task, it proves extremely useful by bringing into play in succession each and every set of muscles. By the majority of teachers this exercise is so conducted as to be regarded as a pleasant means of health exercise, and only so long is it useful. The child that finds light exercise a drag requires close attention lest disease be making inroads when least expected. Hence a teacher should be watchful not to disregard the evident signs which tell of exhaustion, and should act accordingly.

Dancing becomes a means to the same end, but, unfortunately, it is sadly abused. This is not the place to descant at length upon the abuses of dancing, save to warn parents not to permit this exercise to be carried so far that it produces muscular exhaustion rather than tenacity of the muscles. Skating, whether on the ice or on parlor skates, is equally a valuable exercise, but always with the same proviso. Recently we find the addition of lawn tennis, croquet, cricket, and base ball as incentives to out-door exercise. With all of them the constant trouble is to prevent excesses. The great desire for victory carries the players forward until they have long passed the boundary of benefit and they reap an abundant harvest of joints and muscles strained, not to say those graver injuries—heart diseases, blood vessels ruptured, hernia, and the like. The last game—viz., base ball, should be abolished from the list permitted for children. It not only demands too much and prolonged exertion, very destructive to the growing frame, but its dangers of maiming, even killing, its players are so many that it is absolutely unsafe both for performers and spectators.

HOME GOVERNMENT.

The home of a child from its earliest remembrance should be associated with happiness. Health is always the handmaid of happiness. A peevish, fretful child not only discomforts those around it, but is itself constantly the victim of indigestion and the like. Hence it becomes an important duty for the parent to begin the moral education of a child almost at birth. We constantly see how rapidly even an infant becomes the tyrant of the household when its slightest whims and humors are permitted and indulged. Kindness, but also firmness, are demanded in the treatment of children. Decide what is right, what is best, and let that decision be final. Make such decisions in no petulant, hasty spirit. This only leads to fear rather than love, and perhaps to concealment and deception.

Above all, as the child grows older and more observant, be extremely watchful lest your example lead it astray. Remember, a child is ever apt to imitate the actions of those with whom it is constantly associated. Regard these little ones as your most priceless treasures. Study that you may so fashion their homes and their lives that the future will reflect no doubtful or evil results.

SIXTH DEPARTMENT.

TRYING EMERGENCIES.

We know not of what we are capable till the trial comes;—till it comes, perhaps, in a form which makes the strong man quail, and turns the gentler woman into a heroine. MRS. JAMESON.

TRYING EMERGENCIES.

EMERGENCIES will arise. Accidents will occur; and when they occur the prompt action, if it be wisely directed, is that which accomplishes the needed work. An alphabetical arrangement of such cases as are most common is here given. When an emergency does arise, deliberately look for directions in this chapter, and proceed as directed, meanwhile seeking a physician.

Apoplexy.—In apoplexy the patient suddenly falls into a state of stupor or unconsciousness, the pupils of the eyes are dilated, the breathing laborious or snoring, the swallowing difficult, the pulse slow and sometimes irregular, with loss of power in the limbs, and usually a deeply flushed face. *Do not mistake this for intoxication.* In such a case elevate the head and body, loosen the clothing about the neck, place the feet in hot mustard water with mustard over the stomach, apply cold to the head and nape of the neck, and send at once for a physician. If a doctor cannot be obtained quickly, open the bowels by an injection of soap and warm water.

Asthma.—Asthmatic attacks may frequently be cut short in several ways. If the patient be very nervous, let the attention be diverted in any way possible and the breathing will soon become much easier. Another method of relief may be found in administering an emetic; still another, in smoking the asthma cigarettes which are sold generally by

245

the druggists; still another, in drinking one or more cups of strong coffee; still another, in inhaling steam from a basin of hot water into which a tablespoonful of Hoffman's anodyne has been poured, and still another, by giving a full dose of opium, laudanum, or paregoric.

Bites of Dogs, Serpents, etc.—Make haste to suck well the bites of dogs, cats, snakes, and other animals whose bites are poisonous, unless the mouth is sore. In the case of dogs also bind the limb tightly above the bite and burn the wound with a hot iron or needle; besides, capture the dog, if possible, and keep him watched carefully until ascertained whether he is mad or not. In the case of snake bite, after sucking and burning the wound, give whisky or brandy in full doses and keep up the intoxication until the doctor is called.

Bleeding, see Hemorrhages.

Blisters.—All blisters, whether caused by burns, scalds, heat of the sun, Spanish fly, or friction, should be carefully opened near one edge without removing the skin, and then dressed with sweet oil or some mild ointment like simple cerate, cold cream, or cosmoline.

Broken Bones, see Fractures.

Bruises.—First cleanse them; then, until pain is relieved, apply cloths wet with cold water, to which laudanum may be added. After the pain has subsided, warm water dressings will hasten the removal of the discoloration, swelling, and soreness.

Black Eye.—This should be treated as any other bruise. After the swelling is gone, the dark color may be concealed by painting it or by flesh-colored plaster.

Burns and Scalds.—Dust the parts with bicarbonate of soda, or wet with water in which as much of the soda has been placed as can be dissolved. When the burns are so severe that the skin   broken and blisters are raised, open the blisters at one side and swathe the parts with soft linen anointed with simple cerate or saturated with sweet oil, castor oil, or equal parts of linseed oil and limewater.   Burns from acids should be well washed with water.   Burns from caustic alkalies, should be well washed with vinegar and water. When a person's clothing is on fire he should quickly lie down and be wrapped in carpet or something else that will smother the flame.

Choking.—If possible, remove the offending substance at once with the fingers, or with blunt scissors used as forceps, or a loop of small wire bent like a hairpin.   It may be possible to dislodge it by blowing strongly in the ear, or by causing the patient to vomit by tickling the throat.   In a child these efforts may be aided by holding it up by the legs.   If pins, needles, or fish bones get in the throat, they frequently require great care in attempts at removal.   A surgeon had better be called as soon as possible if the body cannot be dislodged at once, and especially if there be difficulty in breathing.

Cholera Morbus.—This affection often requires that something be done at once.   For this purpose, thirty drops of laudanum or two or three teaspoonfuls of paregoric may be given to an adult, or proportionate doses for children.   Also apply over the stomach a mustard plaster or cloths wrung out of hot water and turpentine, and frequently changed. If relief is not soon obtained, seek the advice of a physician.

Colic.—May be treated as above, with the addition of an emetic or purgative, or both, if due to undigested food.

Convulsions in Children.—When these occur, place the child at once in a bath of hot water with mustard added ; apply cold water cloths to the head, move the bowels with an injection of warm water or soapsuds, and give enough sirup of ipecac to vomit, unless this has already occurred.   Con-

vulsions frequently indicate the commencement of some disease; hence it is well to call a physician early.

Contusions, see Bruises.

Croup.—When a child is taken suddenly with the croup
at night, give at once a teaspoonful of sirup of ipecac, or
the same with a few drops of antimonial wine added, or a
teaspoonful of powdered alum followed by a cup of water.
Repeat these soon if necessary to cause vomiting. Warm
water cloths may be applied to the throat if covered with
dry wrappings. Keep the child warm, so that sweating may
be induced, and strive to allay its excitement or fear.

Cuts, see Wounds.

Diarrhœa.—Diarrhœa is most generally caused by an irritation of the bowels, due either to the presence of undigested
food or the remains of a previous constipation. Hence it
is always well to commence treatment by a dose of castor
oil, to which may be added ten drops of laudanum. After
the bowels have been moved, give to an adult ten or fifteen
drops of laudanum after each subsequent movement, stop-
ping its use after a few doses. Half-teaspoonful doses of
ginger in water may be tried. Injections of boiled starch
with twenty or thirty drops of laudanum may be tried. Give
but little opium to children.

Dysentery.—Dysentery may almost certainly be recognized by the griping and bearing-down feeling when the
bowels are moved, and especially if the discharges are slimy
and mixed with blood.

A physician should be consulted without wasting much
time in trying the simpler diarrhœa remedies.

Dislocations.—A dislocation is the displacement of the end
of a bone at the joint; hence there is a deformity of the
joint. The ligaments about the joints are necessarily more
or less torn; hence there is pain. Most of these dislocations

will require the skill of a surgeon ; hence one should be obtained as early as possible, care being taken to make the patient as comfortable as may be by an easy position and cooling and soothing applications to the affected joint.

The following named joints may be easily restored usually by the process given : Dislocations of the fingers are reduced by pulling in the line of the bones with moderate pressure at the affected joint. Retain in place by a small splint loosely bound along the back of the finger and hand.

Dislocation of lower jaw.—Replace this by wrapping the two thumbs well with towels, then thrusting them into the two sides of the patient's mouth, slipping them over the back teeth, at the same time grasping firmly, with the fingers, the two sides of the jaws outside the mouth, and making pressure firmly downward and backward with the thumbs, using the sides of the jaw as a lever. As soon as the jaw is felt to be moving into place, slip the thumbs quickly from off the teeth into the sides of the cheeks to prevent having them crushed by the teeth, which will be drawn together with great force. Afterward, keep the jaw in place by bandaging, so that the lower teeth will be firmly pressed against the upper row.

Dislocation of shoulder.—To reduce this, place the patient on his back, sit down close by his side with foot to his shoulder, remove the shoe and place the foot in his arm-pit, seize the patient's hand and pull firmly, drawing the arm somewhat across the body, and making at the same time, pressure upward and outward with the foot in the arm-pit, If successful, the head of the bone will be heard, or felt, to go in place with a snap. If not soon successful, stop and send for a surgeon. Retain bone in place by bringing the forearm across the chest and securing there by some kind of bandage.

Drowning.—*To prevent drowning.*—When upset in a boat

or thrown into the water and unable to swim, draw the breath in well; keep the mouth tight shut; do not struggle and throw the arms up, but yield quietly to the water; hold the head well up, and stretch out the hands only *below* the water; to throw the hands or feet *up* will pitch the body *below* the water, hands or feet *up* will pitch the body head down, and cause the whole person to go immediately under water. Keep the head *above*, and everything else under water.

To restore the apparently drowned.—As soon as removed from the water, treat the patient instantly on the spot without wasting precious time in removing to a house, unless the weather is intensely cold. Free the neck, chest, and waist of clothing. Place the patient on his face with a cushion under his chest and his arm under his forehead, and make pressure on the back for a moment to force water from the lungs. Clear the mouth with the finger and prevent the tongue from obstructing the windpipe by bringing it well forward, and securing it there by passing a cord well back over its base, bringing the ends out at the corners of the mouth and tying them under the chin. Then turn the patient on the back, with a cushion under the shoulders so as to carry the chin away from the chest and thus extend the neck. Then seek to restore respiration in the following manner, which is generally known as Sylvester's method: place yourself behind the patient's head, seize the arms near the elbows and sweep them around away from the body and bring them together above the head, at the same time giving them a strong pull for a few seconds. This elevates the ribs, enlarges the chest, and thus fills the lungs with air. Next return the arms to their former position beside the chest and make strong pressure against the lower ribs for a moment so as to drive out the air again from the lungs. Repeat this manœuvre about fifteen or sixteen times a minute, and keep it up for a long time, unless natural respiration is secured in the meantime, or it has been established beyond a doubt that the patient is certainly dead.

When the patient begins to breathe, stimulate this by the use of ammonia applied to the nose, by slapping briskly the surface of the body, by dashing water upon the chest or face, and by suiting the artificial to the movement of the natural as nearly as possible. Let some person also commence rubbing the limbs briskly upward so as to aid the feeble circulation ; and secure warmth to the body by warm blankets, warm bricks, bottles of warm water (or anything else that will retain heat), applied to the armpits, over the stomach, and elsewhere about the body. Let some stimulant be given as soon as it can be swallowed, and repeated occasionally until danger is over.

Never attempt to move the patient until fully restored if you can possibly avoid it. Then he should be carefully placed in a warm bed and watched to see that breathing does not suddenly cease. Should this occur, renew the artificial respiration at once.

Ear (*Foreign bodies in*).—If a living insect is in the ear, turn the head to the opposite side and fill the ear with tepid water, oil, or glycerine, and it will soon come to the surface.

A bright light thrown into the ear will also often succeed in bringing it out. Any body that will not swell when moistened with water may probably be removed by syringing the ear thoroughly, with the face held downward.

None but the very gentlest probing of the ear should be attempted by any one but a physician, who understands what a delicate organ he has to deal with.

Earache.—Earaches frequently are caused by diseased teeth. In such cases the quickest remedy is either the extraction of the sinning tooth or the adoption of treatment appropriate for the toothache. Earaches not caused by the teeth may often be relieved by using hot drinks, and a hot hop poultice over the affected ear. A persistent earache most likely indicates some disease of the ear and should always lead to consulting a doctor.

Epileptic Fits.—These are known by pallor of face at first, a peculiar cry, loss of consciousness, then flushing of face and violent convulsions, with foaming at the mouth, rolling of the eyes, and biting of the lips and tongue.

In a fit of this kind, place the patient on the back, with little or no elevation of the head; control his movements only so far as to prevent injury; place a folded towel between the teeth, if possible, to prevent the biting of the tongue.

When the convulsion is over, let the patient rest in some quiet place, having previously taken a slight stimulant if very much exhausted by the violence or length of the fit.

Eye (*Foreign bodies in*).—Dirt in the eye may be washed out by squeezing from a sponge a small stream of tepid water. To wash lime from the eye, use the tepid water moderately acidulated with vinegar or lemon-juice. Cinders and other small particles may be removed generally by touching them with a soft silk or linen handkerchief twisted to a point, or by using a loop of human hair. Metallic particles can often be removed best by the use of a magnet.

To expose the eye more fully, the upper lid may be easily everted by lifting it by the lashes and pressing from above by a slender pencil or stick.

Fainting.—When persons have fainted lay them down with the head as low as possible, loosen the clothing, keep back any crowding that would interfere with plenty of fresh air; sprinkle water over the face, apply hartshorn to the nose, and if too long in recovering consciousness, place heated cloths or plates over the stomach.

Fits in Children, see Convulsions.

Fish-hooks.—When a fish-hook has entered any part of the body, cut off the line, file off the flattened end, and pass the hook on through the flesh like you would a needle in sewing.

Fractures.—Broken bones are easily recognized by the grating of the ends on each other, by the unusual bending of the limb, and by the pain caused by motion at this point. A fracture is called *compound* when the end of the bone protrudes through the skin. Whenever such protrusion is seen, the part should be cleansed and at once covered with adhesive plaster or a piece of linen saturated with white of egg. All fractures should be attended to by a surgeon; consequently the dressings suggested here are only temporary, and intended to protect the parts from further injury.

In fracture of the arm above the elbow, bandage the upper arm to the side of the chest, and place the hand in a sling.

In fracture of the arm below the elbow, bend the arm at the elbow at a right angle, place the thumb uppermost, and bandage it between two padded splints, reaching from elbow to ends of the fingers, one being placed on the back of the arm and the other on the front, and place the hand in a sling.

In fracture of the leg below the knee, extend the leg beside the sound one, giving it the same position; place a pillow beneath from the knee down, fold the sides of the pillow over the leg, and secure it in that position by bandages.

In fracture of the thigh-bone, place the patient on the back in bed, relax the muscles of the leg by drawing the feet up toward the body sufficiently, bind splints to the outer and inner side of the broken thigh; then bind both legs together, and turn patient on the side with the injured limb uppermost.

In fracture of the knee-cap, bind the whole limb to a splint on the back of it, being careful to place a sufficiently large pad beneath the bend of the knee.

In fracture of the collar-bone, place the patient on his back on a hard bed without any pillow.

In fracture of the lower jaw, close the mouth and bandage so as to keep the two rows of teeth together.

In fractures of the skull, lay the patient down and apply cold, wet cloths to the head.

In other fractures, place the patient in the most comfortable position possible, keep him quiet, and apply cold water to prevent swelling.

For splints, pasteboard, leather, shingles, or pieces of cigar-box may be used.

Frostbite.—In frostbite use gentle friction in a warm room, using enough cold water or snow to prevent too rapid reaction and consequent pain in the affected part. If very severe, call a physician, as gangrene may follow.

Gunshot Wounds, see Wounds.

Heatstroke, see Sunstroke.

Hemorrhages.—In hemorrhages from an artery, the blood is bright red, and spurts or jets out from a cut. To stop it, make compression between the wound and the heart.

In venous hemorrhage the blood is dark in color and flows in a steady stream. To stop it, make compression on the side of the wound away from the heart. Hemorrhage from the lungs is bright red and frothy, while that from the stomach is of dark color.

To make thorough compression of a blood-vessel, knot a large handkerchief in the middle, place the knot over the line of the vessel, tie the ends firmly around the limb, thrust a short stick beneath, and twist by turning the stick like you turn an auger.

Hemorrhage from the nose may be stopped generally by snuffing up the nose salt and water, alum and water, or vinegar, or by applying ice between the shoulders or at the back of the neck. Keep head raised.

In hemorrhage from the lungs, place the patient in a sitting posture in bed, giving teaspoonful doses of salt and vinegar every fifteen minutes, and apply ice or cold water to the chest, unless the patient is too weak to bear it.

In hemorrhage from the stomach, broken ice may be swallowed with teaspoonful doses of vinegar.

In hemorrhage from the bowels, use ice-water injections and ice over the abdomen.

Injuries to the Brain.—Blows or falls upon the head are liable to injure the brain in two ways.

Concussion of the brain is recognized by the sickness, faintness, pallor, depression, and confusion of the patient, and is best treated by placing the patient on his back in a quiet, cool place, loosening the clothing, and applying heat to the body and limbs if they be clammy or cold.

Compression of the brain is due to fracture of the skull, generally a portion being depressed. The symptoms and treatment about the same as apoplexy.

Intoxication.—This may be distinguished from apoplexy by the absence of paralysis and of insensibilty of the eye-ball, and by the smell of liquor on the breath.

When sure that the patient is intoxicated and not suffering from apoplexy, an emetic may be given, followed by a dose of some preparation of ammonia.

Vinegar is a very good thing to sober a drunken person.

Insect Stings, see Stings.

Ivy Poisoning.—Treated by the application of cloths saturated with sugar-of-lead water or with a solution of bicarbonate of soda in water.

Lightning Stroke.—Treat with rest and stimulants and warmth applied to the body.

Nausea and Vomiting.—First cleanse the stomach by giving large draughts of warm water, and then give small pieces of ice, a teaspoonful of lime-water, or a half teaspoonful of aromatic spirits of ammonia, or a small quantity of magnesia or baking-soda, and, if necessary, place a mustard plaster over the pit of the stomach.

Nervous Attacks, or Shivering Fits, are treated by hot drinks, heat to the surface of the body, mustard or turpentine over the stomach, and a dose of Hoffman's anodyne or tincture of valerian, if at hand.

Nose (*Foreign bodies in*).—Children are apt to shove up their noses small bodies of different sorts, which may cause serious trouble unless soon removed. Their removal may often be effected by vigorously blowing the nose or by repeated sneezing, produced by snuff, or by tickling the nose with a feather. If these fail, a hair-pin or button-hook may be carefully tried.

Nose-bleed, see Hemorrhages.

Poisons.—*Acids* act as irritant poisons, of which the most common are sulphuric, nitric, muriatic, and oxalic.

For poisoning by any of these, give large quantities of either soda, magnesia, chalk, whitewash, whiting, or plaster. Then provoke vomiting, give bland drinks, rest, and stimulants if required. For *oxalic acid* the best antidote is lime in some form. For *carbolic acid*, vomiting, large draughts of oil or milk, rest, warmth of body, and stimulants.

For the *alkaline poisons*—ammonia, soda, potash, or concentrated lye—give vinegar freely; then provoke vomiting, and give bland drinks, followed by rest, and stimulants if required.

For *arsenic, Paris green*, or *Scheele's green*, give large quantities of milk, white of egg, or flour and water; then vomit;

then give tablespoonful doses of dialyzed iron, followed by a teaspoonful of salt in a cup of water ; vomit again ; give a dose of castor-oil, with rest, and stimulants if needed.

Sugar of lead.—Give Epsom salts, provoke vomiting ; repeat several times ; then give demulcent drinks, followed by castor-oil.

For *corrosive sublimate*, provoke vomiting, give strong tea without milk; repeat these several times, then give milk and raw eggs; follow with à dose of castor-oil, and stimulate if necessary.

For *tartar emetic*, use the same treatment as for corrosive sublimate.

For *phosphorus* (usually from matches), provoke vomiting by giving repeatedly five-grain doses of sulphate of copper, then give a dose of magnesia, but *no oil.*

For *lunar caustic*, give a strong solution of salt and water repeatedly, then vomit.

For *iodine*, vomit, give starch dissolved in water freely, following with bland drinks.

For *opium, laudanum, morphia, paregoric,* and *chloral,* vomit the patient freely and repeatedly, with mustard and warm water; then give strong coffee; keep the patient roused by brisk slapping of the skin, or by moving about, or by the galvanic battery, and use Sylvester's method* of keeping up artificial respiration if necessary.

For *strychnine*, vomit once or twice, give a purgative, and then secure absolute rest in a dark, cool room, free from draughts. Large doses of bromide of potash (thirty grains) or twenty grains of chloral may be given.

For *toadstools or Jamestown (jimson) weed,* produce vomiting and follow by stimulants and external application of heat.

For *decayed meats and vegetables,* empty the stomach, then give a dose of castor-oil and some powdered charcoal.

* See under Drowning, p. 506.

For all poisons the best general emetic is mustard and plenty of warm water, aided, if possible, by the patient's finger thrust down the throat. The best stimulant is strong, hot tea or coffee, to which may be added the alcoholic stimulants. The best bland drinks are milk, beaten raw eggs, gum arabic water, or oil. Demulcent drinks are of the same general character. They are mucilaginous, and so protect the coatings of the stomach from irritants, etc.

Scalds, see Burns.

Shocks.—In violent shock, such as results from severe injuries, lay the patient down, cover warmly, and if cold, apply external heat by using bottles of hot water, hot bricks, or hot flannels, etc. If the patient can swallow, give stimulants; if not, give stimulating injections. A mustard-plaster may be applied to the chest and spine with advantage.

Snake-bites, see Bites.

Spasms, see Convulsions.

Spitting Blood, see Hemorrhages.

Splinters.—Wood splinters, if not too brittle, may generally be extracted by tweezers or forceps by seizing the end and pulling steadily and carefully in the direction opposite that in which they entered. Nature will soon make them easier of extraction by the formation of matter around them. To get hold of a splinter under the nail, cut out a V-shaped portion of the nail above it and then the end can be seized. Splinters of glass unless readily extracted should be left to the skill of the surgeon. When a splinter in the eye cannot be extracted, bathe in cold water and bandage loosely, so as to keep the eye as quiet as possible till the surgeon arrives.

Sprains.—Treat sprains by rest, elevation of the limb, cold, moist applications at first, and afterward either cold or warm, whichever gives the greater degree of comfort. A splint or bandage is sometimes useful.

Stings.—The stings of scorpions, tarantulas, centipedes, bees, wasps, hornets, etc., may be treated best by the application of cloths wet in cold water, or wet mud even. The application of a little ammonia or salt and water will generally give marked relief.

Suffocation.—Treat by quick removal to the open air, loosen the garments, and apply friction and artificial respiration if necessary. To escape injury by the heavier gases, as carbonic acid gas, the gases of mines, wells, etc., strive to keep the head above them. To escape through smoke, cover the head with some article of clothing, and seek the outlet with the head as near the floor as possible.

Sunburn.—For sunburn, use equal parts of bicarbonate of soda and fresh lard or cosmoline.

Sunstroke.—Treat this by removing the clothing, applying ice to the head and arm-pits until the high temperature is lowered and consciousness returns, when it should be discontinued until a rising temperature again calls for it. A cold bath of iced water may be very beneficial.

Toothache.—When due to a hollow tooth, cleanse the cavity with a little dry cotton on a probe or large needle, and then pack into the cavity a wad of cotton which has been dipped in creosote, oil of cloves, or ether. When there is no cavity, try bathing the face and gums with some of the various anodynes.

Unconsciousness.—For the recognition of unconsciousness due to fainting, injuries of the brain, and intoxication, see those subjects. When unconsciousness is due to disease of kidneys there will generally be convulsions, also a smell of urine and a dropsical swelling about the eyes and legs. When there is uncertainty as to the cause of the uncon-

sciousness, lay the patient on his back with the head somewhat raised; and if there be pallor and other signs of
prostration and a cold surface, apply ammonia to the nose,
with heat externally and hot drinks internally. If there
be a hot surface, cold should be used externally and internally.

Wounds.—The first important thing to do is to stop the
hemorrhage according to the directions given under the
head of Hemorrhages. Press tightly between the wound
and heart if the blood is bright red and spurts or jets out;
but if blood is dark and flows slowly and steadily, make
pressure beyond the wound or on both sides of it. For
wounds high up in the arm, press firmly just above and back
of the middle of the collar-bone; and for those high up in
the leg, press over where the artery is found beating in the
groin. For wounds of the head, apply pad over the wound
and bandage tightly.

To temporarily dress incised wounds or clean cuts, bring
the edges of the cut evenly together and fasten by bandages,
adhesive plaster, or pieces of linen saturated in white of egg.
When the chest or abdomen is cut so that the lung or bowels protrude, first cleanse these by gently squeezing over them
tepid water from a sponge, and then carefully place them
back very gently with a soft cloth wet in warm water; if not
able to replace them with such a cloth, wet with warm water
and keep it wet until a surgeon arrives.

Lacerated or torn wounds seldom bleed much. These
should be carefully cleansed of all foreign substances, the
parts placed in position as nearly as possible, and then
treat as bruises with wet cloths sprinkled with laudanum.

Perforated Wounds, such as may be made with a rusty
nail, should be enlarged or kept open by the introduction of
lint, which must be changed three or four times a day, and
the wound should be kept well cleansed.

Gunshot Wounds should always have the care of a surgeon. Temporarily let them be treated by cold, wet cloths, with the addition of laudanum if required. If there be signs of shock, treat according to directions given under that head. About the same general directions may be followed in the treatment of injuries caused by machinery. It may be accepted as a rule, that gunshot wounds, railroad accidents, and machinery accidents are worse than they seem to be. The shock to the system is also very severe in these cases, and is hard to rally from.

In all emergencies, the poorest thing to do is to lose presence of mind and to hesitate when action is needed. Be cool, prompt, decided!

EMERGENCY BY FIRE.

Beyond the class of emergencies already discussed, that by fire is as imperative as any. There may be dangers of this kind where the most pressing duty is flight. One should prepare himself for this by cool contemplation of every new situation in which he sleeps or tarries—where the probable source of danger lies and what is the most available method of escape should be in mind before the emergency arises.

As a rule, however, the party who discovers a fire should give an alarm and then run at it—not from it. Many fires can be smothered out. Far less water will drown a fire than many suppose. A bucket of water applied from a tin dipper to the point of greatest peril will do more good than a barrel of water promiscuously dashed out. Keep cool and put water where it is needed.

In a smoke-filled apartment lie down and creep on the floor. Tie a wet handkerchief over the mouth and nostrils when passing dense smoke. Carry a coil of small but strong rope, with knots along it, when you travel. If needing to escape by it, fasten one end to the bedstead, grasp the rope with a towel, and slide down slowly. Do what you can for others who may share your peril, keeping your presence of mind and assuring others.

RAILROAD ACCIDENTS.

These are generally so sudden that no amount of precaution avails. As a rule for passengers, however, it is best never to jump from a train. That involves more danger than staying aboard, usually. The aisle of the car and near its centre are the safest positions, as a rule. It is bad in collisions to have the feet entangled with the seats. To mount the seat or reach the aisle is generally safer. In any case, keep your presence of mind, without shouting or rashness. None but a foolhardy person allows his head or arms to project from a moving train.

ACCIDENTS ON ICE.

In cold climates every winter has its attendant accidents upon the ice. Prevention here is better than cure, and prevention may be had by the little contrivance shown in the

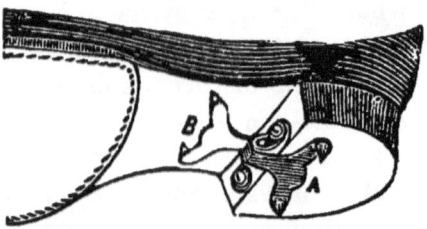

cut and known as the "Detroit Ice Creeper." A represents the creeper in position, ready for use. The dotted line B shows the creeper thrown back entirely out of the way when not in use or walking in-doors. The attachment to the shoe-heel is made by screws. Thus equipped, one may walk firmly on the smoothest ice.

SEVENTH DEPARTMENT.

GAMES AND AMUSEMENTS.

There are some trades that are solitary and exclusive. Authorship is one of these; and perhaps the author is not always a very amusing inmate. But the actor in the private play, the clever and ready wit who makes the charade lively, the musician, the embroideress, the fortune-teller, . . . and the artistic member—these can add to home amusements.

M. E. W. S.

FUN IN THE FRESH AIR.

GAMES, AMUSEMENTS, ETC.

R ECREATION is re—creation. It makes a man feel new. Time immemorial it has been confessed that "all work and no play make Jack a dull boy." The same law holds in children of the larger growth. The taut bow of active manhood must be relaxed at times, or its elasticity will certainly be lost. Splendid surroundings cease to charm and may become monotonous or positively irksome. The softest couch cannot relieve a mind disturbed. For such ills mental panacea is demanded, and this is found in games, amusements, entertainments, and the like.

Any fertile mind can invent something in the nature of a game, or can improve upon existing games. Not, probably, upon the old standard games, however. Chess, for instance, has been studied by the world's master minds, and he is a genius indeed who can add anything thereto. But "the way we play it," as is so often said, is probably the very best way for each special party in the ordinary games, which have not been developed to a perfect method. First, as pre-eminent for combining healthfulness with pleasure, should be considered

OUT-DOOR GAMES.

Archery.—One of the oldest of games is Archery. Originally a means of warfare and the chase, it has survived that use and now flourishes as a pastime. Archery organizations are venerable in England and popular in America.

The " York Round" of Archery consists of seventy-two arrows at one hundred yards, forty-eight arrows at eighty yards, and twenty-four arrows at sixty yards. All public matches shot in Great Britain by gentlemen are decided upon the result of either a single or double York Round.

The " National Round," shot by the ladies of Great Britain at all public meetings, consists of forty-eight arrows at sixty yards and twenty-four arrows at fifty yards. Generally the prizes are awarded upon the result of a Double National Round.

The "Columbia Round," adopted for this country, consists of twenty-four arrows at thirty yards, twenty-four arrows at forty yards, and twenty-four arrows at fifty yards. These distances are well suited to the present state of skill and practice among ladies, and the ranges and division of arrows will be in great favor for the first year or two. It will be then time to consider the matter of extending the ranges.

The points sought in scientific archery are (1) Position; (2) Nocking the arrow, or properly placing it on the string; (3) Drawing the bow, which must be done to the same distance, in the same manner, and in the same time, else irregular hitting will result; (4) Aiming so as to " keep a line " and to hit the target; (5) Loosing the string so that the arrow will fly with power and grace. Finger-gloves, touched in grease, facilitate the loosing.

Bows vary in drawing power, those used in the York Round averaging about fifty pounds. Arrows are twenty-eight inches long, all of the same form, weight, etc. Arrows are pointed so as to enter the target. A slight blunting will vary the flight very materially. Condition of wind must be allowed for, as cross winds, or winds toward or from the target, all affect the flight. Practice under the instruction of archery manuals and expert marksmen will make perfect; and for pleasant, healthful, out-door exercise in which gentlemen and ladies can participate, archery will prove second to none.

Base Ball.—By common consent, Base Ball is our national game. It is, however, a game exclusively for boys and men. It is in no sense a family game. It is attended with so many serious injuries and has been so largely relegated to professional clubs that interest of the better sort has been withdrawn from it to a great extent. Those interested should buy Hutching's *Base Ball Manual*, which contains the rules (of which there are over seventy, and most of them have many specifications), the interpretations of rules, decisions of leagues, record of plays, etc.

Cricket.—This is essentially the national game of England, but it is gaining ground in this land. It is played with single or double wicket, the latter being the true game. The two sides have eleven players each, though a numerical allowance is sometimes made for acknowledged superiority of players. The *in* side remains in until all its members but one have been *put* out. The bowler aims to knock down the wickets, while the batsman protects them by parrying the balls, which are stopped and caught on the field by fielders at various points, while the batsman makes his " runs," interchanging places with the other batsman. Hoyle thus describes the game :

" We will suppose a party of cricketers turning out for an afternoon's sport. Some carry bats, two have cricket balls, and several others bear the stumps of which the wickets are constructed. They come to the place where the wickets are to be set up, or ' pitched.' It is a level field, and the space between the wickets, in particular, is flat as a billiard-table. Now the bowlers advance, and under their direction the wickets are set up. The distance between the wickets is twenty-two yards. The distance between the stumps must be a little less than the diameter of the cricket ball, so that the ball cannot pass between the stumps without touching them and knocking off the bails or little bits of wood placed across the top of the stumps. The companions of the bowler are now dispersed about the field in various positions. . . . They all labor for the same object—namely, to stop the ball when it is struck by the batsman, to catch it (if possible) before it reaches the ground after being delivered from the bat (in which case the batsman is considered *caught out*, and his inning is over), and to throw the ball up, when they have stopped it, to the bowler or wicket-keeper as quickly as possible. The bowler's desire is to knock down the batsman's wicket, while the batsman's province is to defend his wicket by striking away the ball as it is bowled toward him. Beyond this, he has to judge what balls it will be safe for him to strike hard at and what balls he must content himself with *blocking*, or striking down; for on the number of runs he obtains will depend the share he contributes to the success of his side."

For the detailed rules of Cricket, see Hoyle's *Games*. An English publication, James Lillywhite's *Cricketers' Annual*, is full of valuable information.

Croquet.—This game is so well known and so generally played, that no better service can be rendered than—waiving the questions of variety in arrangement and apparatus—to give the generally accepted rules for the play.

THE LAWS OF CROQUET.

1. At the outset two of the party are chosen chiefs, one for each side. These two determine which shall have the first choice of players. Each plays a ball from the starting-point, and he who, with one blow of the mallet, drives his ball nearest the turning-stake wins the first choice.

2. The chief who has won the first choice of players opens the game.

3. Each player at starting must place his ball a mallet's length in front of the starting-stake and opposite the centre of the first arch.

4. A player may play in any attitude he chooses, but in striking he must use only one hand.

5. The ball must be struck with the face of the mallet's head, and the stroke must be a distinct blow, and not a push.

6. The chief who opens the game is followed by the chief of the opposing side, and the other players on each side play alternately in accordance with the colors marked upon the starting-stake.

7. If any players play out of his turn, and the error be discovered and challenged before another player makes a stroke, the opposing side may either compel the delinquent player to replace his ball in its original position, or they may allow it to remain where it was played. But any advantage to himself or disadvantage to his opponents, occasioned by misplay, must be immediately rectified.

8. If the adverse side fail to challenge the misplay before another player has commenced, no penalty is attached, but the offending party cannot use his next turn, having already anticipated it.

9. Should a player, by mistake or otherwise, use a wrong ball, he must suffer the consequences, and not the rightful owner of the ball. If the error be discovered and challenged before the turn is completed, the ball must be restored to the position it occupied previous to the misplay, and any damages sustained by the adverse side by reason of the misplay must be repaired and the offending player deprived of his turn. But if the misplay be not challenged previous to the next player commencing to play, the game proceeds as if no misplay had occurred, and no penalty is attached.

10. Each player continues to play so long as he makes a count in the game; that is, so long as he drives his ball through the next arch in order, strikes the turning-stake in order, or achieves either roquet, croquet, or roquet-croquet, or a combination of two or more of these. Failing to accomplish either of these, he relinquishes his turn to the next player. (See Law 26.)

11. The balls must pass through the arches in their regular consecutive order and in the proper direction of the course. If a ball be driven through an arch out of regular order, or from the wrong side, it does not count any more than if it had passed over any other portion of the ground. When a ball passes properly through an arch it is said to "make its arch."

12. A ball makes its arch when it passes through it in its proper consecutive order, from either of the following causes only :

    I. When it is driven through by a blow from its owner's mallet.

    II. When it passes through from roquet, croquet, roquet-croquet, or ricochet.

    III. When it is driven through by concussion; that is, by a blow from another ball driven against it by roquet, croquet, roquet-croquet, or ricochet.

13. A ball is considered to have passed through its arch if it cannot be touched by the handle of the mallet when moved from the top to the base of the arch, from wire to wire, on the side from which the ball passed.

14. Should a ball be driven only *partially* through its arch in the wrong direction, it is not in a position to be driven back and through in the right direction.

15. If a player can drive his ball through two arches by one stroke, or pass it through an arch and against the turning-stake, he may lay his mallet on the spot where his ball stopped, place it in any direction that is most useful to him, and put his ball at the end of the mallet.

16. Striking the turning stake is equivalent to making an arch, subject to the same conditions, and enjoying the same privileges; with this exceptional advantage, the stake may be struck from any direction. (See Laws 12 and 15.)

17. When a ball has completed the round and has struck the starting-stake, either by a stroke from its owner's mallet or by roquet, roquet-croquet, croquet, or by concussion, it becomes a dead ball, and must be removed from the field.

18. When a ball has completed an entire round with the exception of striking the starting-stake, it becomes a Rover, and may either go out by striking the starting-stake, or may continue its play at large all over the field, subject to the conditions and limitations hereafter specified.

19. A Rover may play upon all the balls one after another, but on no one ball twice in the same turn.

20. A Rover must roquet, roquet-croquet, or croquet in order to continue his play.

21. Should a Rover strike the starting-stake, as specified in Law 17, it becomes a dead ball, and must be removed from the field.

22. When one ball strikes another it is a roquet, and this holds good whether the ball striking it proceeds direct from a stroke of the mallet, or rebounds upon it from a stake, arch, or any other fixed obstacle, or from another ball which it has previously struck.

23. When a ball roquets another, it may strike the roqueted ball again without any intermediate play, but this does not constitute another roquet. If, however, either ball in this second stroke be driven through its proper arch, the arch shall be counted as passed, but the playing ball is not entitled to another stroke.

24. A ball having made a roquet, may either croquet, or roquet-croquet the roqueted ball, or proceed on its round.

25. When a ball roquets two or more balls by one blow of the mallet, it constitutes what is called a ricochet.

26. A ball terminates its tour of play when, without making an arch or striking a turning-stake, it roquets a ball which it has croqueted. (See Law 10.)

27. A ball may only croquet that ball upon which it has made a roquet.

28. A player may croquet any number of balls consecutively; but he cannot croquet the same ball the second time during the same turn without first sending his own ball through the next arch in order, or hitting the turning-stake.

29. A player must perceptibly move the ball he croquets.

30. In making ricochet, a player may croquet the first or all of the balls at his option, but the order of croquet must be the same as that of ricochet.

31. If a ball roquet another, and with the same stroke make its arch, it may croquet the roqueted ball, or refuse to do so, and again roquet it before making the croquet, or it may proceed to make another arch.

32. While executing the croquet, if a ball flinch, the shot is void, and the croqueted ball must be replaced in its former position. The croqueting ball may then proceed with its turn, but it cannot repeat the croquet just missed.

33. The laws of roquet-croquet are precisely the same as those which govern the croquet, and a player may roquet-croquet any ball that has been roqued.

34. After making roquet, a player may take two chances by roquet-croquet.

35. Should a ball in its progress over the ground be interrupted by any one, the player to whom it belongs may either allow it to remain where it stopped after its interruption, or remove it to the point it probably would have reached had no interruption occurred.

36. Should a ball be accidentally displaced, it must be restored to its proper position before the game can proceed.

37. Should an arch or stake lose its upright position from any cause, it must be restored before the play proceeds.

38. No play is permitted outside the limits of the ground. A ball driven beyond the limits must be immediately placed on the ground at the point where it crossed the boundary. A ball so placed may be played upon by friend or foe.

39. If one ball roquets another, and either or both balls go beyond the bounds, either or both shall be replaced, and the roqueting ball may play on the roqued ball the same as if neither had been driven off the bounds.

40. Players on the same side may advise each other upon a stroke, but not assist in making it.

41. The game is finished when all the players on one side have made all the arches and struck the two stakes.

42. The umpire is chosen by the two chiefs.

43. The decision of the umpire is final. His duties are, to decide when balls are fairly struck; to restore balls to their places which have been disturbed by accident; to decide whether a croqueted ball is moved or not, in doubtful cases; and to settle all other disputed points which may arise during the progress of the game.

Lawn Tennis.—Lawn Tennis is the destined game of the future. " How does it compare with croquet?" was asked of an expert in both games. " As a wedding does with a funeral," was the answer.

As in croquet, gentlemen and ladies may play at Tennis; yet in this there is so much of action that for the youthful and vigorous it has special charms.

It should be played on a level, well-cut lawn. Rubber-soled shoes should be worn to insure sure footing and protect the turf. Sets packed in strong boxes can be had from $4.00 to $35.00 in price. The set contains bats, or racquets; regulation balls, net poles, net thirty-six feet long, boundary pegs, lines and runners, mallet, and book of instructions, which gives full directions for constructing the court and conducting the game.

The fact that to play the game requires the set, and that this always includes the printed rules, makes it unnecessary to give rules here. Suffice it to say that the game consists in serving or delivering the ball from the racquet over the net from one court or area into another, the opposing party returning the ball in similar manner. The game may be played by two, three, or four persons. The skill required for correct service, the agility in catching the balls and dexterity in managing them, the opportunity of scoring afforded by good play on your own part and by poor play of the antagonists, combine to make the game very attractive and healthful.

BOARD GAMES.

Chess.—Chess is unquestionably the chief of board games. It is played upon a board containing sixty-four squares,

with two sets of differently colored pieces, or men; each
set having sixteen pieces, of which eight are pawns, having
the same value and moves; the others, with their special
value and moves, being for each set a king, a queen, two
bishops, two knights, and two castles or rooks. Upon this
game volumes of profound depth have been written, and
journals are exclusively devoted to its discussion. In the
brief space here available, so abstruse a game cannot be
discussed with fullness or even fairness. Those interested
need a Chess Manual and the instruction of an expert.

Checkers.—This is an ancient game, a sort of infantile
Chess, played upon the same board, and using twelve pieces
for each side, arranging them on alternate squares in the
three outer rows of the board. The advances are made
from each side by moves on the diagonal squares, the one
having the right to move "jumping" any unprotected
enemy on an adjacent diagonal, so reducing the number of
his opponent's pieces. When a piece reaches the outer
row on its opposite side it becomes a "king," privileged to
move either way. This is "crowned" by placing another
piece on top of it. The one jumping all his opponents first
wins the game. The game for a lively spurt may be re-
versed, the one losing all his pieces first becoming the winner. This is called "Give Away."

Backgammon.—This game is played on the inner side of
the ordinary chess or checker board. It requires fifteen
checker pieces and a set of dice for each of the two players.
The board has twenty-four points colored alternately of two
different colors. The pieces are arranged on eight of the
points for each side, the position of each set corresponding
precisely to that of its opponent. Moves are made as determined by the throwing of dice, each party advancing his
men around the board and aiming at two objects; 1st, to
leave no single piece exposed which might be taken up by

the opponent; 2d, to catch up any exposed piece of the opponent. Pieces can be taken up when they stand alone on a point and the move to be made by the other side reaches that unprotected piece. The piece so taken up cannot resume play until it is re-entered on a point corresponding in number to one on the dice thrown by its owner. When all the pieces of a side have been gathered into the final or home table, the player may throw off any of them from points corresponding to the dice thrown. If he has none to correspond, he must move up the required number of points, or, if this cannot be done, he may play off his next highest piece or pieces, as may be needed. The party first getting all his pieces off wins. If any of the loser's pieces are not then in his home table he is *gammoned*, which is equal to two ordinary beats or *hits*. If the winner throws off all his men before the loser gets his last man to his own side of the board, it is a *backgammon*, equal to three *hits*. The numbers thrown on the dice must be played, unless it is impossible by reason of pre-occupancy of points, when the throw is lost. If doublets be thrown, the player has four moves instead of two.

Russian Backgammon.—In this game all the men are entered into the same table according to the throws. Both sets follow the same route on the board, neither side moving out of the first table till all its men are duly entered, and neither throwing off any men until all of his pieces have reached the terminal table. This game is longer and far more stubborn than the ordinary form.

Bagatelle.—This is to Billiards as Checkers is to Chess— a diminutive member of the same family. He who plays the superior game seldom takes interest in the other. It is played on a board varying in length to suit the desires of purchasers. Cups are set in the board flush with its surface, into which ivory balls are driven with a cue, the plays all being from the opposite end of the board. These cups have different values, upon which the count is made. They vary in number from nine to fifteen. Various games are played on the same, or very similar boards, for which directions are furnished on the purchase of the apparatus.

Other Board Games.—Among the many folding-board games which are deemed specially good may be named Parchesi, Stella, Falconry, Spider and Fly, Go Bang, Russian Tivoli, Fox and Geese, Solitaire, The Captive Princess, Cats and Mice, Ambuscade, Steeple Chase Game, John Gilpin, The Pilgrim's Progress, and The Monopolist.

CARD GAMES.

Aside from the ordinary playing-cards with their almost limitless varieties, there is a splendid assortment of other cards, both instructive and amusing. Every stationer and toy-dealer has these at various prices and with full directions for playing.

MENTAL GAMES.

Dictionary.—A long but familiar word is announced to a company and two minutes are allowed in which to write all the words which can possibly be formed from the letters of the assigned word. Any word of two or more letters is allowed, proper names and foreign terms excepted. Any letter of the assigned word may be used twice or oftener in any written word. At the end of two minutes the writing stops and each list is read. Every word which two or more persons have written is stricken from the lists; every word written by one only counts for the writer as many as there are parties in the game. If five play, each exclusive word counts its writer five, etc. The party announcing the word does not write, but is counted, and directs the reading of the written words in turn from his right.

Post.—This game is well adapted to a large party, and much fun and merriment may be found in it. One of the players is chosen to fill the office of postmaster-general. He in time selects a postman, who has his eyes bandaged for a race. The other players seat themselves in two rows facing each other, along the room, a short distance apart. At the commencement of the game, the postmaster-general gives to each player the name of a town, and if the company is large it is well for him to aid his memory by writing the names of the different places on a piece of paper. All being arranged, the sport begins by the blind postman standing between the rows of chairs and waiting for orders, while the postmaster-general retires to a corner of the room and calls out the names; when so doing the parties bearing them must immediately change seats, and the blind postman endeavors to catch them as they run or get in their place. Should he be successful, and capture one of those changing places, or get in the empty chair, the one caught or excluded from his place becomes the postman. The postmaster always retains his position throughout the game. When a player remains seated after his town is called, he must pay a forfeit or some other penalty imposed by the postmaster. During the game the postmaster will exclaim, " The general post is going ; " then the entire company must change seats, and in the race for a place the postman is certain to find a chair, and leave a companion without one to take his office. We will give an example of this game.

Postmaster: The post is going from Boston to New York.

Boston and New York change places.

Postmaster: The post is going from Trenton to Philadelphia.

Trenton and Philadelphia attempt to change seats, but the postman catches Trenton, and leaves him to take the place of postman.

Postmaster: The post is going from Baltimore to Washington.

Baltimore and Washington change seats.

Postmaster: The post is going from Hartford to New Haven.

Hartford and New Haven try to change places, but the postman gets in Hartford's chair and he must act as postman.

Postmaster: Be quick! The general post is going.

In the confusion of running for a chair, it is quite likely a new postman will be found. Thus the game goes on, affording much pleasure and fun.

Who are you? Who am I?—This game is instructive and pleasant, giving the players an opportunity to gain and give information. One of the company leaves the room, and the others select some noted historical or literary character. The player outside is then recalled; as he enters, the company address him as though he were the person they have named. He also questions them; and the party who leads him to the discovery must in turn retire from the room. For example, as the outside party enters the room, he is greeted with the remarks, "You are truthful," "You are brave." He at once proceeds to question the others in turn.

When and where was I born?

In the 18th century, in Virginia.

For what was I famous?

For military ability, courage, wisdom, good judgment, &c.

Was I a general and then President of the United States?
Yes.

Then, I am George Washington.   •

Another pleasing way to play this game, is by sending two players from the room. They choose some character, and on entering the room, converse together about such person, allowing those in the room to guess the party they personate. The one guessing chooses a companion and leaves the room to enact the next character. Sometimes the parties appear in costume, and act the prominent incidents of the life of the person chosen. Thus by trying different ways to play this game, much instruction and amusement may be gained from it.

The Four Elements.—The party being seated in a circle, the player chosen to commence the game, takes a knotted handkerchief and throws it suddenly into another's lap, calling out at the same time either, " Earth !" " Water !" " Air !" or " Fire !" If " Earth " be called out, the player into whose lap the handkerchief has fallen must name some quadruped before the other can count *ten :* if " Water !" he must name a fish : if "Air !" a bird ; and if " Fire !" he must remain silent. If the player names a wrong animal or speaks when he ought to be silent, he must pay a forfeit and take a turn at throwing the handkerchief; but should he give the correct answer, he must throw the handkerchief back to the first player. This is an exceedingly amusing game ; those who have never joined in it can have no idea of the absurd errors into which the different players fall when called suddenly to name a particular kind of animal.

Key-Game.—This game may be played by any number of persons, who should all, except one, seat themselves on chairs placed in a circle, and he should take his place in the centre of the ring. All the company sitting must next take hold with their left hands of the right wrists of the persons sitting on their left, being careful not to obstruct the grasp by holding the hands. When all have in this manner joined hands, they begin moving them from left to right, making a circular motion and touching each others hands, as if for the purpose of taking something from them. The player in the centre then presents the Key to one of the company, and turns his back, so as to allow it to be privately passed to another, who hands it to a third. Thus it is handed round the ring from one player to another with all imaginable celerity, which task is easily accomplished, on account of the continued motion of the hands of all the players. It is the office of the player in the centre, after allowing time for the Key to be passed to the third or fourth player, to watch its progress and endeavor to seize it in its passage. If he succeeds in his attempt, the person in whose hand it is found, after paying a forfeit, must take his place in the centre, and give and hunt the Key in his turn. Should the seeker fail in discovering the Key in his first attempt, he must continue to search until successful.

Birds Have Feathers.—The company are seated, and each places his hands on his lap. One of the party, chosen as leader, cries out, "Birds have feathers!" and suddenly lifts his hands from his lap; all the company are expected to do likewise. The leader raises his hands each time he calls out anything, but the rest, only when such things as have feathers are named. His object is to catch the others and make them pay forfeits, by raising their hands at the wrong time, which they will do, if not sharp and on the lookout. To illustrate, the leader cries in rapid succession, "Birds have feathers!"—"Ducks have feathers!"—"Chickens have feathers!"—"Geese have feathers!"—"*Dogs* have feathers." In the excitement of the game, some are certain to raise their hands, not remembering that *Dogs* do not possess feathers; and they must pay the number of forfeits agreed upon by the company.

Consequences.—In this game the players are seated round a table, and each supplied with a piece of writing paper and pencil. One player starts by writing a quality of a gentle-

man, "the handsome," "the noble," or whatever may occur
to the mind to apply to a person. All are expected to keep
their eyes on their own paper, not looking at their next
neighbor. The company then fold the top of each paper,
hiding what has been written, and each player passes his
paper to the party on his right, making all the players have
a different paper for the next writing. On this is written
the name of a gentleman; (it is fun to name some one present). The papers are again folded and passed as before,
adding pleasure to the game, as no two persons write consecutive sentences on the same paper. Next write the quality of a lady, fold and pass as before—then the lady's name
where they met—what he said to her—what she said to him
—the consequences, and what the world said. Always fold
and pass the paper at every round of the sentences. One
paper is then given to each person, and they in turn read
the paper in hand. Some startling sentences are found
linked together by different minds. We give these specimens from a choice collection. The talented Mr. Smith and
the handsome Miss Brown met on a railway train. He
said to her, "are you going to Niagara?" She said to him,
"The beauty of the landscape exceeds my anticipations."
The consequence was, "they started homeward to learn the
truth of it," and the world said, "Just as we expected." The
second strip unfolded, reads, "The cross Mr. Snap and the
frivolous Miss Flimsey met in a balloon;" he said to her,
"Love me always?" She said to him, "I will try my best."
The consequence was "An elopement," and the world said,
"How could they?"

Concert.—A noisier game than this could scarcely be
desired by the most boisterous of our young friends. The
players, having selected a "conductor," seat themselves
·round him in a circle. The conductor then assigns to each
a musical instrument, and shows how it is to be played.

When all are provided with their imaginary instruments, the conductor orders them to tune, and by so doing he gives each musician a capital opportunity for making all sorts of discordant noises. When the different instruments have been tuned the conductor waves an unseen baton, and commences humming a lively air, in which he is accompanied by the whole of his band, each player endeavoring to imitate with his hands the different movements made in performing on a real instrument. Occasionally the conductor pretends to play on a certain instrument, and the player to whom it belongs must instantly alter his movements for those of the conductor, and continue to wield the baton until the chief player abandons his instrument. If a player omits to take the conductor's office at the proper time, he must pay a forfeit. The fun of this game depends on the humor of the conductor, and the adroitness with which he relinquishes his baton, and takes up the instruments of the other players.

Yes and No.—After a romp the young people will desire a quiet game, during which they can rest themselves. We advise them to try this pleasant puzzling game. The company take seats and choose one of their number to think of a person or object, while the others try his patience with puzzling questions regarding it. He replies to them with " Yes " or " No," watching himself so as to give no clue to the thought. Each of the party in turn tries to guess what the "thought" is, from the answer given them. If the players are apt and watch closely, they will soon discover the thought, unless it is a very difficult one. After a number of trials, if the word is not guessed, the one chosen may be told, and the same person have the pleasure of giving the company another chance to guess.

How? When? and Where?—This is a good game to test the

guessing quality of a company. One of the number leaves
the room. Those remaining name some object or article to
be guessed by the person outside. It is well to choose
words having double meanings, such as, ark (arc), cord
(chord), flour (flower). This makes the answers more
puzzling and difficult to guess. When the word is decided
upon, the person out of the room is recalled and takes his
march round, going to each in succession and asking them,
"How do you like it?" Take the object named as flour
(flower). The first person may answer, "white;" the next,
"real;" another, "baked," and so on through the company. The questioner keeps trying all the time to find out
the object named. Not doing so, he proceeds to inquire of
each one in turn, "When do you like it?" One person
may reply, "At dinner-time;" another, "in the spring
season." Thus he questions the entire party as before, and
not being sharp in two questions, finally gives a third as a
last resort, and most likely will find out then, as the company, in pity for his dullness, will give hints to put him on
the right track. "Where do you like it?" "At the mill,"
"in the garden," "in clusters," etc. Having guessed three
times and succeeding, he names the person who gave him
light on the subject. He in turn must pay a forfeit and is
sent out of the room, for the company to decide upon
another word. When the party fails to find the word given,
he tries another word.

Hunt the Whistle.—A person who has never seen the game
is elected *hunter;* the others seat themselves in a circle on
the floor. The hunter, having been shown the whistle,
kneels in the centre of the circle, laying his head in the lap
of one of the players until the whistle is concealed. While
he is in this posture, the whistle is to be secretly attached
to the back part of his coat by means of a piece of string
and a bent pin. One of the players then blows the whistle,

and drops it. The hunter, being released, is told to find it, but this is no easy task, as he carries the object of his search about his own person. As the hunter kneels in the centre of the group, the different players blow through the whistle and drop it, as the opportunities occur. The puzzled hunter is sometimes fairly tired out before he discovers the trick that is played upon him.

Proverbs.—In playing this game, the person chosen to guess the proverb retires from the room, while the others remain and name some proverb, such as " A stitch in time saves nine;" "All is not gold that glitters;" "Train up a child in the way he should go;" " A rolling stone gathers no moss," etc. When the proverb is chosen, one of the company gives each person a word of the sentence. The word received must be given in the answer to any question asked by the guesser. We will take the first for example, " A stitch in time saves nine." The first person takes " A ;" the second, " stitch ;" the third, " in ;" the fourth, " time;" the fifth, " saves ;" the last, " nine." The party out of the room is then recalled and begins to question each person, commencing with number one. He enquires, " Have you chosen a difficult proverb ?" " No, I do not think it *a* very hard one to guess." Turning to the next player he asks, " Have you been riding to-day ?" " Yes, but I came home early, that I might put a *stitch* in the dress that was torn." If the questioner is sharp he will see that the answer is so formed as to get the word *stitch* in, and may guess from this the proverb. But he proceeds to number three, and asks, " Do you enjoy playing games ?" " Yes, I have spent many a pleasant hour *in* such amusement." Thus he continues questioning until through the proverb, although he may find out before he comes to the last word. Should he not, he has three times to guess, and if not successful, must leave the room again. If he is fortunate in naming the proverb, he must name the person who gave him the clue, and this one must retire from the room to try his or her guessing abilities.

I Love my Love with an A.—This is a very amusing game if played with zest and earnestness. The interest will be lost, and the sport lose its brightness, if the players are not quick to reply. The object of the game is to rapidly call to mind some epithets beginning with any particular letter of the alphabet. If you cannot do so, a forfeit is the penalty. The company are seated, and all, in turn, express their love for their Love with a word commencing with the letters of the alphabet in rotation. Often the sentences pass round the circle in succession, but generally the last one expressing, calls on one of the party on the other side to quickly respond with the next letter. This keeps up the interest, as each one is on the lookout, fearing to be called on next. For example, the first will say, " I love my Love with an *A*, because he is amiable." The second person continues, " I love my Love with a *B*, because he is bountiful." Then this last one speaking will call on Miss Brown on the opposite side to continue. She will quickly respond, " I love my Love with a *C*, because he is captivating." Should she fail to reply, a forfeit must be paid, and she must call on some one else. Thus the game continues through the alphabet.

Hunt the Ring.—The players form a circle, one standing in the centre of it. Have a long string with a ring on it, held by all the party. The ring is passed quickly from one hand to another along the string, while the player in the centre endeavors to detect into whose hand the ring has passed, and take it from the one holding it. The rest of the players keep the ring going from hand to hand, trying to impress the person inside the ring by their motions that it is with one person, when it may be on the other side of the circle. It takes a sharp look-out and "be quick" to catch it, as it passes rapidly from one to the other. When the ring is found, then the person having it takes the place of seeker and tries his power to catch and find the ring.

What is my Thought like?—The company choose one of their number to think of some person, place or thing, as Washington—Boston—wagon—or whatever strikes the mind first. The company in turn are asked by him or her, "What is my thought like?" They, not knowing the thought, will make odd guesses. For instance, one will say, "Like a locomotive;" the next, "Like a lion," and so on. After the opinions have been collected from all the party, the questioner reveals his thought, and every player has to assign a reason for the answer to the first question, or pay a forfeit. To illustrate: the one who asked, "What is my thought?" says, "George Washington." "Why is Washington like a locomotive?" "Because of his swiftness in the performance of his work." "Why like a lion?" "Because he was brave." Thus the game continues through the circle, affording an opportunity for ingenious answers.

Transpositions.—This game will afford amusement for many an hour and give improvement as well as pleasure. The company being provided with pencil and paper, each, in turn, writes on his or her paper the name of a city, mountain, or some eminent person, &c., transposing the letters so that the word will not be known without some study. It is well to write a few words of explanation after the word. Should the word be a city, state some incident to give the guesser some clue. If a historical person, state some event connected with him, or the country in which he lived. After each one has finished writing, the papers are folded, collected, and put in a basket on the table. After shuffling them together, each one óf the party draws one of the papers from the collection and is expected to decipher the word thereon. If the person cannot do so, a forfeit is the penalty. When each paper has been read, the game begins anew. We give some transpositions of words for those desirious of enjoying this game : Nacci-Ntsnot—the first Christian Emperor (Constantine) ; I ring not sawhivng —the father of American Literature (Washington Irving); Koen-Woyt—a celebrated battle of the Revolutionary War (Yorktown); Lanco-Silrw—a noted British General of the Revolution (Cornwallis) ; Tug-Rafar—the bravest commander of the fleet during the late war (Farragut).

Fruit-Basket.—All the company are seated, except one standing in the centre of the circle, who has charge of the fruit-basket. He gives to each one the name of a fruit to deposit in his basket when called for. The person having such fruit must reply to the request before the holder of basket counts *five*, or pay a forfeit. Every now and then he wishes all the fruits thrown in at once, when the whole circle of players must rise and change places. The holder of basket runs for a chair, and the player left without a place must take charge of the fruit-basket, and give the names of fruit to be again deposited.

Where you were—What you were doing—Whom you were with.—This is a very laughable game, affording sport by the ridiculous combinations given to each person. All the company, except three, are seated in a row. The first of the three starts and whispers to each person " where you were ;" the second following tells " what you were doing ;" while the third gives the name of " whom you were with." After the company have each received these three facts, the leader calls on them to give a report of what they have heard. Should any persons forget, they must pay a forfeit for poor memory. We give some examples.

First person : " I was on the house-top, playing the piano, with Napoleon Bonaparte."

Second person: " I was in the cars, looking through a telescope, with Mr. William St. Clair," (one of the company)

Third person : " I was in a baloon, arranging a wreath of flowers, with Queen Victoria."

We think that our young friends will find much amusement from this game.

The Menagerie.—During a merry set of games, much fun, and surely no harm, can be made by playing an innocent trick on one of the party. We recommend this for your pleasure. The party being seated, the leader addresses them by saying, " I intend starting a Menagerie, and wish each one of you to personate some animal, by making the noise or giving a motion peculiar to them. I will whisper to each one the animal he or she is to represent. When I give the signal, all must rise and give such animal's noise or motion. The lion will roar; the rooster crow ; and so on, when I count three." He then walks to each one and whispers, " Keep quiet," until he comes to the victim of the trick, to whom he whispers, " Ba-a like a sheep." The leader then calls, "Attention ! Look at me, and as I say three, fail not to rise and give the noise of the animal you represent." At the given signal, all " Keep quiet," as requested, except the poor sheep, who rises to his feet, acting and looking very " sheepish." When given to a conceited person, the trick is capital and affords much laughter at his expense.

Initiation—After some quiet, sober games, this " mysterious " one will be enjoyed by all playing it. Three of the company remain in the room, the others (not knowing the secret of the game), retire, and one at a time enters the room to pass through the ordeal of initiation. One of the players remaining inside, seats herself at the piano and commences to play a mournful strain of music; another girl (or boy) stands as door keeper, and with solemn face admits a player. The third one advances to meet the person entering, and in a sober manner blindfolds her, then requests her to point the front finger of her right hand before her and march straight forward. In so doing the blind walker finds her finger caught in the mouth of one of the players. A shout or scream will follow, and the initiation into *that* society is completed.

The admitted member remains in the room, and another player is called to enter, the same joke being played until all are acquainted with the mysteries of the game.

The players inside can themselves determine upon the tricks to be played, and vary them as they desire. Always choose something startling, that will cause the players to scream, and thus excite the curiosity of the company outside of the room, and increase the mystery of the process of initation.

The music should continue, and talking be done in a quiet manner, that the others outside may not hear, and guess the joke of the game. A merry company will always find sport in trying this amusement.

The Hidden Word.—One of the players leaves the room and the others agree upon a word which they must place in all the answers to the questions given them by the outside player on returning to the room. The word chosen should not be a difficult or uncommon word; something naturally placed in any ordinary answer to a question given, such as, "but," "hear," "and," "look," etc. Having decided upon a word, the player is recalled and passes to each one in turn, asking them a question, until the hidden word is guessed. The person giving the clue to the word must then retire and be the next to do the guessing. If the questioner fails to find the word, after enquiring of all the company, he must leave the room again and have another trial. The players should be careful in replying not to place any emphasis on the particular word, or make it prominent in the answer.

The Traveling Secret.—One of the company whispers a sentence to the player on the right. This one, in turn, whispers what was heard to the next one, and so on through the circle, the last person telling it to the first, who repeats aloud what the sentence was when started on its journey and when it returned. Then each player in turn repeats what was heard. It is not often that the secret is the same when reaching home as when starting to go round the trip. No person must repeat the whisper, but should a player fail to catch the secret, one must be invented or given as nearly as possible to what was heard. Some very amusing combinations travel round a circle in this game. Send them rapidly and much fun will be found in receiving and forwarding the secret on its journey.

Words in a Word.—It is necessary that two only of the company should be acquainted with the game. One leaves the room, stating that he or she can return and in a short time tell them the word they agree to use for the game. They decide the word shall be "Love." Then the other player acquainted with the game, tells the first to say "Light;" the second, "Oar;" the third, "Vein," and the fourth, "Ear." The outside person is recalled and on passing to each one receive the words given, and soon informs them that the word is "Love." They must guess how it was found out. By studying you will see that words are taken whose initial letters in rotation form the word selected. Sometimes it is played by all the parties knowing the game, and choosing their own words to form from the one chosen, and the person leaving the room, not knowing how the game is played, must guess the word and art of finding it.

Tasks for Redeeming Forfeits.—When a person in the preceding games fails to accomplish certain tasks, or misses in the sport, he has to pay a forfeit, which may be a glove, ring, or any small article belonging to him, to the player having the office of forfeit keeper. In redeeming these forfeits the players incur certain penances which cannot as a rule be performed without the presence of both sexes.

The manner of redeeming forfeits is this: The forfeit keeper takes his or her place on the chair, while the party chosen as judge to pronounce sentence upon the various persons, sits or kneels on a stool before the forfeit keeper.

The latter holds one of the forfeited articles over the head of the judge (who does not see it), and repeats the following: " Heavy, heavy, what hangs over?" " Is it fine?" (for gentleman), " or superfine?" (for lady), enquires the judge, " Fine," (or superfine, as the case may be). " What shall be done with the owner?" According to the answer given by the holder, a task is given to perform. Having accomplished the task, the article is returned to the owner.

We give some penances which will be found to be pleasant, and laughable to perform.

Journey to Rome.—In this the person whose forfeit is called is required to go round to every person in the room and tell them that he is going on a journey to Rome, and assure them if they have any message or article to send to the Pope, he will be greatly pleased to take it. Every one must give something to the traveler, no matter how large or awkward to carry, (the harder the task the more merriment), until he is literally overloaded with presents. When he has gathered them all, he walks round the room, then to a corner, and deposits them there, having paid for his forfeit.

To Brush off a Dime.—This trick, if well conducted, will

excite great laughter and should be given to a person not knowing it.

The judge shows the owner of the forfeit a dime, and insists that he must brush it off his forehead when placed thereon. Wrap the dime in a wet handkerchief, press it against the forehead, not permitting the person to put his hands to forehead or look in a glass. He will imagine that it is fastened from the feeling of the impression on the forehead, and try in various ways to shake it off, often making himself ludicrous in his persevering efforts to perform the task.

Wit, Beauty and Love.—This is an old-fashioned penance, but it always affords amusement, especially when given to a bashful person. To redeem his or her forfeit, the person must bow to the wittiest, kneel to the prettiest, and kiss the one loved best.

The Knight of the Rueful Countenance.—The player whose forfeit is called is named the "Knight." He must take a lighted candle in his hand, and select some other player to be his attendant, who takes hold of his arm. They march slowly around the room to all the ladies in the company. It is the attendant's office to kiss the hand of each lady, after each kiss to wipe the Knight's mouth with his handkerchief, which he holds in his hand for the purpose. The Knight must carry the candle and not change his rueful countenance to a smile. Should he do so, he must accomplish some other task.

The Bouquet.—The owner of the forfeit must compare each lady to a flower, and explain the points of resemblance. Thus he may liken one lady to a rose, on account of her blushes; another to a snow drop, because she hangs her head so modestly; another to a lily, because she is fair and tall. This penance gives the person who incurs it, a capital opportunity for passing some very pretty compliments, as well as some doubtful ones.

The Barefooted Friar.—This is given to a boy to perform. He is told to put two chairs together, take off his shoes and jump over them. He will, no doubt, be puzzled, think this a difficult task, and dangerous penance, but if he will reflect a moment, he will understand that the shoes, and not the chairs, are to be jumped over.

The Will.—This is a good penance. The player who owns the forfeit, is requested to leave the room; during his absence the others arrange how his property is to be divided. They fix different values to different parts of his body. His head is the chief legacy; the right arm, the second; the left arm, the third, and so on. The penitent is then recalled, passed to his lawyer (chosen from the party), and asked, " As you are desirous of making your will, may I ask you which of these persons is to be your principal legatee ? " The poor victim points to some gentleman or lady. " To whom do you leave the second part of your property ? " The owner of the forfeit points to another person, and so on, until he has willed away his head and limbs. The lawyer then orders the different legatees to seize their property, which they do with great eagerness, one catching his head, another grasping his arm, etc., to the intense astonishment of the owner of these members, and the great amusement of the company.

The Twine-Twister.—Give this penance to a sharp, quick person to repeat to test his or her expertness :

> " When the twister a twisting would twist him a twist,
> For the twisting his twine he three times doth intwist;
> But if one of the twists of the twist doth intwine,
> The twine that intwisteth untwisteth the twine."

Or this one, repeat rapidly :

> " A peacock picked a peck of pepper,
> Did he pick a peck of pepper?
> Yes, he picked a peck of pepper;
> Pick pepper peacock."

The Prison Diet.—First blindfold the person, then bring a glass of water and a tea-spoon. Each one of the party advances and gives the prisoner a drink. He must continue drinking until he guesses the name of the person giving to him. It is not likely he can do this, unless some kindly friend laughs or gives some familiar token known to the prisoner. When the glass is almost emptied, the task is considered ended.

There are many other penalties ; often bright minds in the company can originate some and add to the amusement of the occasion. Some smaller ones are laugh, cry, cough and sneeze in the four corners of the room ; kiss your own shadow six times without laughing ; hop on one foot round the room several times ; pat your head with one hand, and rub your breast with the other at the same time ; pay four compliments to four different persons, avoiding to use the letter *S* in every one ; repeat and compose poetry, or tell an amusing story, etc., etc.

In performing these penalties let good-will and a willing spirit be shown. Often it seems difficult to perform the task, but it will add to the fun and good cheer of the company to take it all in pleasant humor and thus have enjoyment yourself and give amusement to your friends. We trust that many a merry hour will be spent in the playing of these games, and much happiness and profit derived from them.

Twenty Questions.—This game was once so popular among the Cambridge professors that they declared any subject could be reached in ten questions. The company divides into questioners and answerers. After the subject is chosen, questions are asked in some such form as this: Is it animal, vegetable, or mineral? What is its size? To what age does it belong? Is it historical or natural? Is it ancient or modern? etc. A few objects do not belong clearly to either of these classes, or they touch, possibly, on all three; but even these can be mastered. The questioners may consult openly about their question before asking it, but the answerers must be very cautious in consultation lest they disclose too much. Among the more difficult subjects are such as a mummy, a tear, a blush, a smile, an echo, an avalanche, a drought, etc. Puns and evasive answers must not be used.

The Secretary.—All the players sit at a table and are furnished with paper and pencil. Each writes his name, and having folded it back carefully, hands his paper to the secretary, who shuffles the papers, distributes them again, and says, "Character;" whereupon each writes a supposed trait of character. The papers are again folded, reshuffled, and redistributed, when "Future" is announced, and each writes to this idea on his slip. Other points, not to exceed six in all, are named and written upon, and the whole list is then read from each paper, affording a most amusing record.

Rhyming Game.—The leader selects a word capable of many rhymes. Beginning with the first of the company, he says, for example, "I have a word that rhymes with *one*."

"Is it a female recluse?" asks the party addressed.

"No, it is not a *nun*," is replied. Passing on to the second person, this one may ask, "Is it something good to eat?"

"No, it is not a *bun*." The third may ask, "Is it a heavy weight?"

"No, it is not a *ton*." The fourth may ask, "Is it something that makes you laugh?"

"Yes, it is *Fun*."

The party failing to question promptly pays a forfeit; so does the leader if he fail to answer promptly. The party catching his word becomes the new leader.

Acting Game.—Half the players go out of the room and those within decide on a word, telling the others a word with which it rhymes. The outer party then enter and act out a word which they suppose to be correct. For instance, if the word rhymes with *main*, the actors come in with umbrellas, overshoes, waterproofs, stepping carefully, etc., and the inside party says, "No, it is not *rain*." The outs retire to consult, and, returning with bags and baggage, imitate passengers hurrying to get on the cars. "No, it is not *train*." Again they retire, consult, and re-enter. One of them with a mock club strikes a companion, who falls to the ground. "Yes, it is *Slain*." The sides then exchange places. If the word is not guessed, either as announced by its rhyme or as acted, the party failing goes out again.

Crambo.—Each player writes a noun and a question. All are then shuffled, nouns together and questions. Each player then draws one from each set of slips and writes four lines in rhyme, answering the question and introducing the word. The efforts to meet these requirements will provoke an abundance of fun.

FUN IN GENERAL.

Going to Jerusalem.—Place a row of chairs, alternating backs and fronts, and one less in number than the parties in the game. A march tune is then played, and the pilgrims move around the line of chairs. Suddenly the music stops, when each one tries to drop into a seat. Of course one person is left. He retires from the game and a chair is

removed from the line. The music and marching are repeated, and another party is dropped, and so on till one
remains in occupancy of the one chair. This person is victor
in the contest.

Magic Music.—One person leaves the room and the others
agree on something, no matter how difficult if only practicable, which he must do. He enters to music, which is loud
as he nears his point of operation and soft as he departs.
By this modulation he is guided to the thing desired and
almost inevitably does in the end the precise act intended.

Magnetized Cane.—Let a gentleman prepare beforehand
by attaching to his pantaloons, above the knee and from one
leg to the other, a fine black-silk strand about fifteen or
eighteen inches long. Proposing in the company to mag-
netize a cane, let him take such an article and rub it faithfully. Then, standing it erect between his separated knees,
and carefully poising it with his hands, let it lean against
the stretched thread of silk. It will seem to stand alone,
to the amazement of the uninitiated, who will struggle
hard to accomplish the same feat.

The Charmed Quarter.—Let the company select one of three
quarter-dollars and mark it so as to know it certainly. The
other two meanwhile are laid on a marble mantel. Let the
company all handle the piece and examine the mark; then,
having tossed it into a hat—the other two quarters being
lightly tipped into the same receptacle and all shaken up for
an instant—a touch will indicate the marked coin, as by
handling it will have become warm; the others, by lying on
the marble, having become cold. The detection is almost inevitable. If it fail, more "magnetism," imparted by a longer
holding of it in the hand of a spectator, will disclose the
correct coin.

Dynamite.—Cross three wooden toothpicks as if they
were spokes in a wheel, but leave the side spaces larger

than the other two. Cross two other picks over two ends of these and under one of them, so as to bind the five in a

"WOULD I WERE A BOY AGAIN."

tight frame. On this lay a sixth toothpick to represent John Chinaman on his bed. Then apply a match to one end of the frame pieces. This represents the Hoodlum blowing up the Chinaman. When the fire creeps in to the point where the picks cross and bind each other, the spring of the wood will hurl the Chinaman high in the air, illustrating dynamite action, and causing a hearty laugh.

Parlor Magic.—An immense amount of fun can be had by means of the parlor magic, or trick sets, to be had in great variety. Some of the exploits thus attainable are quite puzzling to the observer, especially if the manipulator be dexterous, and, withal, entertaining of speech. Sets of apparatus carry also complete instruction, but practice is needed to make perfect.

Manuals on Games, Amusements, etc.—On all points of home amusement there are valuable treatises or manuals—some large, some small, but all suggestive. If enjoyment is sought in a house, the means of enjoyment must be studied. Study, therefore, to make home happy.

GENERAL HINTS.

So many and so rich are earth's resources, that, when the wisest man has wearied with his discourse, numberless things remain unsaid—yea, quite unthought of—by the sage.

BUFFON.

General Hints.

A FTER the broad scope of this book has been covered, there still remain many things to be said. They are hardly worth discussion ; mere statement is sufficient. They are hints merely on a variety of subjects. Let it not be supposed that every suggestion here given has been subjected to test by the editor of the department. But every one has been culled from a trustworthy source and has been subjected to careful scrutiny. All of them are worth trying; but try them conscientiously. More prescriptions have failed from unskillful handling than from inherent defect. An Irish cook who delayed some fifteen minutes when his master had ordered a soft-boiled egg, excused himself by declaring that it had boiled fast all the time, but showed no signs whatever of becoming soft. So many other domestic manipulators fail.

HINTS FOR THE KITCHEN.

To Keep Meat Fresh.—Take a quart of best vinegar, two ounces of lump sugar, two ounces of salt. Boil these together for a few minutes, and when cold anoint with a brush the meat to be preserved. For fish the mixture is to be applied inside ; for poultry, both in and outside. Or: Place the meat in the centre of a clean earthenware vessel and closely surround it with common charcoal. Or: Cover the meat lightly with bran and hang it in some passage where there is a current of air.

To Make Poultry Tender.—Give the fowl, shortly before killing, a tablespoonful of vinegar.

To Test Mushrooms.—In eatable mushrooms the stalk and top are dirty white and the lower part has a lining of salmon fringe, which changes to russet or brown soon after they are gathered. The poisonous manifest all colors, and those which are dead white above and below should be let alone. Sprinkle salt on the spongy part, and if they turn yellow they are poisonous, but if they become black they are good. Let the salt remain on a little while before you decide on the color. Mushrooms are in season during September and October.

To Keep Flour Sweet.—Insert a triangular tube of boards or tin bored full of small holes, into the centre of the barrel, which allows the air to reach the middle of the meal, and it never gets musty. A barrel of good flour, dry as it appears to be, contains from twelve to sixteen pounds of water.

To Test Coal Oil.—Pour a little oil in an iron spoon and heat it over a lamp until it is moderately warm to the touch. If the oil produces vapor which can be set on fire by a flame held a short distance above the liquid, it is bad.

To Remove Clinkers.—Throw half a dozen broken oyster shells into the fire when the coal is all aglow, and cover them with fresh coal. When all are red hot the clinkers become doughy, and are easily removed.

Cheap Fire-Kindler.—Melt three pounds of rosin in a quart of tar, and stir in as much saw-dust and pulverized charcoal as you can. Spread the mass upon a board till cool, then break into lumps as big as your thumb. Light it with a match.

To Keep a Broom.—If a broom be inserted every week in *boiling suds*, it will be toughened and last much longer, will not cut the carpet, and will remain elastic as a new broom.

To Preserve Oil-cloths.—An oil-cloth should never be scrubbed; but after being swept it should be cleaned with a soft cloth and lukewarm or cold water. Never use soap, or water that is hot. When dry, sponge it over with milk; then wipe with a soft, dry cloth.

To Prevent a Lamp from Smoking.—Soak the wick in vinegar, and dry it well before using.

To Remove Rust from Steel.—Cover with sweet oil, well rubbed on, and let it remain forty-eight hours, then rub with unslacked lime powdered fine.

To Prevent Rust.—Take one pint of fat-oil varnish, mixed with five pints of highly rectified spirits of turpentine, and rub with a sponge on bright stoves or mathematical instruments, and they will never contract spots of rust.

To Freshen Stale Bread or Cake.—Plunge the loaf one instant in cold water and lay it upon a tin in the stove for ten or fifteen minutes. It will be like new bread, without its deleterious qualities. Stale cake is thus made as nice as new cake. Use immediately.

To Soften Hard Water.—Put half an ounce of quicklime in nine quarts of water. This solution in a barrel of hard water will make it soft. A teaspoonful of sal soda will soften from three to four pails of hard water.

Time of Boiling Green Vegetables.—This depends very much upon the age, and how long they have been gathered. The younger and more freshly gathered, the more quickly they are cooked. The following is Miss Parloa's time-table for cooking:

Potatoes, boiled,	30 minutes.	Green Corn,	25 minutes to 1 hour.
Potatoes, baked,	45 minutes.	Asparagus,	15 to 30 minutes.
Sweet Potatoes, boiled,	45 minutes.	Spinach,	1 to 2 hours.
Sweet Potatoes, baked,	1 hour.	Tomatoes, fresh,	1 hour.
Squash, boiled,	25 minutes.	Tomatoes, canned,	30 minutes.
Squash, baked,	45 minutes.	Cabbage,	45 minutes to 2 hours.
Green Peas, boiled,	20 to 40 minutes.	Cauliflower,	1 to 2 hours.
Shell Beans, boiled,	1 hour.	Dandelions,	2 to 3 hours.
String Beans, boiled,	1 to 2 hours.		

Keeping Hams.—After smoking, make coarse cotton cloth sacks so that one ham will go in easily, pack cut hay all around between the sack and the ham, tie the sack at the top, hang in a cool place, and be sure the sacks are whole.

To Make Shirts Glossy.—Take of raw starch, one ounce; gum arabic, one drachm; white of egg, half ounce; soluble glass, quarter of an ounce; water. Make starch into fine cream, dissolve with gum in a little hot water, cool and mix it with the egg, and beat up the mixture with starch liquid; then add the water, glass (solution), and shake together. Moisten the starched linen with a cloth dipped in the liquid, and use polishing iron to develop gloss.

Blackening Stoves.—If a little vinegar or cider is mixed with stove polish it will not take so much rubbing to make the stove bright, and the blackening is not likely to fly off in fine dust.

Musty Coffee and Tea Pots.—These may be cleaned and sweetened by putting wood ashes into them and filling them with cold water. Set on the stove to heat gradually till the water boils. Let it boil a short time, then put aside to cool, when the inside should be faithfully washed and scrubbed in hot soap-suds.

To Clean Pots and Kettles.—When washing greasy pots and kettles, take a handful of meal or bran and rub all around. It absorbs all the grease and leaves them perfectly clean.

To Clean Ceilings Smoked by Kerosene Lamps.—Wash with a sufficiently strong solution of soda in water.

To Prepare a New Iron Kettle for Use.—Fill with clean potato parings; boil them for an hour or more, then wash the kettle with hot water, wipe it dry, and rub it with a little lard; repeat the rubbing half a dozen times after using.

To Remove Fruit Stains.—Procure a bottle of Javelle water. If the stains are wet with this before the articles are put into the wash they will be completely removed. Those who cannot get Javelle water can make a solution of chloride of lime. Four ounces of the chloride of lime is to be put into a quart of water in a bottle, and after thoroughly shaking allow the dregs to settle. The clear liquid will remove the stains. Be careful to thoroughly rinse the article in clear water before bringing it in contact with soap. When Javelle water is used this precaution is not necessary; with chloride of lime liquid it is, or the article will be harsh and stiff.

Washing.—To wash flannels: First, never apply soap directly to any woolen fabric. Make a strong, hot suds and plunge the garment in it. Second, never dip a flannel in cold, or even cool, water, but always hot. Wash first in hot suds and rinse in hot water made very blue. Third, dry flannels as quickly as possible. Wring dry from the second water and hang either in the hot sun or before a brisk fire. When nearly dry, press with a hot iron. None but soft water should be used upon flannels, and resin soap is much inferior to common soft soap, as it hardens the fibres of woolens.

To wash chintz: Take two pounds of rice and boil it in two gallons of water till soft. When done, pour the whole in a tub; let it stand till of about the warmth you use in general for colored linens; then put the chintz in and use the rice instead of soap. Wash it in this till the dirt appears to be out; then boil the same quantity, as above, but strain the rice from the water and mix it in warm, clear water. Wash in this till quite clean; afterward rinse it in the water in which you have boiled the rice. This will answer the end of starch and no dew will affect it and it will be stiff as long as you wear it.

To wash clothes without fading them: Peel Irish potatoes and grate them in cold water. Saturate the articles to be washed in this potato-water and they can then be washed with soap without any running of the color. Oil may be taken out of carpets with this potato-water when simple cold water would make the color run ruinously. This will also set the color in figured black muslins, in colored merinos, in ribbons, and other silk goods. Often the potato-water cleanses sufficiently without the use of soap; but the latter is necessary where there is any grease. When no soap is needed, take the grated potato and rub the goods with a flannel rag.

Sour milk removes iron-rust from white goods.

To make silk which has been wrinkled appear exactly like new, sponge it on the surface with a weak solution of gum arabic or white glue, and iron on the wrong side.

A tablespoonful of black pepper put in the first water in which gray or buff linens are washed will keep them from spotting. It will also keep the colors of colored or black cambrics or muslin from running, and does not harden the water.

To extract ink from cotton, silk, and woolen goods, saturate the spot with spirits of turpentine and let it remain several hours; then rub it between the hands. It will disappear without injuring the color or texture of the fabric. For linen, dip the spotted part in pure tallow and the ink will disappear.

When clothes have acquired an unpleasant odor by being kept from the air, charcoal laid in the folds will remove it.

To take oil or grease from cloth: Drop on the spot some oil of tartar or salt of wormwood which has been left in a damp place until it is fluid; then immediately wash the place with lukewarm soft water and then with cold water, and the spot will disappear.

INDEX.

307